PRAISE F

"Dive in...if you are looking to be charmed and delighted."

— LOCUS

"...[A] knack for creating colorful, instantly memorable characters, and inhuman creatures capable of inspiring awe and wonder."

— NPR BOOKS

"The writing. It is superb. T. Kingfisher, where have you been all my life?"

— THE BOOK SMUGGLERS

PALADIN'S HOPE

PALADIN'S HOPE

BOOK THREE OF THE SAINT OF STEEL

T. KINGFISHER

Paladin's Hope

http://www.tkingfisher.com

Published by Argyll Productions

Dallas, Texas

www.argyllproductions.com

ISBN 978-1-61450-613-3

First Edition Trade Paperback May 2024

For Cousin Amy

CHAPTER 1

It was early morning on the banks of the Elkinslough River. Mist hung heavily over the brown water, turning it briefly pale and disguising the muddiness of the flow. Five men stood on the city-side bank, looking at a corpse.

Four of the men were human, one was not. That member of the group was a gnole, one of the short, stripe-faced badger people. Despite their species and the nearly three foot difference in their height, there was something about both the gnole and one of the men that marked them as similar. They wore identical badges that marked them as members of the city guard, but more than that, they stood alike and they had the same watchful, suspicious air about them.

Two of the remaining men were also similar in the same indefinable fashion. They had impeccable military posture and wore chain and tabards. Their cloaks marked them as servants to a dead god. One was of average height, with dark hair, the other a fraction shorter, with auburn red hair that stood out like fresh blood against the mist.

The last of the five was the only one who did not share a certain martial quality. He was slim and well-groomed and would be considered handsome, but he was also extraordinarily pale, as if he lived his life underground.

It was this fifth man who nudged the corpse with the toe of his boot and said, "Well, if you want my professional opinion, this great goddamn hole in his chest is probably what killed him."

Doctor Piper dealt with corpses and for the most part, he preferred them to the living. He didn't mind living people, he was perfectly happy to meet them and talk to them and even work with them, but corpses never, ever asked stupid questions. You learned to appreciate that when you spent all day analyzing why and how people had died. The dead didn't say things like, "Are you sure he's dead?" when the man's head was half off or, "Dear god, what happened?" when it was bloody obvious that someone had shoved a sword through him. The dead just laid there and got on with being dead.

He definitely preferred them to the city guard. Piper was suspicious of power, particularly power that thought it was the arbiter of justice. He knew Captain Mallory well enough to know that the man was that rarest of creatures, an honest policeman, but that simply meant that his dislike was tempered with pity. Mallory did not engage in graft or extortion and for this sin, he had been assigned the poorest and most crime-riddled quarter of the city, where he could be handily forgotten until his superiors decided they needed someone to blame.

The two paladins were different. Paladins were god-touched and thus could make a much better case for being arbiters of justice, since presumably a higher power was doing the actual arbitration. These two happened to work for the Temple of the White Rat. Stephen, the taller one, he'd met before. The good-looking red-haired fellow was new, but was cut from the same cloth as Stephen, which meant that he might well go into a battle-madness that could level a town but would feel extremely guilty about it afterwards.

The corpse was a corpse. Something very large had punched through the man's body, back to front, exploding ribs outward. Probably it had exploded guts outward too, but after a day or two in the river, most of those bits had gone missing. The fish had gotten a good meal there. They'd gotten his eyes, too. It was fairly gruesome, but you got used to that sort of thing. Normally bodies were brought to Piper's workroom, in a cool subterranean storage room near the Archon's palace, but it was fairly obvious that moving this one would cause it to fall apart, so they'd sent a runner for him to come to the river.

"Any idea what happened to him?" asked Captain Mallory.

Piper shrugged. "If somebody stabbed him in the heart and then tore his chest open, I couldn't tell you." He squatted down. Drowning was always so unpleasant. Things got soggy and bloated. The dead man hadn't been in the water long enough to get truly nasty and the water was cold enough to keep decay to a minimum, but it still wasn't pretty. "I can tell you he's been in the water a day, maybe a day and a half. Not much more than that."

"How do you know?"

Piper nudged the man with his boot again. "The catfish haven't cored him out completely. If he'd been in there for two days, he'd be mostly catfish by weight."

"A human isn't joking," said the gnole constable, nodding to Piper. "A gnole has seen catfish eating." Stephen the paladin rubbed his hand over his face.

"We do have exceedingly voracious catfish," said the redhead, with understandable civic pride.

"What could have made a wound like that?" asked Mallory, refusing to be sidetracked by the local ichthyology.

Piper studied the wound. Even assuming that the local fish population had been at work, there had been a great deal of trauma to begin with. The man's chest looked as if it had exploded outward. "Something big," he said. "Someone help me roll him over?"

The two paladins immediately took an end and flipped the corpse over. Mallory scowled but didn't argue.

The corpse's back was ragged, his head bashed and misshapen. Whatever had taken out his back had gone in at an angle, only just missed the spine, and left a gaping hole the size of Piper's fists. "Most of this is from being banged about after he died," said Piper, squatting down next to the body. It stank, but they always did. He wiped his nose.

"A warhammer could have caused the chest to break outward," said Stephen, "but it doesn't punch a hole in the back like that. Perhaps some kind of maul with a sharpened end?"

"Gored by a bull?" asked the red-head.

"That might do it." Piper nodded up at him. "Didn't catch your name?"

"Galen. Formerly of the Saint of Steel, now I serve the Temple."

"Yes, I figured that much." Piper gave him a brief smile. He really was very good-looking. Cheekbones you could slice cheese on.

"That would be a remarkable bull," said Mallory. "To make a hole that size."

"There's still some aurochs in the woods upstream," said Stephen. "Or a demon could have taken a normal cow. They do like to possess livestock." Mallory grunted.

Piper looked down at the body. He didn't want to do the trick. He could do it, but it was unpleasant and none of these men were stupid and might have questions about why he was touching a dead body with his bare hands and getting a vague expression.

Anyway, it wasn't as if the cause of death was all that mysterious. Piper was pretty sure that the man's last sensation had been of being struck very hard in the back. It might not even have had time to hurt.

He pulled out his dagger and leaned forward, probing at the wound. There was something inside, which might be a very disgruntled catfish, but might be significant. "Hmmm..." Too deep in the wound to get with a dagger. He slid two gloved fingers inside, trying to get a grip on whatever it was. "Aha!"

When he looked up, Stephen was pointedly not looking at him. The paladin had turned slightly green.

"What are you getting squeamish about?" asked Piper. "You've seen dead bodies. You've *made* dead bodies."

"Yes, but I didn't poke around in them afterwards."

"Feh." Piper extracted his prize. "Bone chip. Damn."

"Let me see." Mallory crouched down next to him. "It looks like it, yes."

Piper did not say something sarcastic about being grateful that the guard captain had confirmed what he, a doctor, had already identified. He considered this a great victory of restraint.

"Knocked off by the weapon, then?" asked Galen.

"Seems likely. I was hoping for wood splinters, honestly, then I could tell you it was a sharpened stake or a spear." He turned the bit of bone over in his fingers, frowning. "It's a long chip, though. I won't swear he wasn't impaled on some kind of sharpened bone."

"So it might have been an accident?" asked Mallory hopefully.

"Maybe." Piper shrugged. "I suppose it could have been a supremely bad accident with a supremely pointy tree. Though

I would suspect a very well-polished piece of wood, because trees tend to leave bits of bark in the wounds."

"Could they have simply washed out?" asked Mallory.

"Anything's possible," said Piper, in a tone that hopefully conveyed, "Not a chance in hell." The handsome red-haired paladin hid a smile.

"Why would someone shove a polished stake through him?" asked Mallory, not rising to the bait.

"Maybe they thought he was a vampire."

"A stake the size of a man's thigh, though?" Stephen sounded doubtful.

"Perhaps they wanted to be thorough."

Mallory grunted. The one advantage police had over paladins was that guards had no problem believing that someone would randomly shove pointy logs into other people. Paladins generally took a little longer to get there. Piper suspected that their sense of innocence and moral outrage kept regrowing, possibly through divine means.

"A gnole thinks this is one of the bodies," said the gnole constable.

Piper looked over at the gnole, puzzled, but Mallory grunted again, apparently understanding. "The other two were decapitated," he said.

Both paladins bristled. Piper felt his own stomach sink. "You mean from the smooth men?"

"No, no." Mallory waved his hand. "Different sort of decapitation. Sorry. I realize we're all a bit sensitive about that still."

"Oh good, just a run-of-the-mill beheading," said Galen dryly.

"I hear in other towns, they sometimes go whole weeks without anyone having their heads randomly chopped off," said Piper.

Mallory scowled, and Piper realized too late that the guard

captain was taking that as an insult. "No offense to your men," he added hastily. "Those are all much smaller towns."

"None taken," said Mallory, in much the same tone that Piper had said, *'Anything's possible'.* "I sometimes think of moving to one of those places. But those other two didn't come from here. They washed up on the bank, just like this fellow did. Whatever killed him was upstream."

"A body was in the water the same amount of time," said the gnole constable. He reached out and tapped a claw on the dead man's foot. "A body wore the same kind of boots."

They all duly examined the boots. They were ordinary leather, not particularly distinguished, the kind sewn inside out so that the seams didn't leak.

"Everybody wears leather boots," said Mallory.

The gnole reached up with one hand and smoothed his whiskers down. In a human, it would have been a fussy little gesture. Piper rather suspected that in a gnole, it was the equivalent of taking a deep breath so that you didn't yell. "A job-human wears wooden soles. A rag-and-bone human wears wooden soles. Even a sword-human—" he nodded to the two paladins "—wear wooden soles."

All four humans looked down at their own feet. They were all wearing leather boots with wooden soles. Stephen tapped his foot and it made a characteristic clicking sound.

"Clerks wear leather soles," said Galen thoughtfully. "Lawyers. Priests who don't go outside a great deal. If you're inside and can afford it, you change your shoes. These are indoor shoes, then?"

"So somebody rammed a stake through him indoors..." murmured Stephen.

"Or he went outside not expecting to be long," said Mallory. "Or he couldn't afford a better—no, that doesn't make any sense, wooden soles are cheaper and last longer, leather has to be fitted." He rubbed his face. "All right, Earstripe, you've convinced me. The shoes might be significant."

"Not many bulls goring people indoors," said Galen.

"Thank you for that exceedingly helpful observation, Paladin Galen."

"I live to serve."

"And thank you for your time, doctor," said Mallory, in clear dismissal. "And thank you, gentlemen, for being so kind as to bring Doctor Piper to us. We won't detain you any longer."

"Our honor is to serve," said Stephen, putting a fist over his heart. Unlike Galen, he actually seemed to mean it. Piper felt a wash of secondhand embarrassment.

He took a little extra time standing up, cleaning his gloves first and poking the body a few more times, not because he expected to learn anything but because the dismissal had annoyed him. Still, there wasn't much more that he could do.

"Do you require an escort back, doctor?" asked Stephen.

"No," said Piper. "Since I'm out here, I might as well pick up something for dinner."

"I'm amazed you can think of dinner," muttered Galen. "Or fish."

"The dead are dead," said Piper, not bothering to mention that he definitely wouldn't be eating fish. "The living still need to eat." He nodded to the paladins and the guards and turned away, still thinking vaguely about bone chips and leather soles and things that did not quite add up together.

CHAPTER 2

"Is it just me," asked Galen, as the two paladins left the docks together, "or was Mallory distinctly chilly toward me just now?"

Stephen gave him a thoughtful look. "You've been gone a while," he said.

"Oh, you noticed?"

Stephen rolled his eyes. Galen struck a tragic pose. "Months up north, frozen hellscape, terrible food, actual honest-to-god shapeshifters, and all I get is 'oh, you've been gone a while.' I'll have you know, I nearly died on *multiple* occasions."

"And how is that any different than normal?"

"There were *nuns.*"

"Mmm."

"A round dozen of them. I had to escort them back to their convent, then spend a month lugging rocks around helping them rebuild it. And Istvhan was no help at all. He and his lady love were making calf-eyes at each other the whole time, when they weren't sneaking off every five minutes to play hide-the-bratwurst."

"It's nice that he's happy."

"Disgustingly so." Galen gave up. Stephen did have a sense

of humor, unlike some of the other former paladins, but he was clearly not in a bantering mood. "So what's been happening while I was freezing my balls off?"

"The Bishop," said Stephen.

Galen grinned. Bishop Beartongue was the leader of the Temple of the White Rat within Archenhold. She was a pleasant, soft-spoken older woman who devoted most of her time to solving administrative problems. She also had a mind like a razor and the ruthlessness of a hired killer. Galen would have laid his life down for her without hesitation.

"So what did the Bishop do to get Mallory pissed at her?"

"It's not just Mallory. If you think he's chilly, the other guard captains will give you frostbite. She's been pushing for better recordkeeping by the guard. Wanted someone in each guard station to record arrests, make copies, and keep a central log. Apparently a few too many people have been sitting in cells because the guard 'forgot' how long they'd been in there." Stephen smiled grimly. "Shane was on honor guard duty the day she presented all her arguments to the Archon. Apparently the head of the guard—that's Commander Tamsin now, Commander Burge retired while you were up north—said that he'd be more than happy to do it, he could absolutely understand her concerns, but of course much of the guard was not terribly literate and the budget was stretched thin, so unless she wanted to pay for trained scribes at each guard station, he just didn't see how he could accommodate."

Galen rubbed his hands together in anticipation. "And?"

"Shane says she got that one look—you know, the I-am-taking-your-concerns-very-seriously look—"

"That look terrifies me."

"—and said that *of course* no one could expect the guard to pay for it, but fortunately she and the other temples had recordkeepers ready to go, and since he had given his approval, they would report to work the following day."

Galen let out a low whistle. Then he tried to do math in his head and reached several large numbers. "Wait, but where *did* she get the money? Scribes aren't cheap, and you figure there are...what, a dozen guard posts?"

"Eleven," said Stephen. "Thirty-six scribes, assuming eight hour shifts and an extra to cover in case anyone's out. And she wanted people to record all the records in a central log as well, so forty."

"Where is she getting forty scribes? Are there even forty trained scribes in the city?"

"The Scarlet Guild."

"The prostitutes?"

Stephen chuckled. "That's what *I* said. But it's a field you age out of fairly young, and the Guild has been very concerned with finding gainful employment for members who aren't officially working, in case they decide to start doing unlicensed work somewhere else. You know how the Scarlet Guild is about unlicensed competition. And as Beartongue said, if there's one group of people who can remember names, faces, and respective deviant acts..." He spread his hands. "They don't have to copy illuminated manuscripts or anything, just do basic recordkeeping, and most of them are a lot better at that than the guard. And they aren't going to be appalled at anything they see in a guard station. So the Scarlet Guild is supplying the ladies, who don't charge nearly as much as a scribe."

"Beartongue is a genius. A terrifying genius. Who's footing the bill?"

"The Rat, the Forge God, and the Lady of Grass. And the Dreaming God provided some of their nuns, who are *extremely* literate, and they're training the ladies who want it on the finer points of recordkeeping so that they can hopefully use this as a springboard to other jobs." Stephen shook his head. "And the Scarlet Guild approves of that a *lot*, so they offered to pay the nuns a commission because you know they don't believe in women working for free, so the nuns plowed it back into the project. I'm told the Temple of the Rat has already taken three of the ladies for law clerks and there's a waiting list at the Scarlet Guild to become one of the record girls."

"Saint's teeth." Galen chuckled. "Nuns and whores, doing the good work together. Only the Rat would see that as a great idea. All right. So let me guess...the guards aren't pleased with outsiders checking their records?"

"Oh, it's much worse than that. When the records were spotty, it was a lot easier to extort prisoners and their families." Stephen's expression grew grave. "I knew some of that went on, of course—big city, you expect a certain amount of graft—but I don't think even Beartongue quite knew the level of corruption that was going on. We're hearing of cases where people would get picked up for being drunk, be unable to pay a bribe, and when they got to a magistrate, they were charged with theft and assault. How can you prove the records were altered if the guard are the ones in charge of the records?"

"Oh *hell.*"

"So now a whole lot of guards found themselves out a major source of revenue. A bunch of them quit outright. Even the ones like Mallory who are relatively honest have gotten used to telling themselves that this was just how things worked and the people in jail were undoubtedly guilty of *something*."

"The broadsheets must have had a field day," muttered Galen.

"Oh yes. Caricatures of nuns and prostitutes standing over the downtrodden, holding the guard back with fans and switches. Frankly, I'm surprised that Mallory will even talk to us any longer."

"Why did he, do you think?"

Stephen raised an eyebrow as they turned down the street housing the entrance to the Temple of the White Rat. "He wanted Piper, not us. Piper's the best at what he does, bar none. And Piper happened to be visiting the Temple when word came down."

"Well," murmured Galen, remembering the pale, thoughtful-eyed man. He'd been classically handsome underneath his annoyance, and his hands had been swift and sure as they worked. "Isn't that interesting..."

CHAPTER 3

Two days later, Piper was wrist-deep in a corpse.

This wasn't an unusual situation for him. He spent a lot of time with his hands in corpses. He didn't like it. He didn't dislike it. It was just what he did. He enjoyed putting the mental pieces together about why someone had died, and he liked being able to provide certainty to families, but mostly what he liked was being good at his job.

And Piper was, for reasons he kept to himself, very, *very* good at his job.

This particular corpse was not a difficult problem to solve. He found what he was searching for and carefully pulled the flesh back to reveal it. The man's liver was a horror show, knobbly and puckered, with a growth that looked like a fleshy cauliflower. The man's wife was convinced that he had been poisoned, and arguably he had been, but the poison was self-administered over a long period of time and came in brown glass bottles. Piper sighed. He'd suspected as much, but you had to be thorough.

He cleaned his tools in the little sink in the corner. It connected to a cistern on the roof and the water was cleaner than the sludge in the Elkinslough. He scrubbed his hands down to the elbow as well. It didn't matter as much, perhaps, since he never treated live patients, but it made him feel better not to carry traces of the job home with him.

He was nearly finished when there was a knock on the door.

"Just a moment!" *Now who could that be...?* Normally people made appointments. The families of the bereaved did not get past the door guard, assuming they could even find his work-rooms in the basement of the tower. He wasn't expecting anyone, and lich-doctors didn't get a lot of social calls.

Another, louder knock. Bless it, couldn't they wait? Was it an emergency? No, that was ridiculous: by the time Piper got to a patient, urgency was a thing of the past. He pushed the door open to find the red-haired paladin from the river standing on the other side, his fist raised.

Piper took a step back and lifted his hands defensively. The paladin's eyes went very wide. He had dark green eyes with paler flecks in them, like flawed jade. Very pretty eyes, except for the alarmed expression. Piper looked at the man's raised hand—*oh, right, he'd been knocking*—and then at his own. He was still carrying the bonesaw.

"Um," said the paladin, eyes locked on the saw.

Generally it takes longer for me to make a fool of myself in front of good-looking men. I'm getting more efficient.

"I apologize," said Piper, lowering the bonesaw. "I, err... wasn't expecting a visitor."

He looked down and discovered that he had two visitors. Earstripe the gnole was looking up at him with a bemused expression, although it had to be said that gnoles nearly always looked at humans with bemused expressions, so that might not mean anything.

"Doctor Piper?" said the paladin.

"Yes." He remembered he was wearing his mask and pulled it down. "Sorry. What can I do for you?" He instinctively tried to block their view of the room, even though the constable had undoubtedly seen dead bodies before and the paladin had undoubtedly made a number of bodies dead himself. For some odd reason, there was something different about a body on a slab. Men who thought nothing of sticking a sword into a living human being went green when you stuck a little tiny scalpel into a dead one.

"We were hoping to speak to you, if we may?"

Galen, that was the man's name. Piper hadn't forgotten. It would have been very difficult to forget a face like that, or hair like that, but of course the face came with a name as well. "Yes, of course. Shall we go into my office instead?" He gestured down the hallway with his free hand, glad that he'd already mostly washed up.

The paladin looked at the gnole, who arched his whiskers forward. Interesting. Apparently the gnole was the one who had instigated this visit and Galen was deferring to him. He wondered if the gnole was uncomfortable coming by himself. *Then again, there are still people, even in this day and age, who think gnoles are animals or devils or some other goddamn foolishness. I suppose I might want an escort to talk to someone I didn't know, too.*

"Good, good. Can you—um—look, wait there, I just have to finish washing up." How much blood was there on his apron? And his mask? *Oh dear...*

Piper closed the door and hastily shucked out of his work clothes and into the clean set he kept on hand. There was a scrap of polished tin mirror over the sink, and he checked to make sure he hadn't unthinkingly wiped his wrist across his forehead and left smears. *Looks clear. All right. Stop panicking. This isn't a date, no matter how pretty the paladin is. This is a meeting with a gnole. Probably about that dead body.* Granted, Piper's dating history was not particularly extensive and he had always been terrible at pursuing other men, but he was still pretty sure that the morgue wasn't the place where you were supposed to start.

There were two chairs in his office, plus the one behind his desk. The gnole was sitting. The paladin stood behind him like an honor guard. Piper filed that away mentally with the deference the paladin had shown to the constable earlier. As he moved past Galen to take his seat at the desk, their eyes met briefly. Green eyes narrowed slightly, not unfriendly but definitely weighing. *Wondering if I'm the appropriate person to be talking to? Wondering if I'll help in this...whatever this is? Wondering if I usually run around waving bonesaws at people?*

He sat down behind the table, and pushed a stack of papers aside. "I apologize. I don't usually meet visitors with a bloody saw in hand."

"A gnole has seen worse."

"Of course. Being a constable, you would have."

"Not then." Earstripe gave him a drop-jawed gnole smile. "A gnole worked in a human burrow, before. Old human there used to walk always with hatchet with red paint. Old human said, 'Any nasty buggers who want to rob an old lady will think twice when they see Betsy.' Said it many times."

Both humans in the room digested this. "She sounds very... impressive," said Galen.

"A gnole does not think she was ever robbed."

"I can see that." Piper focused on Earstripe. "Right. Okay. How can I help you?"

The gnole arched his whiskers forward, then nodded human style. "A bone-doctor remembers a dead human on the riverbank?"

Bone-doctor. Well, it was better than a lot of things he'd been called. "Yes, of course, the one impaled on the wooden stake."

The gnole tapped his clawtips together. Piper got the impression that he was choosing his words carefully. "Mallory-captain is not a bad human," he said, sounding a bit defensive. "A gnole is not complaining."

Piper had his own opinions about the city guard, but suspected this wasn't the time. "I have always thought Captain Mallory was honest and did his best for the people he served."

Earstripe relaxed slightly. "Yes. A gnole has been fortunate to serve under Mallory-captain. A gnole would wish to continue to serve. But a gnole has been thinking about the bodies at the riverbank. Can a bone-doctor find the other bodies? The ones with no head?"

Piper sat back, exhaling. "Oof. How long ago were they found?"

"Nine days. Seven days."

Piper shook his head. "They're in the pauper's field by now, if no one claimed them. And I'm not sure how much I could tell from bodies that old, particularly ones soaked in the water. Anyway, the cause of death sounds like it was pretty clear in those cases, so they wouldn't have brought the bodies to me."

The gnole nodded again. "A gnole suspected as much." He turned his head to look at Galen.

"You were right," said the paladin. "I thought it was worth a try, though."

"So you still think they're linked to this third corpse?" said Piper. He was interested despite himself. It was a puzzle, and he'd never been able to resist a puzzle. It was what kept him rummaging around inside the bodies, trying to find answers.

"A gnole smells it."

"There's a smell?" Piper found that interesting. The smooth men had left a very distinctive odor on their victims, and the

Temple of the White Rat had found a perfumer to mix up a facsimile to guide the slewhounds. From what he'd heard, it had actually helped to track down two in Anuket City and another headed to the Dowager's lands.

"Ah. No." Earstripe waved his hands. "Not a real smell. A gnole *senses* it, but a gnole cannot..." He trailed off.

"A metaphorical smell," said Galen.

"Humans can't smell," said Earstripe, sounding philosophical.

"So you've got a hunch they're connected," said Piper.

"Hunch. Yes. A gnole has a hunch."

"And what is your role in all this?" Piper asked, looking over at Galen.

Galen shrugged. "Earstripe felt having a human around would make things go more smoothly. He came to the temple and found me. I agreed to do what I could."

"A human is good at talking to other humans," said Earstripe. He gave an exaggerated human-style shrug, palms up. "A human doesn't always listen to a gnole. And a gnole did not know where to find a bone-doctor, so a sword-human helped."

"I'm sorry I can't help you more," said Piper. "Unfortunately we just don't have the morgue space to keep bodies cold for long." Down here, in the cool stone rooms under the tower, he could get three or four days, sometimes more in winter, as long as they were brought in promptly. A body that had been pulled out of a river nine days ago...no, there was nothing he could have done, except tell them what the person's last sensations had been, and Piper could guess that had been a sudden, surprising pain in the neck. *Well, now, don't assume. He could have been beheaded post-mortem. You don't know.*

And how exactly are you going to explain that? The gnole might not care, but paladins are traditionally somewhat suspicious of wonderworkers, even such marginal talents as mine.

At least Galen was from the Saint of Steel's order. The Hanged Mother's priests would have tied Piper to a stake and set him alight just on general principle. Still, it was best to stay out of these things as much as possible. The profession of the lich-doctors was only a few decades old in Archenhold, and while their word was law within the courts, religious orders were traditionally skeptical of people who carved up the dead for a living.

He nevertheless heard himself saying, "If there's another body, call me as soon as you can, and I might be able to help."

CHAPTER 4

The call came more quickly than he expected. It was a bare two days later when there was a knock on the door and Piper stumbled out of bed and found himself face-to-face with Galen, yet again.

No shirt. Slightly hungover. At least I'm not carrying a bonesaw this time. That's got to be worth something.

"Ah," said the paladin, his eyes flicking down Piper's torso and back up again. "Did I wake you?"

If the man's eyes had registered approval or interest or even acknowledgment, Piper might have considered it a worthwhile way to answer the door, but Galen's face was carefully blank. *Well, I can hardly blame him. The last time he saw skin this pale, it was probably on a dead fish.*

Pain throbbed against Piper's temples. He should not have gotten drunk. He should have stopped after the first few shots, or at least he should have drunk a lot more water. Still, given the circumstances...

"Yes, but don't worry about it." He turned away from the door. "Another corpse?"

The paladin followed him inside his apartments. "Yes. Earstripe says it's another one of the set."

"What does Mallory say?"

"He hasn't told Mallory. I quote, 'A gnole doesn't feel like twisting his own whiskers.'"

Piper grunted. "Sensible." The shirt draped across the back of the chair was clean, insomuch as it hadn't been worn to chop up a corpse. He dragged it on. "Give me a minute."

"I don't think our friend is going to get any deader." The paladin's eyes lingered on the bottle and the single glass next to the chair, but he didn't say anything.

In fact, he so obviously wasn't saying anything that Piper found himself annoyed. "I don't make a habit of it," he growled. "But they brought in a baby last night with a broken neck. The father says she fell; the mother says he shook her. You'd drink too."

"I would," said Galen. There was a bleak sympathy in his eyes, not the shallow kind, but the kind that had been there and remembered. "Which was it?"

The last memory, looking up, her eyes going through that strange lock-and-stare stage that babies went through and so unable to look away from the face looming over hers, everything so much bigger, the mouth open, loudness in her ears and motion she didn't understand and then a popping feeling and...nothing.

His own despair annoyed him. It did the child no good now. "If she'd fallen, I wouldn't be drinking," said Piper. He went to the basin, dumped out tepid water, and splashed it on his face. Galen winced.

"Can they make a charge stick?"

"On my say-so? Yes. As far as the courts are concerned, a lich-doctor is the last word on cause of death. The White Rat will be left representing both sides, but they're used to that." Piper raked his hands through his hair, trying to settle it in something that didn't look like a bird's nest. "Fortunately, I'm an honest man, or something like it." He grimaced at the scrap of mirror. There was nothing to be done about his hair. The polished tin was slightly warped, and he turned his head from side to side, watching his reflection distort. He could just make out the paladin behind him, a pale oval framed by hair the color of...*no, don't start trying to decide what organ at what stage of decomposition is that shade of red. Pick something else. Something that isn't horrible.* Piper wracked his brain for a comparison and finally settled on smoked paprika. He liked smoked paprika. He liked visiting the spice stalls in the market and seeing the rows of jars, the purity of the colors in a dozen shades of orange and umber and scarlet. *Yes. Much better.*

It was probably a good thing that paladins didn't have a reputation as mind readers.

"Okay," he said, giving up on his hair and pulling on a hat. He slung an oilcloth cloak around his shoulders. "Let's see this latest body."

Galen walked a little behind Piper as they made their way to the river. Not many people in this quarter were out at this hour of the morning, and he didn't need to watch the sidewalk closely. Instead he studied the back of the doctor's neck, wondering what to make of him.

Doctor Piper was attractive, certainly. The paladin had noticed that the first time they met. Dark hair, cut very short, and a face that looked young until you saw his eyes. There were lines around those eyes that had nothing to do with laughter.

That first moment when he'd opened the door naked from the waist up had been the kind of shock to the senses that would have reduced a much younger Galen to gibbering idiocy. Piper was lean rather than powerful, but every muscle was in exactly the right place, the lines of his arms smoothly defined, his fingers long and deft. He'd always admired that in other men, ever since he was young. Insomuch as Galen had a type, it was "male, with good hands." His first great love had been another youth at the Saint of Steel's temple, who had not been conventionally attractive but had possessed quite exquisite hands.

Now, Piper certainly was conventionally attractive. *But so pale. Saint's teeth.* Galen had heard poets talk about alabaster skin, but he'd never seen anyone who so closely resembled it. The hollows at Piper's throat and collarbone were almost blue. Understandable given that he worked underground at all hours, but still. As a redhead, Galen was automatically used to being the palest person in any given room, but Piper made him look ruddy and tan. The only darkness across his skin was the fine line of black hair running down his belly and vanishing under the waistband of his pants.

It was a good thing Galen had a lot of experience controlling his expression.

Based on the few conversations they'd had, Galen already suspected that the doctor also had some experience in that department. Half-awake and hung over was the first time he'd seen Piper's expression be anything but cool and sardonic and professional.

Then he'd mentioned the dead child and the lines around his eyes had gone tight and grim. The bitterness in his voice hadn't ended there, either. *Fortunately, I'm an honest man, or something like it.* Galen wondered what lay at the heart of that bitterness.

Piper turned his head, glancing over his shoulder. "Which way?"

"Upriver," said Galen, gesturing. Piper nodded, turning

down the next street. He set a quick pace and did not often look back. A man used to walking alone, Galen guessed.

A handsome man with a hurt looking to be soothed. *Paladin catnip,* his friend Clara would say, laughing. *No, no. You're in no shape to go around fixing anybody's hurts.* The world was full of misery and you had to learn eventually that it wasn't your job to fix all of it. Even when it came in attractively built packages.

They reached the river. Galen took the lead, threading around the piles of fishing nets and jumbled debris on the shore. The Elkinslough flooded now and again, and when it receded, it left all manner of things behind. The mudlarks picked through it for anything valuable, but there was plenty that not even the poorest souls would want. And there, at the end, a small, striped figure with a corpse at his feet.

Earstripe looked up as they approached and put his whiskers forward with clear relief. "A bone-doctor has come," he said. "A gnole is grateful."

"Don't thank me yet," said Piper, kneeling down. "But let's see what we can see."

CHAPTER 5

Piper crouched down over the body. Cause of death was easy to determine. The man was missing most of his pants and all of his left leg. The right leg had a deep diagonal slash across it, bloodless now, at the same height. *Something sliced through here, but he must have had one leg in front of the other.* The fish had eaten away at the stump, so Piper couldn't tell yet how clean the cut had been. They'd gotten the man's genitals as well. *Lovely. Just the thing you want to look at with a hangover.* He wasn't squeamish, of course, but there were proper frames of mind for everything.

He sighed and looked upriver. They were near the edge of the city here, and only a few docks and built-up pilings stood between their position and the land beyond. He watched a mudstilt pick its way along the water's edge, one of the few birds that didn't seem to mind the polluted water. It poked its beak between the stones, walked a few feet, poked again, looking for food. Its belly was bright white and looked absurdly clean compared to its surroundings.

Focus, Piper. They didn't bring you here as a birdwatcher. He dropped his eyes back to the body.

"Same as the others?" asked Earstripe. "Yes?"

"It could be," said Piper. "This one's been in the water about the same amount of time as the others, I think."

"Same kind of death," said Galen.

"The other one was impaled."

"It's still something big hitting him. Only this one was sharp."

"Mmm." Piper was glad he was wearing gloves. He pried apart the lips of the wound on the right leg and examined the bone. There was a notch out of it and some minor splintering. "Yes. Whatever hit him was sharp enough to cut bone, and had a lot of weight behind it."

Galen and the gnole exchanged glances. "A gnole thinks there aren't many things like that."

"Axes," said Galen. "But who can swing an axe and take out a leg and most of the next one like this? And not get hung up on bone?"

"Not a who, tomato-man. A what."

This would have been a very dramatic statement, but Piper was only interested in one part. "Pardon. Tomato-man?"

Galen groaned. "It's the hair," he muttered. "A gnole named me that last year and I hoped maybe he hadn't told anyone, but..."

"A job-gnole told *everyone,*" said Earstripe. Galen ran his hand through his hair which...well, yes, Piper could see the analogy.

"More the color of smoked paprika," he said absently. "But I can see how that doesn't roll off the tongue as well." *And now Galen knows that I've been thinking about his hair. Ah, yes. What a wonderful morning I'm having.*

"Bone-doctor understands," said Earstripe, arching his whiskers forward.

"He gets to be bone-doctor, but I have to be tomato-man?"

"Tomato-man is a job-human," said Earstripe. "Bone-doctor is our priest-human."

"I'm not a priest," said Piper, bemused.

Earstripe flicked his ears. "No, a *priest.*" Piper looked at Galen for explanation.

"Priests and healers are the same caste among gnoles," said Galen. "Also, you're..." He turned to Earstripe and held up his hands over his ears, cupping them forward in imitation of Earstripe. "He? His?"

"Close enough. Humans don't have whiskers." Earstripe's voice dropped on the last word, as if he were bringing up a terrible deformity. "A gnole won't take offense if bone-doctor doesn't."

Piper was completely at sea by this point. "What do whiskers have to do with anything?"

"If you're a gnole, your caste determines whether you're called he, she, it..." Galen spread his hands. "All job-gnoles are *he.* Healers and priests and others who are particularly respected in gnole-society use a word that translates as *our* or *ours.*"

"Ours belongs to all gnoles," interjected Earstripe.

"As a priest-caste human, you're somewhere between a *he* and an *our,* but since you really need whiskers and mobile ears to say that properly in gnolespeech, gnoles generally allow us to use whichever."

"Humans are doing the best they can," said Earstripe, in a tone Piper usually identified with teachers of small children trying to excuse the slowest members of the class. Galen chuckled.

"I'm flattered," said Piper, returning his attention to the corpse. "And in answer to your question, Earstripe, I think that, yes, you could make a good case that this one is tied to the others."

Earstripe nodded, all humor gone. "A gnole thought as much."

"But where are they coming from?" asked Galen, digging his fingers into his hair. "Upstream, but *where?* We've got two fishing settlements upriver, and then it's just rich people's chateaus, but they're empty this time of year. The nobs are all in town for the social season."

"Presumably even the chateaus have staff to keep the rats from getting in," said Piper absently. He gazed into the missing eye sockets. *You know you should do it. There might be something you can use. The last one could have been an accident, but not this one. You have to do it.*

He grimaced and pulled off one of his gloves, holding the wound open with the other hand.

"A bone-doctor thinks something might be in there?"

No, but it's a good explanation. "Worth checking." Piper made sure his knees were firmly planted. You really didn't want to pitch face down over a body. He touched the wound.

Corridor lit by candlelight. Long with pale walls. Something etched on the walls, lines, a shape...He stepped forward. A snick *and then a* woosh *of air and then something struck him hard in the thigh and the world spun around him and his shoulder hit the wall and he was on the floor and his heart was thundering but something was wrong and there was another woosh overhead and another but he couldn't hear it because his heart was beating so loud and...*

Piper withdrew his hand and took a deep breath. A pale corridor lit by candlelight. It didn't look like anything he'd expect to see in a fishing village. How to express that without revealing what he'd done?

"I can't say exactly what caused this, but I do know it's harder to commit murders like this in a small village crowded together on the water than it would be in a chateau where no one is staying for the season," he said. "Poison, strangling, even a stabbing I could see in close quarters, but this is big dramatic stuff with severed limbs."

Galen and Earstripe both nodded. "A gnole has seen things done in tight spaces," said Earstripe, "but a gnole still agrees."

"The city guard's got no authority over the chateaus," said Galen. "If there's a crime out there, it gets reported back here and the paladins or the Archon's people deal with it."

Earstripe grabbed his own whiskers and twisted them savagely. It looked painful. Galen actually reached out a hand as if to stop the gnole, but didn't.

"A gnole goes," muttered Earstripe. "A gnole stays. A gnole tells Mallory-captain. A gnole doesn't." He gave his whiskers another twist.

"You said Mallory wasn't listening," said Piper. He glanced around the riverside, suddenly realizing that there were no other members of the guard here, only Earstripe. Had the gnole not informed his superiors about the body yet?

More twisting. A spate of frustrated gnolespeech.

"Hey," said Galen. This time he did touch Earstripe, though gently, on the back of the hand. "Don't hurt yourself. I'll help you."

Earstripe dropped his grip on his whiskers. "Vig-il-an-ti-ism, tomato-man," he said, enunciating each syllable as if it were a phrase rather than a word. "A gnole leaves the city, a gnole can't arrest anyone."

"No, but I can," said Galen. "And what Mallory doesn't know won't hurt him." He paused. "You won't get credit for the arrest if we keep your name out of it, though."

The gnole shook his head. "A gnole won't get credit anyway. If a human and a gnole are in the same room, a human did the thinking." He curled back his lip. "A gnole is only a slewhound who talks."

Piper actually felt Galen bristle beside him. *I'm surprised his armor didn't rattle.* "Did someone say that to you?" asked the paladin softly. "Give me a name, and they won't say it again."

Earstripe opened his mouth, and then his eyes focused on something behind Piper and he straightened up. Piper had only that much warning before he heard a booming voice shout, *"Constable Earstripe!* What are you doing?"

"Captain Mallory," said Galen. "How nice to see you."

"Paladin Galen. And...Doctor Piper." The captain's eyes narrowed. "Has Earstripe dragged you back down here in pursuit of his ridiculous theory? I told you, Constable, that the lich-doctors are far too busy to waste their time like this."

Piper wiped his hands off and slid on his gloves. He took his time adjusting them before rising to his feet. "On the contrary, Captain," he said, with no idea how to end the sentence, but hoping that inspiration would strike before he got there. "On the contrary. I had requested that the constable inform me of any bodies that had..." *Okay, now is the moment of truth, what's your idea?* He looked down at the corpse, eyes traveling over the puffy skin and the ruin where the fish had gotten the man's genitals. Inspiration, fired by the grisly sight, did not fail. "... been in the water for a lengthy period of time. I am working on a monograph." He met Mallory's eyes squarely.

"...a monograph," said Mallory, eyes flicking from Piper to the gnole and back. Not calling him a liar. Yet.

"Indeed," said Piper. "Most doctors can venture a guess as to how long someone has been dead based on rigor, but after any length of time has passed, it becomes more difficult. Weather, insects, tightness of clothing—everything can change the appearance. We make an educated guess. There are many monographs on the subject, which are helpful, but to date, all of those deal with bodies left on land. We have, at present, no way of telling how long a body has been submerged, beyond our own experience. It is my hope that with enough examples, I will be able to chart the stages of a body's submersion and assist others who may have less experience with drowning victims."

He looked in Mallory's eyes while he said it. *You may be a guard and you may think that gives you some magic insight into human nature, but I have been lying for many years and you do not dare call me out for fear of angering my champions. Like Beartongue. And I outrank you, so far as the courts are concerned, if not the guard themselves.*

Mallory looked back to Earstripe, who shrugged.

"And the paladin is here because...?"

Galen coughed. "My dear captain, perhaps you do not need to know why the good doctor and I happened to already be together at this hour of the morning?"

Captain Mallory did not fluster easily. Piper, however, did. *Oh for the love of...why did he say that? I mean, it's a great cover, but now he'll think...he's supposed to think...* He could feel a flush climbing his face, which probably made the lie more convincing, but *still.*

"I...see," said Mallory.

Galen draped his arm over Piper's shoulders. Piper could feel the weight of muscle and mail across his neck. He could not look at Galen. He couldn't. He wouldn't. His blush was completely out of control.

It wasn't that he cared if Mallory knew that he preferred men. It wasn't exactly a secret, and very few people in Archenhold were going to care anyway. Several past Archons had taken male consorts and at least one had married his husband, and since the populace had much bigger concerns—like the expansionist tendencies of the city-state across the river—it had quickly become a non-issue.

It was just that it had been *so* long and Galen was *so* good-looking and...well...

"I was not informed of this," said Mallory.

"I didn't think it was any of your business," said Galen brightly.

"I *meant,*" said the captain, with icy clarity, "that Earstripe was to be procuring bodies for the doctor."

"A gnole isn't procuring," said Earstripe, speaking up. "A doctor wanted to look, that's all. A gnole sent a runner to the guardhouse first, and stayed with the body."

"Still. I was not informed."

"Honestly," said Piper, and had to clear his throat, because Galen was very close and his arm was warm against the cold air of the river and when he breathed, Piper could feel the other man's mailed ribcage against his side, "honestly it didn't occur to me that you'd care."

And you wouldn't care, if you weren't looking for some reason to be mad at Earstripe. Do you not like that he's investigating this on his own, or that he's a gnole? Do you not like that the White Rat is involved?

It might be that latter. The White Rat's tame paladins were helpful, sometimes. One had been instrumental in cracking the problem of the smooth men. But they also had served the god known as the Saint of Steel, and when their god had died, they had run mad. Even now, people treated them as not-quite-tame beasts who might suddenly turn and bite. The fact that no one knew why the god had died didn't help.

Mind you, if you could bring me a body, I could probably find out what His last sensations were...

Piper had never said as much. He might spend more time with the dead than with the living, but he wasn't completely lost to all tact. Also, did gods even have bodies?

Mallory grunted, and it occurred to Piper that the issue might be much less complicated. The Rat's social workers certainly did a great deal of good for the people that the guard was supposed to be protecting. But one of the Rat's chief duties was providing legal counsel, and guards did not much care for that at all. Depending on which way the wind was currently blowing, the guard captain might simply be annoyed at the Rat and anyone associated with it, including Piper.

"If you're quite finished..." said Mallory, apparently deciding to move things along.

"I'm not, actually. Pala—Galen, can you turn the body over for me?"

"Of course, love." Galen released him and bent to roll the corpse over. Piper know that the *love* was purely to make the act look better, but he felt the blush reach his ears anyway. He would never call anyone *love* in public. It wasn't his nature. *Also, this is fake. Also, he's really goddamn good-looking.*

That hair. Really deep red, not the ferocious carrot color most people got stuck with. And his eyes were probably actually hazel but that much red really drew out the green in them. And he had freckles—was there a redhead alive without freckles?—but only a few dusted across his skin and that was deeply unfair, given what your average redhead had to deal with. Were there other freckles elsewhere on his skin? Where? How far down did they go?

Piper stared at the body on the ground and thought fixedly about fish eating someone's genitals.

The corpse didn't look much better from the back, but then, they never did. Piper took more notes than he would ever use, even if he *were* writing a monograph, just to see if he could outlast Mallory. Earstripe stood in solemn silence. So did Galen.

Eventually, he had to admit that Captain Mallory was willing to wait quite a long time to give Earstripe a dressing down. He put his notebook away and nodded to the gnole.

"Thank you so much for informing me. This will be very valuable."

Earstripe nodded. Piper turned to Galen. *Say something convincing.* "I appreciate you humoring me. Would you like to walk me back home, then?"

"Naturally," said Galen. "We can get that breakfast you promised me." He winked. They strolled arm in arm away from the river, and made it nearly to the street before they heard Mallory's voice raised behind them.

CHAPTER 6

"Think Earstripe will be okay?" asked Piper, as they walked. They were still arm in arm, which Piper had apparently forgotten, even though Galen hadn't. There was more muscle lining the doctor's forearms than he would have expected. *Well, he's out there sawing through ribcages. That's got to take a certain amount of strength.*

"I hope so." Galen grimaced. "I know he was going behind Mallory's back, and no commander appreciates that."

"You think he believed us?"

"What, that we're screwing like crazed weasels?"

Piper blushed again. Galen didn't know whether to feel guilty or crow with triumph. *Stop. That's unkind. He might not even be interested in other men.* Galen would bet his eyeteeth that wasn't the case, but you did find some men who wouldn't admit to it, for whatever reason. *Really, though, how often do you find a grown man who blushes like a maiden? It's adorable.*

"I *meant,*" said Piper, withdrawing his arm from Galen's, "that Earstripe called us because I'm writing a monograph."

"Oh, he absolutely thinks we're lying, but there's just enough chance we're not, and he's a fair enough man, that

Earstripe will get out of the worst of it. He'll pretend he's coming down on Earstripe for not informing him that you wanted to see the bodies though."

"How is that fair?"

"For a policeman, that's about as good as it gets."

The doctor scowled. "I do not like policemen."

Galen raised an eyebrow. "I thought you worked with them a lot."

"How else would I know them well enough to dislike them?" Piper shook his head. "I prefer working with your people, honestly."

"Paladins?"

"The White Rat. Although I suppose paladins, too. At least you've got a god in your head who will stop you if you decide to rough people up."

Galen said nothing. He had not had a god like that since the summer solstice five years ago, when the Saint of Steel had died. It seemed like a good time to change the subject. "*Would* you like to get breakfast?"

Piper gave him a quick, startled look. Galen spread his hands and attempted to look charming and harmless, which was a bit of a struggle when you were carrying a sword longer than the other person's thigh.

"I feel like death warmed over," said the doctor, "and the thought of food is nauseating. That's probably a sign I should eat, or at least drink something non-alcoholic. What do you suggest?"

"I know just the place."

Galen started to lead the way, but Piper held up a hand. "Let me wash up first," he said. "I've had my hands in a corpse and that doesn't go well with toast."

They detoured to a public pump. There was a bucket of mostly clean sand there for scrubbing, but Piper ignored it, pulling out a brick of soap and washing up with that. Galen worked the pump handle a few times to give him water to work with. He turned his gloves inside out and used the sand on them, however, then tucked both damp gloves into his bag. "Right," he said, when he had finished this rather elaborate washing up. "That'll do."

"Mmm," said Galen. Saint's balls, the man's hands were also extremely pale. It was amazing he didn't have rickets. *He needs to spend more time outside, not in that basement.*

For all that, Piper looked to be in good shape. He was no soldier, but he had those lovely long-fingered hands and smoothly muscled forearms. Galen wondered how much muscle it took to sling bodies around. *Probably quite a lot. Every corpse I've ever dealt with has been a lot of dead weight, and he didn't seem to have an assistant helping him.*

"How do you get the bodies down to your workshop?" he asked abruptly.

If the change of topic surprised Piper, he didn't show it. "There's an old shaft that runs down under the wall from outside. Fairly steep, but you can get a wheeled cart down it. We bring the bodies in through there."

Galen did some mental calculations. "Odd place for a shaft."

"It really is. Supposedly it was the remains of a tunnel dug by sappers during some war a few hundred years ago, but let's say that I'm very, very skeptical."

They had reached the hole-in-the-wall public house that Galen had selected. He held the door open. "Oh?"

"It's much deeper than it needs to be to get under the wall, and everything's been smoothed. Now, I grant you, I'm working out of what was probably an old wine cellar, and you can make a case they were bringing barrels in, but that's not where the tunnel stops."

Galen paused. "It isn't?"

"Nope." Piper squinted at the menu on the wall. "What's good?"

"Toast, egg, and pork scrapings. And the tea is strong enough to kill an ox."

"Sounds dreadful. I'll take it, minus the pork scrapings."

"You sure? They're better than they sound."

"I don't think I can handle meat at this hour."

Galen placed the order and took two mugs of tea, then steered Piper to one of the tables. It was still early enough that most of the other customers were either late workers or carousers from the night before. "So where does the tunnel stop?"

Piper took a slug of tea and grimaced, then set the mug down. "An ivory door."

"A *what?*"

"You ever seen a wonder engine?"

"Those big statues they find that the ancients left behind? No, but I saw plenty of clocktaurs back in the day."

"Made of the same stuff. Looks like ivory, but much harder."

Galen grimaced. He'd been twenty when the clocktaurs came through, and fighting against Anuket City's monstrous mechanical legions had been his first taste of battle. Also his first taste of the battle tide. The Saint of Steel had taken him up barely a month after the war started. Then Archenhold had surrendered and he and the rest of the Saint's chosen had to choose between standing idly by and going to the Dowager's City, to the south, to hold the line against the clocktaurs.

And then it had ended as abruptly as it started. The clocktaurs went out of control and the demons bound inside turned on each other. He'd helped the Dreaming God's paladins mop up a few stragglers that survived, and they were still gigantic and made of strange bone gears, but if you hit them with hammers long enough, they went down.

You had to boil the pieces to stop the gears turning, though. It was nauseating.

The notion that there was a door made of that horrible ivory under the city was deeply unsettling. "And it's just down there? What's on the other side?"

"No idea. Can't get the door open. You know what that material is like." Piper drank his tea with the grim expression of a man taking medicine. "My predecessor said he'd tried everything, but it's more like a wonder engine than a clocktaur. You can't even dent the stuff. Fire is supposed to work, if you can get it hot enough, but that's not really feasible in a closed corridor."

Galen nodded. Clocktaurs would burn at about the temperature used to temper steel, but it was nearly impossible to get the fire hot enough on a battlefield. The Forge God's people had tried rigging something up with portable bellows, but the only way to make it work was to have one of the forge-priests practically standing on the clocktaur's head. They'd had better luck with the Forge God's rare paladins, who could swing a hammer long after even a berserker like Galen had to stop.

"Anyway," Piper was saying, "when the war started, the Archon had it bricked up in a couple of places, just in case there was something on the other side. Apparently there wasn't. Eventually they opened the far end again, because it bothered people to see the body wagons coming through the administrative areas." He stared into the dregs of the tea. "Or it bothered them to see the grave-gnoles, take your pick."

Galen gave a humorless huff of laughter. Grave-gnoles, the lowest caste of gnolekind, were swathed from head to toe in old burial shrouds, and tended to unsettle both humans and other gnoles. That didn't stop either species from employing them to dig graves and move the dead, of course.

"Have you seen the door?" asked Galen.

Piper didn't meet his eyes.

"You have, haven't you?"

Piper looked around guiltily. "Look, once I found out what was past the bricks, I had to at least look. And they didn't do a very good job with the mortar anyway. I left it better than I found it when I bricked it up again."

Galen leaned forward. "And?"

Piper sighed. "And it's a door, all right. Set flat into the wall. You can see the seams, but they're barely a hairsbreadth. You can't get a knife blade in. I broke two scalpels on it and stopped. They're too expensive to waste on a bit of idle curiosity."

"What do you think is behind it?"

"Water," said Piper unexpectedly. He looked up as a grim-faced servitor dropped two stacks of toast on the table, drowning in egg yolk and, in Galen's case, bits of blackened meat. "Ah, thank you."

"Water?" asked Galen, helping himself to toast.

"It's well below the level of the river. High water marks on the walls, and there's about six inches worth of standing water down there. I'm surprised the tunnel isn't filled, but I suspect that whatever structure is behind the door may be blocking off the worst of it." Piper shrugged.

"And nobody's broken it open looking for treasure," murmured Galen. "Surprising."

"I don't think the ancients actually left very many treasures." Piper gazed at the toast like a man approaching the gallows. "Sure, everybody with a blanket of junk will try and sell you one, but have you ever heard of a real one? Something that wasn't a wonder engine, or a bit of mysterious wall?"

"Once."

Piper looked up from his toast, startled.

"We escorted two dedicates of the Many-Armed God from

where they had been excavating back to their temple. What they found looked like a carved lizard with one white eye. About as long as your thumb. The mouth opened and if you pressed the eye, a little flame would come out." He spread his hands. "The dedicates were more excited about the scraps of fabric it was wrapped in than they were about the carving. One said that it was a finer weave than anything we could make. And I'll tell you one odd thing about it..."

It was Piper's turn to lean forward. Galen was pleased to see that he'd eaten most of a piece of toast, almost without noticing.

"Part of it was melted."

"Melted?"

"The fabric. One corner of it had been singed, and it didn't burn, it melted like wax."

"...Huh."

"I know, right? But I grant you, that's the only treasure I've ever seen that I believed was real. The people from the temple were thrilled by what looks like bits of trash from the same site. I could believe they'd pay money for them, but it's not the kind of thing someone trying to make a quick coin would recognize."

Piper nodded. "If there was any trash around the door, it's long gone, particularly given that the tunnel has been flooded before. I suspect it was more prone to that before the city got built up around it. There's a decent neighborhood by the entrance now, with actual storm drains. Figure that the door was underwater for most of its history, and once it dried out, the only people who knew or cared were my predecessor and the Archon's people. There's probably things like that all over the place. How long was Anuket City around before somebody dug up their damn wonder engine?"

"Fair enough." Galen took the last slice of toast and finished it off. Piper finally noticed that he'd been eating his and gazed at it with dismay.

"Glad you're feeling better," Galen said. "For a moment there, when you were feeling around in that wound, I thought you were going to faint."

Piper grunted, staring down at his toast. "Just a hangover," he said after a moment. "My head was pounding."

"Mmm." Galen nudged a fresh mug of tea toward him, and thought that the interesting thing about having watched Piper lie to Mallory was how easy it was to tell that he was lying now.

CHAPTER 7

It was only a day later that there was a knock. It came from low on the door, and Piper, who had been half-expecting it, knew to look down when he opened the door.

Earstripe looked tired. He was wearing many fewer rags than he had been before, and though he was still well covered, he looked smaller and more frail. "A gnole is not a guard-gnole any longer," he said, without preamble.

"I'm sorry," said Piper. *Oh damn, now what do I say? This is hard enough with a human.* He found himself wishing that Galen was here, someone who understood the gnoles a little better. He didn't want to say something so utterly wrong that he offended Earstripe or drove him away. He held the door open. "Would you like to come in?"

The gnole nodded. Piper ushered him in. "Do gnoles...ah... drink alcohol?"

"Only sweet."

"Damn." Piper had always preferred the smokier whiskeys himself. He tried to remember if there was something in the cupboard that might work, a mead or a fruit brandy or something. "I'm sorry, Earstripe, I don't think I have anything."

Earstripe waved a hand. "A gnole doesn't mind. A gnole didn't come for that, bone-doctor."

Piper sat down opposite him. "Go on."

Earstripe met Piper's eyes squarely. "I need your help," he said.

Piper blinked.

"Too many bodies. There are too many. I am going up the river to look. I know something is going on, no matter what Mallory-captain says."

Every word was carefully chosen, but Piper could hear desperation underlying them. The change in Earstripe's syntax startled him more than he cared to admit. *Did I somehow think he was unintelligent because of the way he sounded before? Even though I know better?*

Perhaps. But how worried is he now, that he dare not take any chances with a human misunderstanding him?

"Do you think you can find the killer?" he asked.

"A...I have to try."

"Going upriver could be dangerous," Piper said.

"Yes." Earstripe lifted his hands as if to begin twisting his whiskers, then smoothed them down instead. "Tomato-man has offered to help," he added. "Galen-Paladin. The Rat-priests, they will listen to a paladin. They listen to you too, yes? Bone-doctor?"

"Sometimes," said Piper. He knew where this was going now. *Yes, of course. He's going to ask me to come with them. And he thinks he has one shot at this, so he is using the most formal human language he can, and staring me in the eye even though I can tell he doesn't like doing it.*

His first instinct was to refuse. He worked in a little stone room underground, not on far-flung trips into danger. *I am not equipped for this. I cannot fight and my conversational skills are limited to things like, "Did you know that blowfly eggs only take a day to hatch into maggots?" I am no good for this sort of thing.*

Galen was going. Galen with his easy smile and some kind of secret in his eyes. Piper had laid awake thinking of those eyes and the arm Galen had laid across his shoulders, the strength of muscle and sinew and safety.

Galen is going. And Earstripe needs your help.

He took a deep breath. Perhaps it was inevitable. Perhaps it had been since the first morning on the riverbank, looking at a body with a gaping wound in its chest. "You need me to come with you," he said.

"You would help a gnole, bone-doctor. You would help the dead."

"There's no helping the dead," said Piper wearily, "but I'll come anyway. Just in case we can help a few more of the living."

It was barely dawn when they left the city. Piper couldn't shake the feeling that there was something clandestine about their trip. *We're not doing anything illegal. We get to leave the city. I arranged for a replacement for a bit, I'm not leaving my job. And Earstripe left the guard, that doesn't make him a prisoner.*

Earstripe walked beside him. There was a new swatch of fabric draped across one shoulder. It was bright turquoise. Piper wondered if it meant anything. *Congratulations on leaving the guard? Shame on you for leaving the guard?*

Maybe it just meant that the gnole had gone shopping. Piper didn't pretend to understand the details of the dress code among the nobility, and those were other humans. Trying to comprehend gnole fashion was probably a lost cause. *For all I know, their eyes are as different as their noses, and there's markings that I can't even see.*

There was still a great deal of traffic at this hour of the day, but most of it was flowing into the city of Archon's Glory, not out. Wagons passed them, probably full of eggs and milk to feed the city's appetites. Piper picked out women carrying baskets of vegetables and cages of live chickens. A fisherman went by with a string of eels on a pole over his shoulder. Hardly anyone was going the other way.

They passed human guards stationed at the gate, who eyed the trio expressionlessly.

Do they recognize Earstripe? Do they know that he's going to investigate something outside the city? Will they try to stop him?

No. No, it's not illegal. And I'm hardly a prisoner in Archon's Glory. Paladins are allowed to investigate things, and we have a paladin with us.

He glanced over his shoulder at the paladin in question. Galen walked a little behind them and to the left, one hand on his sword hilt. He did not look at the guards, but his eyes were always moving, scanning from one person to the next, obviously looking for threats.

Does he think someone's going to attack us? Would the guard retaliate against Earstripe? Wasn't sacking him enough?

"Are you expecting trouble?" he asked quietly, when they were out of earshot of the gate.

"I'm always expecting trouble," said Galen easily. "But no, not really. Should I be?"

"I don't know. The way you were looking, I wondered."

"I don't think the real trouble will start for a while yet."

"A gnole thinks a gnole has had plenty of trouble already."

"Sorry, Earstripe."

"Eh. Humans can't smell."

No trouble found them. They left the city behind, and then the little village of merchants and stables outside the city, and then the outlying farms. It was cold and the road was still dusty. Eventually, Galen reached into his pack and took out a drop spindle and began spinning handfuls of wool into thread while he walked, a surprisingly domestic activity for a paladin.

Piper switched his pack to the other shoulder and wondered if they were simply going to walk all the way to the various manor houses, and what they would do when they got there.

"Sorry," he said, when he had to call a rest for the third time. "I'm not used to forced marches." He gave a weak smile and tried not to think about how Galen must despise him for being a soft city-dweller. *Of course, he lives in the city too, it's just that I don't spend hours a day marching around and smacking things with swords. And to think, I believed I was actually fit before this...*

"Don't worry," said Galen, sounding much too cheerful for the early hour and the brisk pace. "We've got a ride waiting at an inn a few miles ahead."

"A ride?"

Galen grinned. "An old friend of mine. You'll like him."

They reached the inn at midday. Galen was glad to arrive. He could tell that Piper was not enjoying the walk. *Which is down to equipment as much as anything else. He hasn't had to optimize the straps on his pack so they're absolutely comfortable after the third mile, and his shoes are probably fine for standing for hours, but not so good for walking on uneven road.*

He didn't say anything, because the doctor was clearly embarrassed by his inability to match the pace of the other two, and Galen suspected it would come out condescending. Fortunately, he'd already arranged for a solution before he was even aware of the problem.

The gnole waiting outside the inn was older than Earstripe and the dark stripes on his face were mottled with brown and gray as well as black. "Brindle!" called Galen, waving.

"Tomato-man," said Brindle, lifting a hand. "You made it." He gave a drop-jawed gnole grin to Earstripe and said something in liquid gnolespeech. Earstripe replied and they both arched their whiskers forward.

"You two know each other?" asked Galen.

"A guard-gnole is family," said Brindle proudly.

Earstripe sagged and muttered something. Brindle asked a sharp question and his ears went back. Galen and Piper exchanged worried looks. Earstripe scuffed the ground with his foot.

Brindle straightened. "A *gnole* is family," he said, then leaned over and licked Earstripe between the eyes. He turned to Galen. "Brought a wagon," he said. "And an *ox*."

"Not a mule?" Galen had travelled for weeks with Brindle the prior autumn, during which the gnole had been saddled with a wagon drawn by mules. Brindle had very strong opinions about mules and their inferiority to the noble ox.

"Tomato-man thinks he is amusing." Brindle rolled his eyes and turned to Piper. "A human has a name?"

"A human is a bone-doctor," said Earstripe, before Piper could reply.

"Oho!" Brindle flicked his ears and studied Piper with great interest. "A human is ours, then?"

"Err..." Piper tried to remember how the complicated gnole pronouns worked.

Galen looked amused. To Brindle, he said, "Doctor Piper is *he*, among humans. Because we can't smell."

Brindle looked skeptical. Earstripe explained something, involving many hand gestures and ear positions. Brindle finally nodded and said to Piper, "A gnole will call a bone-doctor what he wishes, but a bone-doctor has a gnole's respect."

That seemed to settle that, so far as everyone was concerned. Piper wondered if there was a book available on gnole language for humans and made a note to pursue the matter when he returned to the city.

Assuming we ever return, and aren't killed by some murderer out in the wilderness who is impaling people or chopping their legs off.

"Is this the same ox you rescued in Morstone?" asked Galen.

"An ox is, yes." Brindle patted the animal's flank with pride. "An ox is called *Wise-nose.*" He scrambled up onto the wagon seat and tapped the animal's flank with his stick, and they were off.

The ox's top speed was approximately three miles an hour, which suited Piper fine. He no longer felt as if he was slowing the party down. The two humans walked alongside or sat in the back of the wagon. Earstripe sat up front, next to Brindle, the two of them with their heads close together, chatting.

"Do you think Earstripe is all right?" asked Piper softly. "He and Brindle, I mean? It seems like being a guard-gnole was important."

"I don't know. Though I do know Brindle, and once he said, 'A gnole is family,' as far as he was concerned, that *ended* the matter. Earstripe may feel a bit differently about it, though."

"I wish we could help," said Piper. "But we know so little about them, and I feel like we could easily make it worse." He thought back again to Earstripe's sudden switch in language when he'd asked Piper for help, and how startling it had been. "Or at least leave him having to reassure the dimwitted humans, and I can't imagine he needs that right now."

Galen chuckled. "Spoken like a man who's been there himself."

"I think every doctor has been at some point. You give someone bad news and then the person with them panics, and the patient winds up having to reassure the person who isn't even sick. It's part of the reason I prefer working with the dead."

"Ah..." Galen nodded. "You worked with live ones first, then?"

"I did. But I'm a great deal better with the dead." That was as much as Piper wished to say about the matter. His particular trick had given him a great advantage when identifying cause of death. At first he had hated it and tried to avoid using it. Later, he had simply been grateful for that advantage. Anything to stop working with the living. *They feel too many things and they want you to feel them, too. And half the time you cannot save them, no matter what you do, but you cannot tell them that.*

And they act as if you are a fool or a god, and honestly, sometimes you feel like both.

It had all been too much. Too many feelings. Too many emotions. He had fought for a post where there were only the dead, who felt nothing any longer, and he had won it, and everything had gotten so much easier.

"Even the ones who die by violence?" asked Galen, looking at him with those flawed jade eyes.

"Even then. Sometimes I can help get a little justice. And even if I can't, they're not suffering any longer."

CHAPTER 8

The wagon was large and mostly empty, despite several crates that Piper guessed were full of food for the ox. Plenty of room to stretch out. The Temple had included a pair of thick bedrolls. Piper had somehow assumed they'd be staying at inns and hadn't thought to pack any, so when evening came, he was grateful for the foresight. He took the small lamp from his pack and lit it.

"Ah!" said Galen, stepping up onto the back of the wagon. "You brought a lamp?"

Piper nodded, setting it in place atop a crate of provisions. "In my line of work, you always need light, and there's hardly ever enough."

"Ingenious design." Galen moved past him, bent over to clear the ceiling, and inspected it. A short little chimney, a glass hood, and an extremely wide base to keep it from tipping over.

"They use them on ships," said Piper, "for reading charts below decks." He unrolled his bedroll on one side of the wagon, leaving plenty of room for Galen on the other. *And I suppose that means we'll be sleeping together. In a sense.*

A purely platonic sense.

Yes. Purely platonic, of course.

He sat down cross-legged on his bedroll and wondered if he should start undressing or if there was something else you did when camping out on the road. He settled for pulling his boots off.

"I was surprised you came along on this trip," said Galen, startling him.

Piper looked up. "Why, because I'm a city boy?"

Looking up was a mistake. The lamplight woke fiery highlights in Galen's hair and fell kindly across the sharp planes of his face, softening the lines of worry. There was a sharp dip in the center of his upper lip, and Piper had a mad urge to run his finger across it.

To distract himself, he said, "I may not be used to staying on the road instead of at inns, but I learn quickly. Just tell me if I'm about to walk off a cliff or set myself on fire."

Galen shook his head. "It's not that," he said. "This could be dangerous. We may have a murderer, or more than one."

"As opposed to the city, which is notoriously free of murderers?"

The paladin gave a short huff of laughter. "All right, that's true enough."

Slightly offended that Galen thought so little of him, Piper began stripping off his gloves. "I may not be a warrior, or even a guard-gnole, but I'm not completely helpless. People have broken into the morgue before."

Galen was quiet for a little time, digesting that. Then: "Why would someone break into a morgue?"

"To hide a cause of death. Or in this case to steal the papers where I wrote it down." Piper shrugged. "They tend to back off when you wave a bonesaw at them." He kept his voice light and amused, even if the memory made his mouth go dry. The burglar had tried to hit him over the head and Piper knew intimately, even if most people didn't, just what damage a blow to the head could cause. He'd heard it in time to dodge sideways and then he'd picked up the bonesaw and started screaming and the burglar had panicked and bolted.

He folded his gloves on the crate beside the lamp, and loosened the ties of his shirt. Galen watched him in silence, and Piper had no idea what the man was thinking. He could feel a blush starting to rise. *Does he think I'm undressing for him? Did he think I was bragging about the burglar? Am I overthinking this?*

"Believe me," he said, talking to fill the awkward silence, "I'm not going to jump into any fights. You're the one with the sword. I'm perfectly happy to let you use it while I stand back and wring my hands and worry about infections."

Galen chuckled. "Don't worry. The Saint of Steel left us all very hard to kill. I'd much prefer to be the one in front with a sword."

"I'll keep that in mind." He pulled his shirt off over his head. *Not the pants. I guess I'll just sleep in my pants.*

"Anyway," said Galen, "sleep well. I'll see you in the morning." He picked up his bedroll and turned toward the back of the wagon.

"You're sleeping outside?" said Piper. "But I thought—I mean, there's plenty of room—"

Galen flashed him a quick smile, though it didn't reach his eyes. "I'll be fine. I'm used to it. Sleeping underneath the wagon keeps the frost off."

"But it's still cold..." Piper trailed off as Galen pushed the cloth flap aside, swung himself over the back of the wagon and was gone into the dark.

He stared at the flap for a moment, then quietly finished folding his shirt. Piper blew out the lamp and lay down on his blankets, trying not to feel as if he'd been rejected for something he hadn't even been offering.

. . .

Galen lay under the wagon and felt like a right bastard.

He'd seen the flash of hurt in Piper's eyes as he left. The poor man probably thought he'd driven Galen away somehow. Nothing was further from the truth.

Hell, when the doctor bit the index finger of his glove to pull it off, Galen had briefly lost the power of speech. The slide of leather over skin, barely audible, made him want to howl like a dog. It had taken an effort of will to focus on what Piper had been saying, about someone attacking him in the morgue, and then he *had* been able to focus because he needed to find out who these people were and hunt them down in the streets.

Then the man had started on the shirt, and Saint's black and bloody tongue, Galen wasn't made of stone. He'd seen Piper shirtless before, when he'd woken the man up, and the memory of dark hair and smooth muscle was still fresh, but it wasn't the same as actually watching him undress. There had been absolutely nothing intentionally seductive about those long fingers working the ties on his shirt, and Galen was still rock hard before he'd gotten the first knot untied.

But Galen couldn't stay. He couldn't sleep next to a stranger, not without explaining that if he started yelling in his sleep, under no circumstances was Piper to touch him, or even get too close. And that was a conversation that he just didn't want to have. Not right now. Maybe not ever. Prospective bedmates tended to get very alarmed when they learned that you were capable of horrific violence in your sleep.

Hi, you're very sexy, incidentally I'm a berserker and if you touch me during a nightmare I'll break your arm, wanna bone?

His lips twisted. No, that rarely went over well.

Besides, it might not happen. It's been over a month since the last nightmare. Brindle knew all about it and would handle matters if it happened, but if he didn't have to explain to Piper that he was, incidentally, sometimes a raving madman, so much the better.

The thing that no one warned you about insanity was how incredibly *tedious* it was. You were always having to explain yourself and apologize, over and over, and you got so tired of being crazy. And Galen, at least, was always crazy in the same way, so he was just repeating the same explanation over and over.

Not that I particularly want my madness to develop any exciting new manifestations, but Saint's teeth, it's tiresome.

He'd gotten better, anyway. Mostly better. Right after the god had died, waking him up during a nightmare would send him into a berserker fit. Fortunately, the Temple of the Rat had taken the liberty of strapping the broken paladins down until they woke from their comas, which had turned out to be providential. After that, Galen had taken to strapping himself down, but the healers got very upset by it and lectured him about nerve damage in his hands. But the nightmares had faded over time, and it went from every night to every few nights, to every few weeks. If someone woke him while he screamed, they'd still probably get a black eye, but the tide didn't rise and it stopped there. It was...manageable. When the Rat sent Istvhan out after the smooth men, Galen had gone with him and slept in a tent alone, and strangely, that had helped even more.

But he still didn't feel like explaining this to Piper. Not tonight. Not with the image of the doctor stripping off his gloves still fresh in his brain. *Whatever will happen with him will happen. But it would be unconscionable to put someone in danger just because I'd like to get in their pants.*

He was doing the right thing, and he knew it. He told himself this four or five times, while picturing those long fingers in vivid detail. Then he got up and took a walk because there was only so much that mortal flesh could bear.

They reached the fishing village the next afternoon. Piper could smell it long before he saw it, which squared with his limited experience with fishing villages. He thanked the White Rat that the cold air meant the smell carried slightly less than it would have in summer.

"So how does this work?" he asked, as the village came into view. They were about half a mile off the main road out of Archon's Glory, right up against the river. The river bent and split here, with a narrow channel that cut off part of the bend and left an island not much bigger than a city block behind. The fishing village was built on pilings that crossed the channel, two or three stories high in some places. "Do we just walk up and say, 'excuse me, have you fished any corpses up recently?'"

"We will attempt to be subtle," said Galen.

Piper raised an eyebrow. His experience with paladins was admittedly somewhat limited, but *subtle* was not the first phrase that came to mind.

"Gnoles will ask gnoles," said Earstripe. "Gnoles will tell gnoles what humans won't tell humans. If a killer is here, a gnole will warn other gnoles."

"Assuming the killer's a human," said Piper.

Both Brindle and Earstripe looked at him sharply. Then Earstripe gave a half-nod. "Yes. A gnole was assuming that." Brindle studied his claws.

"I mean no offense," said Piper hastily. "Just..."

"No," said Earstripe. "No, bone-doctor is correct. Could be. A gnole should not assume. "

Galen snapped his fingers. "Actually, yes. Bone-doctor *is*

correct." He flashed a grin at Piper, and despite his rejection the night before, Piper felt his stomach turn over. "We *are* going to go in and ask 'excuse me, have you fished up any corpses recently?' Or at least I am, and you are going to roll your eyes behind me and act as if this is all a colossal waste of your time, and I shall act like a public servant with just enough brains to fill a thimble, sent on a make-work job by his superiors."

"A paladin, lying? I am shocked, sir. *Shocked.*"

"Where's the lie?" Galen's grin broadened. "Earstripe is in charge of our little jaunt, and he's sent me on this mission to ask questions. I shall say exactly that, and what other humans assume is their problem, not mine."

"And the brains to fill a thimble?"

"Oh, that part's true enough. Paladins can't afford to be terribly bright, you know. Otherwise we'd start to think too much about what we were doing, and fret ourselves into apostasy."

Piper let that pass. "It could work. If the killer is here, and thinks we're unlikely to turn him up, he may be careless. And if there *are* corpses..."

"Then people understandably alarmed at having caught one will certainly be eager to tell us all about it," said Galen. "The public always feels better when they have someone to complain to." He nodded to Earstripe. "With your permission?"

Earstripe gave the paladin a thoughtful sniff, nostrils working. "A gnole permits," he said. "A gnole agrees."

"A gnole wonders what will turn up..." muttered Brindle, and turned the ox toward the village.

CHAPTER 9

Galen watched Piper and thought dark thoughts. Dark, mostly carnal thoughts.

The carnality wasn't the problem. Galen had taken plenty of lovers over the years and generally felt that sex was only as complicated as you chose to make it. He wanted to slide his hands over Piper's chest and follow that line of dark hair downward until he reached the promised land. He wanted to see what those long, clever fingers could do when they were wrapped around his cock. He wanted...well, he wanted a lot of things, and while it would have been a trifle awkward with the gnoles just outside, probably overhearing everything and rolling their eyes at each other about the silliness of human mating, Galen had worked with worse situations.

The problem was that he liked Piper a bit too much and he was starting to worry about him.

There wasn't anything outwardly wrong. The man made jokes and laughed and listened to the gnoles and asked intelligent questions. He let Galen and Earstripe take the lead in the investigations, and he'd played his role perfectly in the fishing village, wearing a much put-upon expression. "Corpses," Galen heard him say to an elderly matron, "are rather beyond my power to fix, despite what the gentleman here seems to think. But this salve you're making intrigues me..." And the matron, who was boiling up a concoction that stank like the inside of a flounder, grinned at him and invited him to sit down and before long they were deep into a technical discussion of the various uses for fish oil.

By the time they left the village, Piper probably knew more about how to use fish oil for medicinal purposes than the fish did. When they were ready to leave the next morning, though, the doctor had vanished.

Galen finally tracked him down in a small, shabby room, writing furiously, with an overturned crate as a desk. There were two women in the room with him, one older, one young with her face turned away in clear embarrassment.

"Right," said the doctor, as the paladin filled the doorway. He blew on the ink to dry it. "You take this to Doctor Lizbet on Pope Street. Can you remember that?"

The older woman repeated it back to him. "She can help, you say?"

"If anyone can."

The young woman swallowed hard. "We don't got the money," she whispered.

"It won't cost you anything," said Piper. "You give her this note. And if you can't afford an inn, go to the Temple of the White Rat and tell them Piper sent you. They'll put you up for a few days in the petitioners' lodging."

The older woman looked up at him with too-bright eyes. "The gods take care of you, son."

The corner of Piper's lip twisted up. "I hope so," he said, "but until then, we've got to take care of each other."

"What was that all about?" asked Galen in an undertone, as they met up with Earstripe and left the village.

"A damned mess. After childbirth, some women suffer a tear or a hole down there and it's in the worst possible place to heal cleanly. Turns into a fistula. It's...not good."

"Not something you can treat, I take it."

Piper snorted. "If I had enough poppy milk to put her in a stupor, and some specialized equipment so that I could see what the hell I was doing, and about three more sets of hands... and even then, Lizbet would do it better. A lot better. I've done it once, and that was on a corpse."

Galen had no idea how to respond to that. "Will she be all right?"

"I don't know," said Piper honestly. "Even with the best care in the world, it's barely an even chance. Maybe not even that. But she's willing to try, because the alternative is worse."

"Worse?"

"A lot of smell, a lot of discharge, a lot of pain, a lot of mess. Forever. No more children, if she wants more. Probably no more husband, whether she wants him or not." Piper lifted his hands, let them fall again.

"Poor girl."

"Indeed." He sounded exasperated. "If they'd just get better care immediately afterward...but no, everybody gets it in their head that childbirth is natural and any fool could do it. Cows give birth, so why not people? And so I see more new mothers on the slab, or old women who have been living with something like this for years..." He shook his head, lip curling. "Sorry, I'll stop. Nobody wants to hear me ranting about this, least of all me."

And that was the bit that troubled Galen. Piper clearly felt passionately about this, but he seemed annoyed by his own passion. As if his own emotions were an imposition. *On the other hand, he's probably right that most people aren't quite pleased to hear sudden diatribes about fistulas. Still.*

"The Rat's healers can't treat things like that?" he asked, hoping to draw the doctor out a little.

"The Rat's healers are stretched thin." Piper frowned. "Not as thin as they are in other places, perhaps, but for extremely specialized surgeries, it's still hard."

"And this doctor can treat her for free?" Galen had a suspicion, but couldn't resist confirming.

"Not exactly, but she owes me a favor." Piper gave him a sidelong look, as if not certain how he'd react. "That is..."

"You might as well tell me," said Galen. "I've probably heard worse."

"I found cadavers for her to practice her technique on."

Galen frowned. "You can't possibly be a resurrectionist. Beartongue would have your balls." While the White Rat was occasionally remarkably flexible, not many priests approved of the illicit trade in grave-robbing to provide doctors with cadavers.

"I most certainly am *not,*" said Piper. "But if I got someone in on the slab who had a fistula...well, I sent a discreet word round to Lizbet. The family got the body back, with no visible changes and she got the practice in. *Did* get the practice in, anyway. It only took a few. And because of that, there's a lot of women she can help."

"That seems fair," said Galen. "It's not as if you're selling organs to black-market charm-makers."

"Yes, well. It's *not* ethical, and I know it, and god help me, it genuinely is a slippery slope. Start thinking you have the right to do things to people's bodies in a good cause, and you're halfway to hell and picking up speed. But I also don't know what I could have done any differently." He hunched his shoulders. "I've asked the Bishop about how we could do it, if we could offer financial compensation in return, but that ends up with poor families selling their loved one's cadavers or even more people stealing them for money, and it's just...really not a good idea."

Earstripe, who had listened to this in silence, shook his head. "A gnole thinks humans worry too much about dead humans, not enough about live ones."

"You're not wrong there," said Piper. "One more thing we're peculiar about. Any luck with tracking down our particular dead humans?"

The gnole shook his head. "No bodies. No humans acting strange." He paused, then added, "No more than usual, for humans." Brindle snorted.

"Well, it's only the first stop," said Galen. "And murders like this seem like they'd be done in isolation."

"Most of the fisherfolk wear heavy boots everywhere," said Piper. "No leather soles." The definition of *inside* and *outside* had been rather fluid as well, and by Piper's standards, damned cold.

Earstripe nodded to him. "A gnole noticed that, too."

"So we're agreed the bodies probably aren't coming from there, then?"

Nods all around. Brindle had an ear cocked toward them, but didn't comment.

"The chateaus were probably always more likely," offered Galen. "The sort of place where you swap out shoes to save the carpets."

Earstripe twisted his whiskers until Brindle made a chuffing sound at him and he stopped. "A gnole is thinking chateaus will be harder," he said. "A human walks up and asks a butler-human about dead bodies, butler-human gets very..." He paused, clearly searching for an appropriate word. "Mallory-captain says *shirty*."

This had already occurred to Galen and he wasn't sure what to do about it. "I suppose we go up and...hmm...could we tell them that there's been some suspicious activity reported in the area and ask if they've seen anything out of the ordinary? Give them an opening to mention bodies if they want to?"

"If you phrase it in a lot of civic duty and we're-just-checking-up-on-people," said Piper, "I suppose it might work?"

"If we could get in and talk to the servants," said Galen, "we might get somewhere. Or at least see if anything sets off warning bells. But that's going to depend entirely on who answers the door."

"Fancy houses don't hire gnoles," said Brindle. It didn't sound like he considered this a burning injustice so much as a matter of poor taste. "Can't go asking gnoles. Could maybe visit a stable, follow nose, but don't know if it'll help."

CHAPTER 10

It could have gone better. The first house had a butler who said, in icy tones, that there had been no suspicious activity of any kind, unless one counted disreputable sorts coming to the door. His expression left little doubt as to exactly who he was referring to. The second house was staffed by a caretaker who seemed to think that Galen was trying to run a protection racket, and was demanding money to keep the suspicious activity from happening to him. The third house had no one home at all, so far as they could see.

They caught a lucky break with the fourth house. The caretaker was garrulous and extremely bored. "Ah, well, it's a skeleton crew on now," he said. "Come in, come in! Have a bite to eat. Tell me all the news from the city." He made a sweeping gesture that included both humans and gnoles, although Brindle opted to stay with the ox.

Unfortunately, while he pulled out a selection of cold food in the kitchen and called in the two gardeners who were out working on the grounds, he didn't actually know anything useful. Galen didn't get any sense that he was hiding any information. The most that he could offer was that occasionally a cow got loose from the fields and turned up in the gardens, and that the baker's boy kept obstinately making full deliveries, even when they'd told him to stop. "Said I wasn't paying for a whole house worth of bread," he said, gesticulating with the end of a loaf, "but I don't like to short change him, because the lord's cook doesn't do plain baking. Flatly refuses. Take a few loaves with you, will you? Otherwise it'll go to waste. Even the chickens are getting sick of it."

"Well, I can't say that was useful, but it was certainly profitable," said Piper, setting a sack full of round loaves into the wagon. "If we're lucky, maybe the next house will have a feud with the cheesemaker."

The next fine house was abandoned. So was the one after that. "I didn't realize so many of these places were in such poor condition," murmured Piper.

"Big house is expensive," was Brindle's opinion. "Maybe too expensive."

Galen nodded. "And if they're entailed to a title you might not be able to sell them, even if you can't keep them up."

The one after that didn't look promising either. The roof had a precarious slant and several of the windows had boards over them. Piper had already mentally dismissed the place when Earstripe called a halt. "Smoke from a chimney," he said, pointing.

"So it is." They left Brindle and the ox at the road, and hiked up the long drive to the chateau. It was even less promising up close, although someone had made an effort to keep the weeds clear of the front entrance.

Galen knocked loudly, waited for a few moments, then knocked again. He had just lifted his fist for the third time when the door was yanked open and a man blinked at them in surprise.

"Are you the clerk?" he asked. His gaze swept down, taking

in the sword and the surcoat over the armor. Then he spotted Piper behind Galen's shoulder. "Are *you* the clerk? I didn't think the roads had gotten that bad, that you'd need to hire a guard..." He trailed off in the face of the men's incomprehension. "Err...are you here about the ad?"

"No," said Galen. "We're in the area investigating some suspicious activity and wanted to ask if you'd seen anything."

"Suspicious?" He blinked again. He had a certain owlish quality, Piper thought, rather short and sturdy, with large, watery eyes. "Good heavens! Come in, come in." He stepped back into the hall. "I'm sorry, I'm Thomas. I mean, I'm not sorry that I'm Thomas, I'm sorry that I thought you were here because I'd placed an ad for a clerk."

"You needed someone to manage the estate?" asked Piper politely. Privately he thought that the man was rather more in need of a carpenter, or perhaps a fleet of them.

"Oh my, yes. It's this dreadful chateau, you understand." He waved in a gesture that encompassed the building, outside and in. "It's falling apart and it's simply full of all this horrid furniture that the last generation wasn't able to sell off, but now they're antiques so perhaps someone will want to buy them. But I haven't any idea what's here, so someone needs to document it all, and probably there's paperwork somewhere and then if I'm lucky, one of the dear departed family actually left some money or property that isn't falling down. But you can't get anyone to stay out here, of course, so I post the ads..."

They crowded into the hall. Thomas blinked at Earstripe, but didn't comment. Once inside, the decay was even more obvious. This had clearly been a very impressive building in the distant past, with wallpaper on the walls, but it had fallen down or been haphazardly ripped away in shreds.

Piper saw movement past Thomas's shoulder. A heavyset woman stood in the doorway behind him. She had a curiously blank face, but she met Piper's eyes and mouthed words. He missed part of the first word as Thomas moved, but the second one looked like "away."

Get away? Go away?

It seemed rather odd. His surprise must have shown on his face because Thomas turned, following his gaze, and said, "Missus Hardy? Is there a problem?"

"Wanted to see if your guests fancied tea," said Missus Hardy, in a flat, uninflected monotone.

"Tea would be lovely." Thomas beamed at the trio. "Please, come into the parlor. Err...forgive the state of the furniture. And the walls. Actually, forgive the state of the whole place. I inherited it from my grandfather, you see, and he hadn't done any upkeep at all, and now it's all falling apart. The floors are still sound enough, but you go into the east wing and you're taking your life in your hands."

Piper followed Galen into the parlor. The wallpaper was in slightly better shape here, but not by much, and the furniture had blankets thrown over it to hide the state of the upholstery. The two humans sat on a long sofa, with Earstripe sitting upright between them, his ears tense. He still hadn't spoken. Piper wondered what he was thinking.

"So you say there's suspicious goings-on?" asked Thomas, leaning forward. "What sort? It's not arson, is it?"

"No, not arson." Galen launched into his prepared speech. Thomas listened with apparent interest, making small noises of alarm.

"Well," he said finally, "that is all quite terrible. But I'm afraid I can't help you. I don't see anyone regularly except my housekeeper and the boy who delivers supplies. And clerks if I can get them." He sighed. "They never stay long, I'm afraid. I can't pay much and this isn't exactly a social whirl out here in the countryside."

Missus Hardy came in with a tray of tea and set it down. She moved with short, halting steps and her face never changed. She left again without asking if they needed anything else. The teacups were mismatched and there was a large chip out of the teapot that made Thomas's pouring rather haphazard.

"Why are you concerned about arson in particular?" asked Earstripe, in his most careful diction.

Thomas was so startled he nearly dropped the teapot. "I beg your pardon!" he gasped, mopping up the tea. "I didn't expect—that is—oh dear. I'm sorry! You startled me."

He didn't realize Earstripe could talk, thought Piper. *He has either been out here since before the gnoles arrived in Archenhold or came from somewhere else. I wonder which one it is, or if these people truly have so little contact with gnoles that they don't know anything about them.*

"Arson," repeated Earstripe, cutting through the man's babbled apologies.

"Oh. Yes. Well." Thomas gestured toward the house again. "It's a firetrap, obviously. Of course, the roof leaks, so we've plenty of buckets of water around in case that happens, but..." He trailed off, his eyes moving to Piper. "You said you were a doctor?"

"Of sorts, yes," said Piper, hoping that he wasn't going to have to advise the man about his piles or something equally messy.

The man's eyes lit up with sudden excitement and he bobbed his head, looking even more like an owl than usual. "An educated man, though? You know about the ancients, yes?"

"A little," said Piper, surprised at the conversational shift. "I've seen plenty of things that people claimed belonged to the ancients, and a few that actually did." *Galen said to try and get these people talking, so here goes...* "There's a door in a passageway in the city that I've inspected closely, but it's sealed tight. Made of the same material as a wonder engine, though."

"Yes. Yes! Let me show you!" Thomas jumped to his feet. "Follow me."

He led the trio to the kitchen, where Missus Hardy was bending over the hearth, to a set of stairs leading down. "This is so exciting! I never get to show anyone my discovery."

Piper and Galen traded looks. Earstripe looked at both of them and muttered something under his breath about humans.

The stairs led, not surprisingly, to a cellar. It was dark and the stones were slick with moisture, as one might expect this close to the river. Earstripe's nose worked furiously. Galen peered into the shadows, possibly looking for attackers.

Thomas picked up an oil lantern at the base of the stairs and fiddled with the knobs until it brightened. "Here, it's easier if one of you takes this..." Piper, fully aware that he was the least useful one in a fight, took the lamp. *I suppose if this strange man turns on us, I can at least throw burning oil on him...*

He had no idea what to think about Thomas. The man was clearly a bit peculiar, but there was a large distance between "peculiar" and "murdering people and dumping their bodies in the river." *And if you lived alone in a gigantic crumbling house with a grim housekeeper for company, you might get a bit peculiar too.*

Missus Hardy the housekeeper still troubled him. Who told guests to *go away*? Was she trying to warn them or scare them off?

Thomas finished adjusting a second lantern and strode off, head held high. "Ignore the mess," he said, over his shoulder. "There used to be a very nice wine cellar down here, but my grandfather's creditors ransacked the place about fifty years ago. I haven't had time to put it right."

"Well, it's only been fifty years..." murmured Galen.

They threaded around smashed shelves and jumbled furniture. The oil lamps illuminated dark openings in the stone walls but shed no light on the rooms beyond.

"Large down here," said Galen.

"Oh, yes." Thomas laughed, although it came out as more of a titter. "Yes, indeed."

Piper did not care for tittering. It was almost always a bad sign. If you got a murder victim on the slab and one of the family was a titterer, nine times out of ten, they were the ones who'd put the knife in. He'd told the Temple of the Rat that once, and Bishop Beartongue—who had only been a Deacon in those days—had rolled her eyes and said that he was not allowed to pre-judge people because he didn't like their laugh. *Though in fairness, she did apologize once we turned up his collection of teeth.*

Still. Presumably plenty of people also tittered in the absence of a dead body. Piper just wouldn't have run across them. *Your sample is skewed, that's all.*

"A gnole smells the river."

"Oh yes." Thomas waved toward one of the distant walls. "There's a water stair over there. Used by smugglers back in Grandfather's day. That's how he lost all his money, you understand. He was a very bad smuggler, I'm afraid. Paid a fortune for what was supposed to be brandy and then it turned out to be pickled eels. He sold the eels and made enough money to run away to Delta, but he never set foot in Archenhold again."

Dead bodies could have been dumped by the water stair. Of course, the manor's also right on the damn river, so it's not like access is a concern.

"Here we go," said Thomas. "Down the steps here. Watch your step, it gets very slick." He led the way down a set of roughly mortared brick steps. Piper, having had to learn to mortar a brick wall in recent memory, was pretty sure that the craftsmanship was the work of a fellow amateur. Rope threaded through two iron rings on the wall served as a crude railing.

The steps went down perhaps six feet, and then stopped. The floor was damp and layered with sacking and loose boards. The whole area smelled of algae and rot.

Thomas lifted his lamp and shined the light down the hallway. Galen stopped and Piper nearly ran into his back. The paladin let out a low whistle.

"*This* is what I've been studying," said their host proudly.

Piper had to crane his neck to see around Galen. It was a short hallway, perhaps ten feet long, though the ceiling was very high. But it was the door at the end of the hall that had captured everyone's attention. Earstripe's ears strained so far forward that it looked painful.

Piper recognized the door at once. He'd seen one like it before, on the other side of the brick wall in the tunnel that ran by his workroom.

Unlike that door, this one was open.

CHAPTER 11

"This is something made by the ancients," said Piper. "Like a wonder engine."

"Yes, exactly!" Thomas beamed at him. "You recognize it?"

"I saw a wonder engine once," said Piper. "The one in Moldoban." Galen noticed that he didn't volunteer anything more about the door in Archon's Glory.

"Oh, yes," said Thomas. "I haven't been there, but I've heard of it. This isn't a wonder engine though. It's a series of corridors." He waved toward the door. "The builders put a wine cellar right next to it two centuries ago. Another three feet to the left, and they'd have found it. Or rather, they'd have found a wall, and then you follow the wall down far enough and you reach the door. But here, here, come inside!"

The corridor beyond the door was about the same size as the one before, the floor made of something that looked like stone, the walls the same pale ivory as the door. On the left side stood another closed door, and at the far end, an open one.

There were also a half dozen perfectly normal barrels lined up along the wall.

"Lamp oil, water, and food," said Thomas. "In case the door were to close on me."

"Does it close?" asked Galen warily.

"Hasn't yet. But I prefer to be safe rather than sorry." Thomas tapped one of the barrels, which had a box of unlit tapers atop it. "Anyway, it's just easier having it here rather than having to go dig around in the cellar. If you'll leave your lantern here, though, Doctor? This next bit is really more impressive without too much light. Mister Earstripe, would you take a candle, though? I don't think I'll drop my lantern, but this isn't the sort of place that you want to be completely in the dark." Earstripe grunted, but lit the candle from the lantern. Piper set his lantern down on the ground.

"You see why I worry about arson," said Thomas. "If the house were to burn down on top of this..."

Piper and Galen both nodded. Fire was the only thing that seemed to destroy the ivory material, and only a strong, hot fire at that. A burning building might well do it. "Where does that door go?" asked Piper, nodding to the one set in the wall. The closed door looked almost exactly like the one he knew.

"I have no idea," admitted Thomas. "It doesn't open. I haven't figured out a way to get it open, short of trying to burn the whole place down. Maybe when I've explored all the rest of the tunnels, I'll come back to it, but there's so much to see and do already..." He ran his free hand through his hair, beaming with childlike glee. "I can't wait to show you! Hardly anyone understands about the ancients!"

He stepped through the door at the far end, and the others followed. Piper stopped dead, then whispered, "Oh, sweet gods..."

It took Galen a minute to realize what had impressed the doctor. It was much brighter in this hallway, but it wasn't until he saw the lack of shadows on the floor that he realized why.

The walls were lighting up. Against the ceiling, spaced every foot or so, were triangular patches that glowed with a soft, diffuse, almost watery light. The light grew as he watched, growing brighter and brighter, until it outshone Earstripe's candle.

"It's working," breathed Piper. "From so long ago, and it's still working. It's glowing."

"Yes!" Thomas swung around so excitedly that he threatened to splash lamp oil. "It's still working! You understand!"

"The wonder engines still work," said Piper, "but something like this...I've never even heard of such a thing."

"Oh, there's more!" Thomas was practically vibrating in place. "Wait until you see!" He hurried down the short corridor to another door set in the wall. This one was closed, but there was a large block on the wall beside it, protruding out about half an inch.

"Once I open the door, you'll have about thirty seconds to come inside," said Thomas cheerfully. "I suggest you don't linger. And once you're in, do not, under any circumstances, step away from the wall."

Galen looked at Piper. Piper looked at Galen. Earstripe's ears eased backward.

"Is this dangerous?" asked Galen.

"No more so than a cliff edge," said Thomas. "I'll go first. Just don't dawdle, and stay out of the center of the room." He set his hand on the block and pushed. It moved inward with a click and the door slid open. He stepped forward. The other three exchanged another set of helpless glances and followed.

The room inside was perhaps twice as wide as the corridor, leading to another open ivory door. The walls, floor and ceiling were made of the same familiar ivory material. Rather more worrisome, there was an enormous bloody splatter across the floor and a series of drag marks leading to the door they'd entered.

"...um," said Piper. "Uh. Okay, this may sound rude, Thomas, but I can't help but notice there's a giant blood stain on your floor here."

"Yes," said Thomas absently. He was staring up at the ceiling. "Don't worry, it's from a pig."

The door suddenly slid closed behind them. Earstripe leaped for it, but couldn't get his claws around it. The door across the room also snapped shut. Earstripe turned toward it, but Thomas threw an arm out before him. "No, don't go forward. Wait for six minutes."

By the ceiling, the walls began to glow.

"The door will stay closed for twenty-eight minutes," said Thomas. "I timed it."

"And something happens in six minutes," said Piper. "You timed that, too?"

"Oh yes. It's really quite amazing. Better demonstrated than explained, though."

"A gnole does *not* like this," muttered Earstripe. Galen agreed heartily.

The walls, once Galen actually looked at them, were not quite smooth. Delicate lines, barely wider than a human hair, crossed and recrossed the bone-colored surface. Most were perfectly straight, running across the ceiling and the walls, but occasionally they would break off at right angles. *Decoration? Seams? Marks from furniture or equipment that used to be there?* His eyes followed one from the far door, cutting a neat square around the corner, and down to the floor where it got lost under bloodstains.

"You're saying you butchered a pig down here," said Galen, wondering if this sounded completely absurd to anyone else.

"Not butchered, no. Dragged it back upstairs and did that.

Imagine butchering anything in this room!" Thomas tittered, which did nothing to soothe Galen's nerves. He always hated tittering.

Is this man completely deranged? What is going on here? He took a step back and angled his body between Thomas and Piper, just in case something dangerous happened.

Perhaps the motion alerted Thomas to his fears, because the man smiled apologetically. "I'm sorry, I don't mean to be mysterious. This is truly extraordinary and I want you to experience it the way I did. Then maybe you'll understand what it's like. Just another few minutes, I promise. But do *not* cross the room."

Earstripe's ears were laid flat against his skull now. Galen didn't blame him in the slightest. *What does he expect to happen?*

"Any minute now..."

Click.

Whoosh.

A wall of ivory fell from the ceiling and slashed down to the floor, cutting the room in half. Piper cried out in surprise. Earstripe yipped. Galen stepped backward, blocking Piper into the corner, one hand going for his sword.

"There!" said Thomas, satisfied. "There, you see?"

"What the *hell* is that?" shouted Galen.

"I don't know!" crowed Thomas. "Isn't it amazing? The ancients made it. It's thousands of years old, just like the lights, and it still works."

"Works?" said Piper, from somewhere behind Galen's left shoulder.

"The mechanism. The door still opens, the blade still falls. Oh, it's quite safe now. It won't reset until someone opens the entry door from the other side." Proving that he believed what he said, Thomas strode forward into the room.

No one else moved. Galen watched the man walk up to the

enormous wall and pat it almost affectionately. "Look at it!" he said. "It'll retract back up in another few minutes, so look now."

Piper stirred behind him. Galen was reluctant to let the doctor out of the relative safety of the corner, but...well... *What are you really going to do against something like that falling from the ceiling? Do you think you're going to block it with your sword*? He stepped aside.

The doctor joined Thomas at the blade. Galen grimly followed, even though his nerves were screaming. Earstripe stayed by the doorway, his ears still flat.

The ivory wall had not quite touched the floor. The bottom tapered like a wedge, into an edge as sharp as an axe blade. *That's what it is, the world's biggest axe blade. If you were standing under that when it fell...* His eyes were drawn to the blood stain, which was neatly bisected by the wall. *Ah. Yes.*

"Fascinating," said Piper. He touched the surface with his gloved fingertips. Galen's nerves jangled, but nothing happened.

Up close, the wall was cut with many small holes, an elaborate filigree. The surface itself was not smooth, but had a swirling texture, shapes repeating themselves in dozens of variations, dripping with lozenges and soft-sided hexagons and sagging many-armed spirals.

"Did someone carve this?" said Piper, half to himself.

"That's what I can't decide," said Thomas, clearly excited to share his enthusiasm with someone else. "Dedicated artisans have carved stranger things. But it doesn't look carved, does it?"

Piper shook his head. "It looks...*grown.*"

"Exactly!"

"The clocktaurs were like that," said Galen. "Covered in thousands of little gears. But nobody ever carved the gears, they just grew like that. Their insides were full of gears that actually worked, but then the outside was crusted with them too. As if the wonder engine just had an idea of gears and kept building it outward without stopping."

Piper flashed him an admiring look and despite his nerves, it warmed Galen's heart. And other places.

"Yes," said the doctor. "Yes, of course. The ancients sometimes just grew things into a shape. If you asked a wonder engine to grow a wall, and didn't care what it looked like, maybe you'd get something like this."

"Reminds a gnole of bees," said Earstripe. He abandoned his doorway reluctantly and came to stand beside them. He tapped one claw on the ivory and it made a soft *tok!* sound.

"Bees?"

"Burrow keeps bees." Earstripe gazed up at the strange wall. "Make a...a..." He spoke a gnole word, ears flicking. "A gnole doesn't know human words. Bees make honey, make more bees, in sheets?"

"A hive?" hazarded Galen.

"Hive is a bee's house's, yes?" Earstripe grimaced. "Bees make a hive in a tree, or a gnole makes a box for a hive. Inside the hive, though? Sheets of honey. Wax. If sheets are in a box, sheets are the shape of the box. If sheets are in a tree, sheets are the shape of a tree. Still little bee cells, over and over still the same, but fits a different shape."

Piper was already nodding. "Like sheets of honeycomb. The same repeating patterns." He ran his fingertips over a pattern of lozenges. "Only instead of wax, whatever they used made ivory. They just had to build a frame and let the...the ivory bees... fill it."

"What kind of insect makes ivory instead of wax?" asked Galen, bemused.

"Not one we know of. And this is all just a conjecture." Piper grinned at him, and it occurred to Galen that the doctor was actually enjoying this. *I'm glad someone is, I suppose.* "But imagine if there were. Or perhaps not insects, perhaps something like...like..." He made grasping motions with his free hand, as if trying to pluck a thought out of the air.

The wall quivered. Everyone stepped back hurriedly, except for Thomas. As they watched, the gigantic blade retracted smoothly into the ceiling with only a soft whistle of air. Two narrow flaps that had been pushed aside snapped back into place, leaving the ceiling marked only by a narrow line that blended in with the rest of the markings on the walls.

The far door opened.

"There we go," said Thomas. He made for the open door.

"Are there more of these rooms?" asked Galen, struggling to keep his voice from rising. He could feel the black tide around his feet, tugging at him, whispering that there was danger, and he fought it down. *There's danger, but it's nothing you can fight with a sword. This is like crossing a narrow bridge or skirting a cliff face. Running mad with a sword will not help anyone and will probably get you killed.* The tide backed off grudgingly.

"Oh yes," said Thomas. "At least six that I've been able to reach. Don't worry, it's all quite safe. Well, as long as you stand in the right place, anyway. And the traps won't bother you going back the other way at all. We'll just have to wait for the doors to open. In fact, that click you heard? If you listen very closely, you can hear a kind of soft whirring right before the click. I think that's the mechanism firing up."

Stepping under the line of the blade was utterly nerve wracking. Galen focused on his breathing. *You have charged into a room full of enemies with only a knife before*, he told himself. *That was more dangerous than this.*

Yes, but you had a chance of killing those enemies. How do you kill a wall made of the hardest stuff you know?

During the Clocktaur War, they had tried any number of ways of dispatching the clocktaurs. Sledgehammers worked if you had enough men and enough sledgehammers, but you always broke dozens of hammers doing it, and the men wielding those hammers said their shoulders were never the same again. Divine blacksmiths of the Forge God ultimately proved the most effective, probably because their god had a certain sympathy for the joints of His chosen.

In the end, if you could dig in the dirt, the best method turned out to be to dig a giant pit and then just roll massive stones down onto the clocktaurs. Siege towers were swiftly repurposed into ramps that could be dragged to the edge of the pits. It took many, many stones.

When the Dreaming God's paladins cleaned up the remaining clocktaurs in the years that followed, they went out with the Saint of Steel's paladins and a few of the Forge God's people. Galen and his brothers dropped immense weighted nets on the clocktaurs and the smiths went for the legs. You just had to get them down long enough for the Dreaming God's paladins to get hands on them and get the demon out of them.

"Right!" said Thomas. They passed through the door and into another corridor, identical to the first one, except for the lack of barrels. "Now, the next room—"

"We're going into more of these rooms?" Galen was not pleased about this at all. "Is there some point to this?"

Thomas looked briefly stumped. "Don't you want to see them?"

"Are you asking if I *want* to stand in rooms where *giant blades fall on my head?"*

"When you say it like that, it sounds weird," said Piper. "But isn't this fascinating?"

"And horribly dangerous!"

"Oh no, not nearly as much as it looks," said Thomas hastily. "As long as you don't do anything foolish like run into the middle of the room. That triggers all the traps immediately.

Now, this next room for example? Perfectly safe if you stand in the corners this time. Here, I'll show you." He palmed the switch beside the door and it slid open. "Come on, follow me, you have six minutes..."

Galen wanted to scream. Intellectually, he knew that this was probably not nearly so dangerous as it seemed, but his nerves were ringing like church bells and the battle tide wanted to rise but there was nothing to attack.

"Up against the corner, scoot, scoot," said Thomas, making shooing gestures. Galen grimly herded Piper into the corner. Thomas stood on the other side of the room, still beaming like a proud father, beckoning to Earstripe.

"A gnole thinks ancients were crazy," muttered Earstripe, heading toward the corner.

"I'm sure it makes perfect sense if we only knew what they were using it for," called Piper. "I mean, a mill must seem like some kind of horrible torture device if you don't know about grinding grain."

"A gnole thinks our bone-doctor may be crazy too."

"Exactly!" said Thomas, ignoring the gnole. "We just don't know what it's for. Now, my personal theory—and this is only a theory—is that it's meant for some kind of religious pilgrimage."

"The Church of Sharp Falling Objects?" asked Galen.

"Not quite that, my good man. We have no writing from the ancients, so we can't know as to their scriptures, but imagine a kind of proving ground where the acolyte has read the holy texts and knows where to stand. Imagine the act of faith, to kneel in the proper place while blades come down around you."

"Imagine the mess, if you don't remember the text correctly."

"It's only a theory," said Thomas, sounding slightly hurt. "I could be completely wrong, of course. But imagine such a pilgrimage, through multiple rooms, stopping to pray at each place, until arriving at last at...well, whatever they arrive at."

"You don't know?" asked Piper.

"Not—oh, hang on, nearly time. Do make sure you're in the corner, please."

Galen set his feet, Piper wedged into the corner behind him yet again. "We seem to keep doing this," said the doctor.

"Because we keep going into these rooms."

Click. Click. The walls slashed down again. This one came down at an angle, three feet away. There was technically plenty of space, but Galen felt a chill wash of adrenaline nonetheless. His fingers were locked on his sword hilt. He shoved backward even farther, his back against Piper's chest. Piper lost his balance and grabbed for him, one hand on his arm and one at his waist.

If we weren't in an ancient death-trap, I could really enjoy this part.

"It's the same as the other one," Piper said, craning his neck over Galen's shoulder.

"Yes, and I hate it. We're going back."

Piper squirmed, trying to wriggle out of the corner, and Galen had to close his eyes. Adrenaline turned to arousal much too easily and there was a very attractive man moving against his back and this was *not* the time, not at *all* the time—

Piper stilled so suddenly that Galen feared he'd fainted. *I can't have been pushing him that hard. No, he's breathing fine.* He half-turned, and then Piper's breath was warm in his ear, and there were too many shadows to read the man's eyes, but he could see a line of white around the irises.

He's frightened. Galen felt a sudden mad urge to gather the man up in his arms and protect him from whatever had alarmed him. *Yeah, that will certainly work well when he's frightened of giant blades falling from the ceiling.*

"We can't leave," the doctor said, very softly.

It took Galen a moment to make sense of the words. "What?"

The lights that Thomas and Earstripe were carrying cast beams of light through the holes in the walls, leaving a pattern of cut-out shadows across the walls. Piper's lips were almost against his cheek. "We can't," he whispered, "because this is where those men died."

CHAPTER 12

"Are you sure?" asked Galen, just as softly. Piper nodded. "How do you know?"

Piper's breath caught. "I'll explain later," he whispered. "But it was in a room like this one."

"He said that was a pig."

"We don't know it wasn't. Shhh, act normal. The wall's about to come up."

The last thing Galen wanted to do was act normal, but if Piper was right, they were down in a labyrinth with someone who was probably a murderer. *Although you don't know that,* he told himself. *They might have been his assistants. Or burglars.*

Though those bodies didn't get dumped into the river by themselves, now did they?

Either way, act normal. Don't let him think you suspect. He's clearly excited to talk to Piper, but if he gets the impression you know what's happening, he may turn on you. And since this is his dungeon, that's the last thing we want.

The wall slid up. Thomas stepped out of the corner. "Just one more!" he promised. "This one's easy."

"Easy?" said Galen, with false heartiness. "Easy how?"

"Easy in that nothing happens. I think it was meant to be filled with poison gas." Thomas sounded much too excited by the prospect. "But it must have broken down over the centuries, because now nothing much happens. There's a little bit of a hiss from some nozzles and then the door opens."

"If nothing happens, do we really have to see it?" asked Galen.

"Oh, but you must! The technology is really quite ingenious. The nozzles look like seashells. Come, come, it's very safe. I've been in that room a hundred times."

Galen and Earstripe exchanged glances. Galen knew that gnoles were much better at reading body language than humans—their language was based on it—but he didn't know how to express as complex a concept as this. He settled for jerking his chin toward Thomas's back and giving Earstripe a very intense look.

The gnole shrugged. "Door back is closed anyway, tomato-man. Might as well."

Galen stepped away from the wall, one hand on Piper's arm. "Are you feeling all right?"

"I've been better." Piper's already pale skin had gone unusually ashen. He shook his head a few times, raking his hands through his hair. The candle in Earstripe's hand cast shadows from beneath and left his eye sockets as dark and shadowed as a skull.

Thomas was waiting for them in the hallway. This one was turned ninety degrees, with a door at either end. Piper cleared his throat and said, in something approximating his old enthusiasm, "Does this lead to two different rooms?"

"Yes! Though the gas room is much more interesting. The other room is just another one where blades fall from the ceiling, though they do it in lengthwise thirds." He started toward the left door.

Earstripe held up a hand. "Smells like death," he said.

Galen stiffened, waiting for Thomas to react, but the man only sighed. "Oh dear. Yes, it's the pig, I expect."

"*Another* pig?"

"It's really the most efficient way," Thomas said. "I get a couple of shoats from one of the local farmers and then I put them in the room and close the door. When the door opens again, even though the trap has reset, I can usually tell more or less what happened. Unless the pig is still alive, of course, but when that happens, I just close up the door again and wait. And once I know, it's easy enough to wait out the trap and then pull the dead pig out. But one of the doors past this one has a pit that runs across the middle of the room, and the pig fell in the pit, and then once the pit closed up...well, six minutes isn't a lot of time to haul a dead pig out of a hole in the ground. So it's still there. The smell was a lot worse a few weeks ago, believe me."

"That is...efficient, yes," said Galen, trying to keep his voice entirely neutral. He wondered if there was really a pig down there, or if there was another victim in a pit somewhere, like the ones that had washed up on the riverbank. *Can Earstripe smell the difference between a decaying pig and a decaying human?* He wished there was some way to ask without alerting Thomas.

"Anyway, this is the last room we'll do," said Thomas. He palmed the door switch and strolled inside. "No need to stand anywhere for this one."

This room looked slightly different than the others, the walls lined with round shapes that resembled a snail shell, each with a circular hole in the middle. Galen found himself gravitating to the corner despite Thomas's reassurances. *Not that the corner is necessarily safe, mind you.* Earstripe had his shoulders hunched and kept pawing at his nose, although Galen couldn't smell anything yet. Piper went to one of the round openings and peered into it, which was unsettling to watch. *It's not likely that there's a spring-loaded arrow in there, or an eel that's going to shoot out and latch onto his face, but there's something about staring into holes...*

"Aren't they interesting? I wish I could see the mechanism inside." Thomas lifted the lantern and then cursed as oil sloshed from side to side. "Oh, blast!" He squatted down and set the lantern beside him. "No, don't worry, just me being clumsy...should have dealt with the wick earlier, but I was so excited to show people the rooms..."

He crouched in the doorway, still muttering to himself, and began disassembling the lantern. Galen's nerves were jangling again. "Could you please not put your eyeball against that thing when it starts clicking?" he said testily.

"I wasn't putting my eyeball against it," said Piper. "Thomas, have you slid a probe into these holes? How deep are they?"

"One and three-quarter inches, give or take," said Thomas, and then, without so much as a pause, he pitched backward through the doorway.

Galen lunged forward on instinct, not sure if he was catching Thomas before he fell or grabbing him before he ran. The door was already closing and he barely got a hand around the edge, then had to yank it back or lose his fingers. The room was plunged into darkness, broken only by Earstripe's candle.

Click.

Click.

Light began to leak from the walls.

"Thomas!" yelled Galen, pounding on the door. "Let us out!" *Stupid. Stupid. I should have been watching him more closely,*

I knew he was a murderer, but I was so busy making sure that he didn't think we suspected him that I didn't move fast enough.

"You're fine!" Thomas's voice was muffled by the door. "It'll open in twenty-eight minutes, don't worry. And the gas really doesn't work."

"Why did you shut us in here?"

"The pigs never get past the pit trap," said Thomas. He sounded as if this was perfectly reasonable. "I have to use humans past that. Incidentally, the pit trap is the next one on the right. There's two stages to it, though. First it's on this side, then it's by the far door. If you stand in a line in the dead middle of the room and don't panic, you'll be fine."

"What?!"

"The middle of the room! Look, there's a set of triangles on the floor. If everybody stands in a triangle, they'll be fine. Be sure you do the righthand room, though. The lefthand one is full of spikes, and nobody ever gets past that one. I have lost more pigs that way..."

Galen slammed his fist into the door again.

Piper joined him. "We're not running your gauntlet, Thomas," he shouted. "We're just going to wait until these doors open and come out."

"I know you'll try that, so I'm afraid I'm going to shut you in here," said Thomas, sounding apologetic. "I am sorry, Doctor Piper. You seem like someone who could appreciate the mystery, and I hate to have to use these tactics. But you've also got a much better chance of getting through than any of the others did! Certainly better than the pigs! And think what we'll learn!"

Hissssss.... Air puffed from the nozzles. Galen held his breath. Piper put his sleeve over his nose.

"Don't worry," called the muffled voice, "it really won't do anything. I've been in there lots of times. I think probably the gas was lighter than air, so the penitent would have to lie flat to escape it."

"A gnole doesn't smell anything," said Earstripe. Galen let his breath out again, cautiously, then began to pound his fist on the door in impotent fury. "You can't think you'll get away with this! People will come looking for us!"

"Yes," said Thomas. "That'll be useful. I can always use more test subjects if you don't get to the end. I don't actually know where the end *is*, you understand, though my theory is that you'll eventually reach the sanctum sanctorum, and then the exit is the door next to the entryway, so you'll wind up back in the cellar. So that's a good reason for you to try and get through, isn't it? To make it through before you run out of water or light. I shouldn't want to try it in the dark." He tittered again.

Galen snarled. The battle tide wanted to rise, but it had no target. Even a divine berserker did not know how to fight an unbreakable door. "When I get out of here, I'm going to wring your neck!"

"I hope not, but I'll be going now, just in case. Good luck! I really am rooting for you. Remember, stand in the triangles!"

And after that, despite Galen's bluster and Piper's pleas, there was no further answer from the other side of the door.

Galen put his back to the wall, slid down it, and said, "I'm an idiot."

"No more than I am," said Piper, joining him.

"Yes, but guarding people from murderers is my job. And I was so busy watching him to see if he had a weapon that I walked into this like a lamb."

"A gnole did too, tomato-man." Earstripe's ears were flat against his skull. "A gnole kept smelling, but a human only smelled excited, not guilty."

"Oh, good," said Galen, "he's a remorseless murderer. That makes me feel better."

Piper tried to head off the recriminations before they got any farther. "Look, what could we have done? As soon as we refused to go any farther, he would have trapped us. He knows the place. We don't."

"I could have held a sword to his throat."

"In which case he could have just taken us into a room with a blade and told us to stand in the wrong place, so that you got chopped in half and he didn't."

"Mmmm."

Piper gave up. Paladins wallowed in guilt as a form of meditative exercise. There was only so much you could do. "The door opens back up in twenty minutes."

"So he said."

"Well. There's that. But if he actually wants us to find the traps for him, presumably he would give us as much information as possible."

"Or he could just be a garden-variety murderer who enjoys watching people get chopped to bits by ancient death machines."

"How is it that I work with dead bodies all day and *I'm* the optimist?"

That won him an exasperated smile. Then Galen's green eyes narrowed suddenly. "But you knew. How did you know that this was where those men died?"

"Oh. That." Piper looked away and rested the back of his head against the wall. "I suppose you deserve an explanation." He toyed with the idea of lying, then discarded it. Withholding information could be dangerous. And they were in a death trap. *And if the paladin gets antsy about me being a wonderworker...well, I'll refer him to Bishop Beartongue, I suppose.*

There was no way of telling how religious types would react

to his admittedly minor magical talent. It wasn't very impressive, but it was related to the dead, and people tended to get very anxious about anything that smacked of necromancy. It was hard enough just being a lich-doctor.

Some priests, like those of the Hanged Motherhood, would want him burned at the stake for witchcraft, although that wasn't much distinction since they would have burned the world if they could have found sufficient kindling and a big enough stake. And then again, you had the White Rat's people, whose only concern was how you could use such a talent to solve problems. *Galen works for the Rat now, no matter who he once served. They're not a burning order. Perhaps it will be all right.*

"I'm a wonderworker," he confessed. "Not much of one. If I touch a dead body, I can see what they saw as they died."

He didn't look at either one of his companions. The air nozzles had stopped hissing, and as he watched, the far door slid open.

"You can watch them die?" said Galen, his voice determinedly neutral.

"Not watch. I'm on the inside, seeing what they saw and feeling whatever emotions they felt. Only the last few seconds, usually." He added, almost plaintively, "The Bishop knows."

There was a long, long silence, and then Galen said, "That's what you were doing on the body at the waterfront. When you took off your gloves." Piper looked up, nodding. Sudden knowledge flared in the paladin's eyes, and he said softly, "And the baby." Piper had to look away.

Galen reached out and gripped his shoulder. Living flesh, no death on it. It warmed Piper more than he wanted to admit.

Earstripe flicked his ears sharply. "Can a bone-doctor eat meat?"

Piper shook his head. "Mostly, no. Eggs are fine, they're almost never fertilized. The more rendered it is, the less likely it is to set me off. Grease doesn't bother me. I can eat a cake baked with lard, or a jelly that started its life as hooves. And shellfish is fine. I don't think clams and oysters are smart enough to know they're dead." He tapped one gloved finger against the other. "And tanned leather doesn't remember anything either."

"But if a bone-doctor bit into a steak...?"

"I am intimately acquainted with the last moments of a number of cows," said Piper glumly. "Every time someone mixes up an order. There's nothing to destroy a nice evening like suddenly being in a slaughterhouse and watching a hammer land between your eyes." He paused then added, "Most of them don't mind much, I have to say. They're confused because they're not in a place they recognize, but they aren't scared of dying the way we are. But *I* know what's happening."

He'd also run into a couple of dried fish in the village—there had been almost no way to avoid them, they were on every possible surface—and had started coughing every time as he relived the dry-land drowning. He was pretty sure at least one of the fisherfolk thought he'd had consumption.

Galen and Earstripe sat in silence for a few minutes, and then finally Galen said, "Saint's *balls,* what a horrible talent that must be."

Piper snorted and finally dared to look over at the paladin again. There was no condemnation in those green eyes, which was a relief. "It's not fantastic, no. But in my line of work, sometimes it's useful."

"A gnole thinks it is useful now, bone-doctor."

Piper snorted. "I didn't recognize the spot soon enough to get us out of here."

"Not that." Earstripe made a short chopping motion with one hand. "Smelling bodies, yeah? Something dead up ahead. You find a body, you touch a body, maybe you know what killed it. Maybe you know where to stand, yeah?"

Piper inhaled sharply. "He said it was a pig up ahead."

"He also locked us in a death trap," said Galen, "so I think his truthfulness may be in question." He rose to his feet. "Come on. I'm sure the front door is locked, but we had better check anyway."

CHAPTER 13

The first door was indeed closed and locked. They crossed back through the rooms warily, waiting for the traps, but apparently Thomas had been telling the truth and they only worked when one entered through the front door. The short hallway at the end was dark and the door was sealed as tight as the doors of heaven. Tighter, probably. Galen knew at least a few people who were probably going to heaven, but he didn't know anyone who was getting through that door.

Their host had left them a neat pile of waterskins, a box of matches, the other lantern, and a note that read: *Remember, the righthand door. Stand on the triangles. Good luck!* in such cheery handwriting that Galen felt like snarling.

"Damnation," he muttered. He made several attempts to open the door, bashing it with his shoulder, digging the blade of his eating knife into the narrow seam. The door did not move a fraction and he broke the tip off his knife. He hadn't really hoped for more, but it still felt like a blow to the gut.

"Well," he said, eyeing the broken tip. "Now what do we do? Try to go through the maze, or try to break down the door?"

Piper shook his head. "I've tried to break down this kind of door before, and I had a crowbar and a hammer and anything else I could think of to try."

"Brindle will notice when we don't come out," said Galen.

"If a human doesn't try to kill a gnole."

Galen winced. "He's one of the toughest people I know," he said. "And he'll be suspicious. I think he'll probably get away, and try to bring help."

"Maybe," said Piper, "but can they help find us when they get here?" He rapped the door. "Thomas can just say the door doesn't open. Nobody would think he was lying."

The silence got deeper and glummer. Piper was the one to break it. "I say we go on, and try to get out. We're smart, we have some experience, and...well...the alternative isn't great."

"Better than starving to death," said Earstripe. He opened one of the barrels, revealing apples packed in straw. The one next to it held water.

None of them said what probably all of them were thinking —that there might not even *be* a way out, that this might be a maze with no end. Who knew why the ancients did anything? Who knew why they had left this line of traps waiting for the unwary? Galen pushed this thought aside. *All we can do is hope.* Years ago, he might have prayed, but the Saint was gone and hope was all that any of them had left. "Unanimous, then. All right. Everyone drink up and take a load of lamp oil and candles, and let's see how far we get."

The way back was easy enough, now that they knew what to expect. The blades falling still made Galen jump. Piper put a hand on his shoulder and the paladin summoned a rueful smile for him, but Piper could tell that it was a strain. The muscle under his fingers was drawn as tight as a bowstring.

Not that I'm doing much better, mind you.

They reached the last door and all three of them stared at it.

Piper set a hand on the smooth surface. "Stand on the triangles, he said."

"He *said* that," said Galen. "Do we trust he was telling the truth?"

Piper gnawed on his lower lip. "I think he wants us to live as long as possible," he said slowly. "If he's running us through this maze to test the traps, there's no point in telling us something that will kill us right off the bat."

"Unless he's simply a murderer who enjoys the thought of people dying."

"...there's that." Piper nodded. "Maybe we shouldn't all go?"

They argued for several minutes about who was going into the pit trap room. It was probably a credit to each of them as individuals that they were all willing to sacrifice themselves, but it didn't make deciding any easier.

"I'm the one who's trusting that Thomas wants to know how the traps work."

"A gnole brought humans on a tailless snake hunt." (Piper filed '*tailless snake hunt*' away to ask about later.)

"I'm a paladin."

In the end, it was the last one that carried the day. "Really," said Galen, a small smile playing over his lips, "somebody has to take the stupid risks. That's what I'm *for.*"

"You're for more than that," said Piper sharply.

"Not really, no. Even when my god was alive, that's what we were for."

Piper wanted to grab Galen and shake him and yell that he was worth more than bait for a trap, but this did not seem like the proper time and also he wasn't sure how to do it without insulting the late Saint of Steel. So he gritted his teeth and let Galen walk through the door while his nerves screamed at him to follow.

"The smell's a lot worse in here," Galen called. "I don't see any bodies, though. Nor blood stains."

"Are there triangles on the floor?"

"Probably. There's everything else."

Thirty seconds later, the door closed. *Click.* Earstripe heaved a massive sigh. Piper rested his forehead against the wall, his stomach churning. He thought he might be ill. The cool ivory against his skin helped, but not much.

Twenty-eight minutes.

If Thomas had lied, then Galen could be dead in six. They wouldn't know until after the fact.

Indistinct words came through the door. Was Galen calling that he had found the triangles? Screaming that there was poison gas that worked this time, and he was about to die? Piper curled his hands into fists, resisting the urge to hammer on the door. It wouldn't help, and what if Galen came back to find out what the problem was and became trapped?

Earstripe sat down. Piper almost yelled at him to stop being disrespectful, which made no sense at all. *Calm down. Standing or sitting makes no difference. You could stand on your head for twenty-eight minutes and it wouldn't change anything that happens in that room.*

Pretend this is a bedside vigil, and you are waiting to see if the patient recovers. You're good at that.

He sat down as well. Vigil. Yes. He understood those. You went in and you drenched everything in alcohol and you prayed you didn't nick an artery and you got out your needle and gut and you prayed some more and when you were done, you closed everything up as best you could and dumped more alcohol over it and then you waited to see if they lived or died.

It was so much easier with the dead. You couldn't hurt the dead. You never had to second guess yourself. Nothing you did or didn't do could make it any worse.

(Tell people you wished you were dead, though, and they thought you were suicidal. It was too much trouble to try to explain that you were fine being alive, you just envied the dead their composure.)

"How long has it been?" he asked. Earstripe shrugged.

Ten minutes? Surely more than six. Surely Galen was dead or not dead by now.

Someone thumped on the door. Piper nearly fainted from relief, and then thumped back. "He's alive!"

"Sounds that way," said Earstripe.

It was much easier after that. Piper leaned against the wall, resisting the temptation to keep pounding on the door just to hear the paladin respond. The minutes stretched by. Earstripe sat down and had a good scratch. Piper thought about pacing, but decided against it.

A minor eternity later, the door slid open. Galen stood framed in it. Piper jumped forward and threw his arms around the paladin. "You're alive!"

"Ah...yes. Yes, I am." Piper felt the other man's chuckle vibrate through his chest. "I'm alive. And there was even a dead pig."

It occurred to Piper that he had just flung himself into Galen's arms like a long-lost lover, rather than like a friendly acquaintance and travel companion. He stepped back, feeling a blush already starting to climb his neck. "I...uh..."

"No, no, I love it when handsome men hug me for not being dead." Galen paused, grinning at Piper. "Although if you want to hug the pig too, that's going to be a little more difficult."

"I shall skip the pig," said Piper, with as much dignity as he could muster under the circumstances. His ears felt hot. *Now why did I do that? I knew he couldn't be dead, he thumped on the door and everything, so what the hell is wrong with me?*

Galen hadn't seemed to mind.

"Right," said the paladin. "The floor is made of what look like interlocking tiles. Most of them snap down, starting from this side. Some of them don't. It's incredibly nerve-wracking, but the tile itself is about eighteen inches square, so you can stand on it easily enough. I understand why the pigs panicked, though."

Piper and Earstripe nodded. "A gnole wants to get this over with," muttered Earstripe.

They stepped through the door. Galen led them to the correct spot, holding up the lantern and pointing out the safe tiles. "There, there, and there. And now hold on."

Piper listened for the mechanical click of the door. The lights came up.

The clicking started up again, but this time it was staggered —*click-a-click-a-click-a-click!* The floor fell away behind him. Piper fought the urge to lunge forward as the pit raced toward his heels.

"Steady," said Galen beside him. Piper closed his eyes.

The clicking stopped. When he opened his eyes again, the floor behind him was completely gone.

"The rest will go in a minute," said Galen. Piper nodded. Earstripe might as well have been a marble statue of a gnole.

Click-a-click-a-click-a-click...

"A gnole does not like to watch that," said Earstripe.

Piper didn't much like it either, but he forced himself to look, even though his heart was thumping in his chest. He had to admit that the design was ingenious. Each tile folded downward, leaving a narrow, wickedly sharp edge facing up. Anyone standing on the wrong tile would either fall down into the pit itself or find themselves literally on a razor's edge.

"...and there's the pig," said Galen, pointing.

"I had been wondering why he didn't just carry a pig over the pit," Piper said, "but I suppose you couldn't very well balance here for five minutes with a panicking hog, could you?"

"I wouldn't want to."

Piper's gaze was drawn back to the darkness. "Look there," he said, crouching down.

Galen made a small noise of alarm. "Don't fall in."

"I'm fine. But look—chunks of ivory. And are those gears?"

"More over on this side, too. Couple of them."

Galen knelt down cautiously on his own square. "I don't... wait, yes. That looks familiar." He scowled. "It looks like part of a goddamn clocktaur."

"Couldn't fit a clocktaur through the door, tomato-man."

"No, of course not. Although if you were going to kill one, those giant falling blades would probably work a treat." He frowned. "This can't be some kind of clocktaur killing device. It's just not big enough. But if it was about twice as large..."

"Maybe they used to have small clocktaurs," said Piper thoughtfully. "I suppose if you have the capacity to make a sword, it follows that you can make a dagger just as easily."

"But why would you need this whole maze just to kill them off? You could do it with one room full of blades."

"That's an *excellent* question." Piper stretched out his hand and touched one of the razors. He felt the skin on his fingertip part and hastily pulled it back. "It's incredibly sharp. Whatever this stuff is, it doesn't dull over time. Fascinating. It must be some property of the material. It doesn't oxidize, so rust doesn't build up, even though the air is clearly being refreshed regularly. There must be some kind of ventilation system that's still running, since the rooms aren't full of bad air. I wonder how they managed that?"

"You're *enjoying* this," said Galen accusingly.

"I am *not.* It's just fascinating, that's all." Piper huffed. "Obviously I'd rather be observing it with an easy way out and fewer dead pigs." He wondered if the door below his workshop led to something like this, instead of water, as he'd suspected.

Speaking of water, there was a sudden liquid sound. Piper looked over and saw that Earstripe was urinating off the side of his tile into the pit.

"What?" said the gnole. "A gnole had to go."

"You're pissing on ancient technology!"

"Ancient humans did not provide toilets for a gnole."

"Yes, but—"

"A gnole will aim for the dead pig, if it makes a human feel better."

"Besides," said Galen, "if those are clocktaur bits, urine's not going to hurt them. Trust me on this one."

"You pissed on a clocktaur?"

"What can I say? War is hell."

Piper paused. "Did it do anything to the clocktaurs?"

"Made them slightly damp? You can't drown the things anyway, they just walk along the bottom of the moat."

Piper shook his head. "Incredible. And they were powered by demons, the paladins say. Err, different paladins, that is."

"The Dreaming God's people," said Galen. "They'd know." He chuckled. "They're not the sharpest, even by our admittedly low standards, but what they don't know about demons isn't worth knowing. And god, are they pretty."

"*So* pretty," said Piper, almost involuntarily. Galen flashed him a broad grin, but whatever remark he was about to make was lost as the pit tiles snapped upright again. The far door ground open.

They crowded into the hallway nervously, even though the hallways had, so far, been entirely safe. The triangular lights came up. There was only one door this time, on the lefthand wall.

"Are we turning?" asked Galen. "Is this the halfway point?"

"Possibly," said Piper. "Or there could be switchbacks. We have no idea what the layout of this place really is. It might be spiraling around a central point."

"Our charming host thought that one closed door in the wall outside was the exit," said Galen.

"A gnole thinks that human dances with snakes."

"What does that mean?"

"You know...?" Earstripe made swooping gestures with his hands, wiggling his whiskers.

Piper and Galen looked at each other, then back at Earstripe. The gnole sighed. "Humans can't smell." He reached out and touched the panel beside the door.

It slid open onto darkness.

CHAPTER 14

A smell of decay rolled out. "There's a dead body in there," said Galen, holding up the lantern. Earstripe mumbled something, grabbing his nose.

Piper took a deep breath and lunged past him. Galen cursed, grabbing for him, but the doctor said, "I'm coming back!"

"But if you go halfway—!"

"I won't!"

The corpse was only about a third of the way inside the room. The corpse's head was rather farther away. Galen followed Piper, ready to pick him up bodily and throw him through the doorway if he had to. But the doctor only leaned down and touched the body. He stiffened, inhaled sharply—Galen swore and reached for him—but then he straightened up and turned back, nearly running into Galen.

"Sorry, I—"

"Go, go! Apologize later!"

Piper ran for the door. They got through and it was at least ten seconds before the door finally closed, which made Galen feel as if he'd been acting irrationally, which only annoyed him further.

"Don't take risks like that," he said, through gritted teeth.

"We agreed I was going to do the trick—"

"I'll drag the corpse back for you!" snapped Galen. "Just...no more running into death traps." This came out much more angry than he wanted it to. He took a deep breath and added, in as pleasant a tone as he could manage, "I'm sorry. I don't mean to yell. It's not that I don't think you're capable. I just..."

Piper's a grown adult. He's not a soldier under your command. Stop acting like you have the right to order him around.

Galen half-wanted to give the man a dressing-down as if he were a raw recruit, and the other half wanted to wrap him in cotton wool like a hollow egg. "So, the body," he said, trying to change the subject.

Lines drew taut around Piper's eyes, and Galen cursed himself again. *You're yelling at him when he just watched a man die. What's wrong with you?*

"More blade walls, I think," said Piper. "Two of them meeting horizontally, right at neck height. I'm not sure exactly how tall that is, but if we crouch down, we should be all right."

"I'll go in," said Galen.

"But we don't know if there's more blades. There could be another set."

"Is a corpse cut in any other direction?" asked Earstripe.

"No, but they would have fallen down after the first one. If there's another blade, at hip height, say, he wouldn't have been around to see it."

"A human lies flat," Earstripe suggested. "By corpse. Then we know."

"I love lying flat in congealed blood," muttered Galen. "Really. One of my favorite things."

"I don't mind," said Piper. "I've seen a lot of blood. I can go."

"And relive the man's death for six minutes?" asked Galen.

"It would stop when I stop touching him."

Galen shook his head. "You're not expendable," he said. "If I die, you've still got a chance of getting through the trap by touching *my* corpse. If *you* die, we're back to dumb luck."

Piper looked like he wanted to argue, but couldn't. "Fine," he muttered. "Just...don't die."

"I'll try to avoid it."

Unfortunately, they still had twenty-eight minutes until the door opened again, which was awkward, since Galen was still kicking himself for acting like an imperious ass.

"Did you ever do the...ah...trick...with one of the smooth men?" asked Galen, when the silence had gotten almost palpable and he had to break it.

Piper shook his head. "The bodies just knew that there was a terrible pain in their necks. The clay heads, once you had them out, didn't do anything." He swallowed, looking suddenly pale. Galen wondered what he was remembering. *Probably being scared shitless. I would be, in his situation.*

"Did you ever try with one actually in a body?"

"I offered," he admitted. "To your bishop. Beartongue. She knows about the trick. That's why I probably can't ever be fired from my job. Not that people haven't tried. The word of a lich-doctor is practically law in a courtroom, and a couple of times I've testified to things that were...oh...not politically expedient for various parties. They would have loved to send me back to the gutter, setting up a shingle to pull teeth and treat pox. But the Temple's had my back, and she made those problems go away."

"It's what the Rat does," said Galen, with bleak amusement. "They solve problems." He was one of those problems, and the Rat had solved it, as well as someone like him could be solved. They could do nothing for his night terrors, but they had given him a job to do, and a place for him and his brothers to recover what shreds of their sanity they still could. Some of them had even put themselves back together well enough to love and be loved. *Mind you, some of us are lucky to have achieved 'fuck and be fucked.' I don't see myself getting much past that...*

Piper was still talking. "Anyway. I offered to touch a live one. Beartongue said no. Said that there was a chance they might be able to jump down a connection like that, and she wasn't throwing away her favorite lich-doctor on a chance. I won't say that I wasn't relieved."

"Ah. So that's why you work with the White Rat, then."

"Yes, in a roundabout fashion. Technically, I am employed by the court system as a consult to the courts. There aren't many lich-doctors and there's a fair amount of competition for the posts, even knowing that people will give you a wide berth once they learn what you do for a living. But you get the tricky cases where people don't know how someone died, and I was, thanks to my talent, good enough at it to get one of the few openings. Then we had a case where everyone thought it was murder, and I could tell it wasn't—they'd found the suspect standing over the body, and he'd been hit on the head, but I *felt* him have a heart attack—and no one wanted to listen to me. I was only an apprentice then, and my predecessor was making the declarations. He thought it was the head wound, but the man had been dying before he ever got hit. But the Rat was representing the accused, and Beartongue was the lawyer—she was only a solicitor sacrosanct, they hadn't made her the Bishop yet. I managed to pounce on her outside the courtroom and blurted out the whole story. To her credit, she didn't think I was a raving lunatic. She did insist on testing my ability, but once I'd proved it to her satisfaction, she backed me. Managed to do it without having my talent exposed in court, which I was grateful for. The suspect was acting in self-defense, and she went free. We've been working together, unofficially, ever since."

"Makes sense." Galen could just imagine Beartongue rubbing her hands together with unbridled glee at discovering Piper's grisly talent.

"So that's how you become a lich-doctor. How do you become a paladin?" asked Piper.

Ah, I should have seen that coming. Well, turnabout is fair play. "Depends on the paladin. Which god do you want?"

"Pick one." Piper smiled, and Galen was grateful, because it meant that he could pretend for a little while that they weren't talking about him.

"Ah, well. If you're with the Dreaming God, you have to be pretty and incapable of being tempted by demons. Also...I won't say *dumb,* because they aren't really, but very, *very* straightforward. They're a type. A good-looking type, mind you, but a type."

"I've seen them," said Piper. "They were all very pretty, now that you mention it."

"I know. It's unfair. The one I know—Jorges, good guy—says it's so that they can't be tempted by demons who offer to make them beautiful. The vast majority of demons wind up possessing farm animals, though, and they aren't smart, so I suspect the Dreaming God is just shallow like that."

Piper laughed. "Well, if you're a god..."

"Indeed. Meanwhile, if you're with the Forge God, you train as a blacksmith-priest. At the end of it, most of them stay smiths, but occasionally the god picks one as a paladin. I don't think even they know what the criteria are. Most of them don't actually *want* to be paladins, as far as I can tell." *Who would, really? You kill and kill and keep on killing, either for the god or so that you can keep on living yourself. If someone came back and gave me the chance not to be a berserker at all...* He realized that Piper was waiting for him to finish the thought and coughed.

"The Forge-God's people tend to be very dedicated smiths, and having to go around and fight people and act as backup for other paladins means they don't have much time for that. The ones I knew were constantly busy with their hands. They had to take up portable hobbies. One crocheted." He chuckled. "Stephen—you know him—my brother in arms, he knits. Those two had some fine old fights about which was a better thing to do with yarn."

"Odd to think of knitting paladins," said Piper.

"Particularly berserkers. But it's an easy thing to do when traveling. You've seen me using a drop spindle, haven't you? I give him all the thread."

"Odd to think of paladins making thread, for that matter."

"Ah, but you didn't grow up in my family." Galen smiled. "My grandmother was a weaver. The children got drop spindles as soon as they could hold something in their hands. I was spinning thread practically before I could walk. Still do. It seems wasteful just to sit around."

"From a family of weavers, eh? A long way to becoming a paladin."

"Not really. My mother was a priestess of the Saint, you see. A genuinely god-touched one. My father, I am afraid, could not bear to come second in my mother's life, and left when I was young."

Piper's face held sympathy but no pity, which Galen appreciated. "Hard for a human to compete with a god."

The words struck him much harder than the doctor could realize. He had lashed out at Stephen once, to his disgrace. "Trying to replace what we've lost, are you? I didn't think you'd try to find it between a woman's thighs."

"It isn't like that," Stephen had said. "You cannot ask a

woman to compete with a god. But we can still love someone and be loved. Even as broken as we are."

The memory still filled him with shame, though he knew that Stephen had forgiven him, probably before the echoes had died. His fellow broken paladin had found love against long odds. Galen did not begrudge him that, exactly. Stephen deserved love if anyone did. No, it was...envy. Envy, because Stephen had not been at Hallowbind. Envy, because Stephen deserved it, and after Hallowbind, Galen never would again.

In the death throes of the Saint of Steel, the god-touched priests had died outright or killed themselves or fallen into death-like comas from which they did not wake. Galen did not know which one his mother had done. The high priest of her temple had burned it to the ground, screaming about a pyre fit for a god. The paladins though, had turned on anyone around them, each one taken by the battle-tide, trying to fight the world that had taken their god away.

Stephen had been lucky. He and Shane and Istvhan had been travelling with two paladins of the Dreaming God, who had fought them off. Galen and Marcus had been less fortunate. There had been a dozen paladins meeting with local men near the town of Hallowbind. No one knew how many local men there had been. They had only found two left hands. The broken paladins had torn them to shreds and when they could not find another enemy, they had turned on each other. The survivors had fallen comatose when they could no longer fight, but only Marcus and Galen had woken up again.

He remembered almost nothing of Hallowbind, but what little he did remember was enough to turn his dreams into screaming horrors.

"And you were chosen?"

"I was. I went for a soldier as a lad, and the god took me a month later. Fortunately, I knew what the berserker fit was, so I just turned around and went home."

"All right, that's doctors and paladins," said Piper. "Earstripe?"

Earstripe sighed. "Ask."

"Why did you join the city guard?"

The gnole shrugged. "Burrow said to join. Guard not always good to gnoles. Blame gnoles for things. If a guard is a gnole, that guard can speak up." He picked at a loose thread on one of his rags. "A gnole was a rag-and-bone gnoll, but she was good at human speaking." His diction shifted noticeably, becoming more precise, taking care with each syllable. "Burrow said to become a guard-gnole. Become a *job-gnole.*"

"Ah." Galen knew enough about the gnole caste system to know that would be a step up for Earstripe. "If you became a guard, you'd be promoted."

"Would have to be," said Earstripe. "Some gnoles won't listen to a rag-and-bone gnole. Would listen to a job-gnole." It was always hard to tell, but Galen thought there was a bleak edge to his amusement. "Now gnoles listen to a guard-gnole, but guard-humans don't always listen. Mallory-captain doesn't listen now."

"So you struck out on your own to try to solve this," said Piper. "To save these humans, when the guard wouldn't listen to you. But why?"

"God's stripes." Earstripe shook his head in disbelief. "Bone-doctor would save some gnole, yes? If some gnole was hurt?"

"Of course," said Piper. "If I could."

"And tomato-man would save some gnole?" He swung his muzzle toward Galen. "If some gnole needed big human with a sword?"

"Yes, of course."

Earstripe spread his hands, claws gleaming. "A gnole saves some human. Same thing." He took a deep breath, clearly choosing his words carefully. "A gnole's compassion does not require *fur.*"

"Right," said Piper, into the horribly uncomfortable silence that followed. "I've just put my foot in it. Earstripe, I apologize. I shouldn't have questioned why you'd help humans. You're a good person."

Earstripe shrugged. "Eh. Humans can't smell," he said.

Piper looked at Galen.

"That's how they say we're too ignorant for gnoles to take offense," said Galen, faintly amused. Brindle said it frequently. As far as Galen could tell, gnoles viewed humanity as a race of ignorant, powerful toddlers, some of which were likable enough, but none of which were particularly bright.

"A human is good at what a human is good at," said Earstripe in a conciliatory fashion. "Build high walls, hit monster with sword, write words down on paper. A gnole doesn't expect a human to be good at gnole speaking."

There was a clicking sound from inside the door and the panel on the wall popped out an inch.

"Time to go," said Galen. "I'll knock when I can. Although I suppose you'll hear the screaming if I get it wrong."

Piper winced. Galen squared his shoulders and went in to face his fate.

CHAPTER 15

He'd been close to dead bodies before. Often he was the one who had made them dead. But there was a difference between a battle and lying down on the floor next to a headless corpse, particularly one that had been decaying for a couple of weeks.

At least there were no flies. That was worth something. And it was cool down here, so the smell was only horrible instead of intolerable.

I wonder how many people died here, and how far they got in the rooms. Let's see, if Thomas pulled the corpses and dumped them in the river, we could have already had the headless one, probably the one with the leg chopped off, depending on the angle, and...hmm, yes, he mentioned a room full of spikes, that would explain the one that had been gored...he must not have been willing to pull this one out. Couldn't figure out exactly how he died, and didn't want to risk it.

The lights came up. His view of the corpse got better. He turned his head the other way. If he was going to die, he didn't want his last view to be the stump of a rotting neck.

He had a sudden intense wish to confess his sins and be absolved. A priest would have been nice. Another paladin would have been even better. Unfortunately he had a gnole and a doctor, one of whom probably wouldn't be impressed by his sins and the other of which featured far too prominently in them.

Would Piper be able to tell what he'd been thinking when he died? Should he think something as a message? What sort of thing? *It's not your fault? You're very sexy and I regret not jumping your bones?*

No, don't be ridiculous. The best thing you could think is probably, "There's another blade right about here."

His nose itched. He wanted to scratch it, but had a dreadful feeling that doing so might mean losing a hand.

Click.

Two blades came from overhead, just as Piper had seen. They met with an almost infinitesimal *snick* overhead.

Perhaps thirty seconds later, just when someone who had crouched down would have been feeling relieved and maybe straightening up a little, a second set closed like jaws, about eighteen inches away from his face.

"Clever," said Galen, because the alternative was to piss himself. "Very clever."

The light through the holes in the blades mingled with the flickering of the oil lamp. It was like looking up through a supremely deadly cheese.

It's a good thing you're a paladin, because you would never have made it as a poet. A deadly cheese? Really?

Six minutes was an interminably long time to wait to scratch one's nose. It felt like hours. He finally slid his hand up and scratched because possibly losing a hand was preferable to another minute with his nose on fire.

He had just sagged with relief when the blades slid back. Galen caught a glimpse of a third set above the rest. *Ah. In case someone was quick enough to jump on top of the first set. Even more clever.*

He waited another minute, just to be sure, then sat up. He could hear knocking on the door and scrambled to his feet to go alert his companions that he was still alive.

"You were right!" he yelled through the door. "There was another blade."

"Are you hurt?" Piper yelled back.

"No!"

"Good!"

He wandered over to the open doorway on the far side of the room, though he wasn't willing to go through it just yet. The door might not close behind him, but he didn't quite understand the rules and he wasn't going to risk it. He settled for leaning out and looking both ways.

There was only one door on the opposite wall. It was identical to all the others. Well, he hadn't really expected anything else.

He busied himself searching the body as well as he could, given its advanced state of unpleasantness. Male, young enough not to have any gray hair. Piper could undoubtedly tell a great deal more. Leather shoes. The only thing in his pockets was a stub of pencil. No money, nothing identifying.

He relayed all this to the others when the door finally opened. "Pick a spot and lie down," he said. "It's easy enough, just unsettling."

They picked spots. Galen watched Piper, as rigid as a corpse, and wondered if it was safe to reach out and take the other man's hand. *Safe from blades, maybe. Safe from more than that...?*

He did it anyway. Piper gave him a startled but gratified look, then jumped as the first blades closed. "There's another one coming," said Galen. "Don't sit up."

"That won't be a problem," said Piper. "I appear to be completely paralyzed." Galen squeezed his fingers reassuringly.

"Still more clearance than some gnole-burrows," said Earstripe. The second blade snapped. Piper jumped again, his gloved fingers closing convulsively on Galen's. "Slightly less than gnole-burrow now," Earstripe observed.

"Now would be a terrible time to discover that I'm claustrophobic," said Piper.

"Are you?"

"Definitely not. I work underground in a stone box full of dead bodies. Claustrophobia would be very bad for my career."

"I can see that."

"It's not the tight spaces I mind, it's the giant killing blades making the spaces so tight."

"That seems very logical." Galen stroked his thumb over Piper's knuckles. The kidskin was very fine and he could feel the bones of the other man's hand.

The blades retracted and Galen released the doctor's grip reluctantly. (Did he imagine it, or was Piper a little slow as well?) Gnole and paladin clustered around the headless body, while Piper inspected the head in the corner.

"Male. Twenties, I'd say. Good diet, probably from a reasonably well-off family."

"How can you tell that?"

"He's still got all his teeth," said Piper. "None of the usual markers of malnutrition. He'd be on the tall side, too."

"If a human's head were still attached, anyway," muttered Earstripe.

"I'll put my professional reputation on the line and say that was a recent development."

The gnole snorted. "Leather shoes, like the others," said Galen, pointing. "And all he had in his pockets was a pencil."

Earstripe held up one of the dead man's hands. It moved stiffly, but even with the dark stain of settled blood, Galen could see the ink stains on the man's fingers. "A gnole thinks a clerk, maybe."

"Down here taking notes?" guessed Piper. "Thomas talked about hiring a clerk. Suppose he hired this one, then shut him in, just like us?" Earstripe nodded to him.

"Other humans might have been the same," the gnole said. "Couldn't tell about fingers, though."

"No, the water damage was too much," murmured Piper. "It would make sense. He lures people in using their intellectual curiosity." His lips twisted self-deprecatingly.

"It wasn't just you," said Galen. "We're both down here with you, remember?"

He could tell that he hadn't convinced the doctor, but Piper nodded jerkily and went to the far door. All three of them stepped out into the hall, tensed for the rules of the place to change, but nothing happened except for the greenish lights flicking to life on the wall.

"Do we try the next door then?" asked Piper.

"No," said Earstripe. "We rest." He sat down, leaning against the wall. "A gnole and humans did much today, much running, much alarm. Need sleep, or start making mistakes, yeah?"

"Sleep?" said Piper, sounding astonished.

"He's right," said Galen.

"I'm sure he is, but it seems so strange to sleep after all of this."

"You get used to it." Galen sat down as well, stretching his legs out in front of him. "Sometimes we'd have hours before launching an attack, and the smartest thing to do was to take a catnap. It was hard to learn at first, though."

"I can imagine."

"I don't think I could sleep just yet, though."

"No, me neither." Piper sat down next to him and sighed.

"My brain will start hammering me with guilt or second-guessing all the ways I could have stopped this."

"You couldn't have known."

"Bah." Piper shrugged. "That wasn't a call to try and convince me. It's the usual foolishness, nothing more."

"Why do you do that?" asked Galen.

"Do what?"

"Dismiss your own feelings like that. As if they're an annoyance."

"Mostly because they are." Piper waved his hand at the ivory doorway. "And really, we're stuck in a bizarre death maze where I'm feeling our way along trying to figure out what makes the dead bodies dead before it makes us dead. This isn't really the optimal time to be delving into my feelings, is it?"

Galen laughed softly. "Well, you've got me there. But also we're not going anywhere in a hurry, so we've got plenty of time."

"I can think of a great many things I'd rather do with my last hours on earth."

Galen wondered if the doctor had meant that flirtatiously. Had that been a meaningful look? Was it worth spending his last hours on earth feeling horribly awkward if it hadn't been?

Sure, I can charge the enemy bare-handed and screaming without a qualm, but can I ask a handsome man if I can kiss him without breaking into a cold sweat? Apparently not.

"Humans could try going to *sleep.*"

"Sorry, Earstripe..." The gnole grumbled something in their general direction and rolled over.

"Anyway," said Piper, more quietly, "it's not like there's some deep dark well of misery and torment that I'm sitting on. I'm just so tired of it all. Having to be responsible for someone else's emotions is fine and good for friends and lovers, but as a job? Day in and day out, scared people who are either so cowed you have to tease out their symptoms or so full of bluster that you're waiting for a kick to the head? It's exhausting. Some people can do it. Me, I just got worn down."

The word *lovers* had licked down Galen's spine and he had to shake himself free. "So you decided to work with the dead."

"Between that and my little trick, it seemed the best fit. The only emotions I have to deal with are mine and the occasional family of the deceased, and by the time they get to me, they've usually gone through the initial shock and we take refuge in courtesies." He sighed. "Every now and again they want to yell at me because I'm telling them a story different than the one they told themselves, but somebody from the Rat is usually there to handle it. The Rat's full of good people."

"And yours?"

"My what?"

"Your feelings?"

"Oh, *those.*" Piper waved his hand, as if dismissing a mosquito. "I have them, obviously. I'm not a clockwork creature out of Anuket City. But ideally, I keep my life arranged so that it doesn't get out of hand."

"Even happiness? Joy?"

Piper tilted his head toward Galen, his dark eyes lighting with amusement. "How many men really suffer from a surfeit of unbridled joy in their lives?"

"I really hope somebody somewhere is," said Galen. "Make up for the rest of us who are just muddling along, you know?"

Piper laughed. Damnation, he was attractive when he laughed. Regardless of his feelings about...well...feelings...he had no problem laughing, and Galen found himself watching the movement of the doctor's tongue against his lower teeth and feeling quite a few things himself.

"I'm more curious about what this place was meant to be," said Piper, obviously ready to change the subject. He waved his hand, taking in the ivory walls. "Why build this? What was it meant to be?"

"Crazy humans building a crazy thing," muttered Earstripe. Galen knew from experience that gnoles had about fifty words that all translated as *crazy,* none of which actually involved mental illness, which they called *head-sick.* He wondered which version of *crazy* the gnoles considered the ancients, and how it varied from all the others.

"Possibly, but all the wonder engines seem to have a purpose, even if we don't always know why." Piper leaned his head back against the wall, chin tilted up. Galen's eyes traced the long column of his throat, the dark stubble coming in around the edge of the clipped beard. He could imagine how the skin would feel against his lips, the roughness turning to smoothness lower down his neck. "Some kind of torture chamber?"

Torture chamber cut Galen's imagination off at the ankles. He looked away. "It doesn't feel right for one of those," he said.

"It doesn't?"

Galen sighed. "Have either of you ever seen one?"

"A torture chamber?" Piper shook his head. "I've had some bodies come in that were pretty badly treated," he said. "But I don't go out in the field like that." There was a hollowness to his tone that Galen knew too well.

Earstripe sat up, abandoning the pretense of sleep. "A gnole saw a den where a human lived," he said. "A human called himself a doctor. A human who didn't want anyone to get better." He paused, then said, obviously reluctantly, "Not-doctor's den looked like bone-doctor's den."

Piper winced. "Was he stopped?"

"Yes. A human got away, found gnoles. Gnoles hid a human, got guard-gnole, guard-gnole brought others. Not-doctor went out window, fell." Earstripe stared at his claws.

Galen wondered if the man had really fallen. Gnoles were much more practical in some regards than humans.

"Was the person who escaped all right?" asked Piper softly.

Earstripe shrugged. "Don't know any human would be *all right* after. A human healed up. A human stayed in gnole burrow for a long time. Couldn't look at other humans. A gnole took a human to another burrow, out of the city, no humans, only gnoles. Don't know after that."

Galen sighed. He could understand that. "I've seen one," he said. "We'd been called in to clear out a...a mess, frankly. A bandit group that turned into a cult, or a cult that took to raiding, take your pick. The leader kept an actual torture chamber. It felt different than this." He lifted his head, scanning the plain ivory walls with their faint etched lines. "It felt like it was waiting." Even now, he could remember the iron machines, the spikes, the screws, the stained leather straps. Things that he understood the use of immediately, and other things that he had never learned and didn't want to know. All the devices had oozed malevolence, but worse, they had a kind of terrible inanimate patience, as if they knew their time would come again.

The paladins had burned and smashed everything in the place, but even that hadn't felt like enough. The Saints of Steel weren't big into blessings, but there was a priest of the Forge God with them, who had prayed over the site for a day straight. Galen had never seen the woman look so haggard. Even the battle hadn't affected her as much.

"It's the forging," she had said, when Istvhan had asked. Istvhan always asked. "Someone wrought those machines, brought them into being. Devices that exist only to draw pain from flesh. Once a thing is made, it exists in the mind of the world. The next one is easier to make, and the next one after that."

"Some of those machines have existed for a long time," said

Judith, who didn't talk about her past. Galen had served beside the other paladin for nearly a decade at that point, and still didn't know where she came from.

The Forge God's priest had sighed. "I know," she had said. They were all sitting around the fire that night, and the orange light could not seem to illuminate the deep hollows of her eyes. "The first takes a twisted genius. The hundredth can be done by any blacksmith. It is why our first lesson is always to be careful of what you make."

He shook away the memory and tried to explain what the Forge God's priest had said, but didn't know how much he managed to convey to Piper and Earstripe. "This doesn't feel like that," he said. "This place feels like it will kill you and then you'll be dead. Just dead. It isn't trying to carve you up in little increments. You don't have time to panic or see what's happening to you. It isn't *evil.* It's just *here.*"

"You're right," said Piper. "You've put your finger on it. This doesn't feel cruel, exactly. It feels like a test."

"Bad human said it was religious."

"I can't swear it isn't," said Piper. "It'd be a pretty odd one, though, wouldn't it? Usually you just have to put on a mask and crawl through some caves on your knees."

"A little self-flagellation, a lot of candles," agreed Galen.

"Human religion is crazy," said Earstripe with finality. "A gnole wants to sleep. Humans sleep too. A gnole doesn't want humans dying because they stayed awake chattering."

"Yes, Mother," said Galen.

"Hmmph! Wipe paws, too."

Piper snickered. He slid off his outer tunic and balled it up into a pillow. Galen knew there was no point in standing watch, but it was hard to close his eyes nonetheless.

Once he did, though, he fell asleep instantly, pulled down into dark and drowning dreams.

CHAPTER 16

Piper woke because someone shrieked in his ear.

He shot upright, convinced that they were under attack or the building was on fire or possibly there were wolves or all three at once. For a moment he could not remember where he was, but the watery light on ivory walls snapped him back to reality. *No wolves, not on fire—is it Thomas? Has he come back to kill us?* He looked around wildly. Earstripe was on his feet, teeth bared. And Galen...

Galen lay on his side, eyes tightly closed, his face screwed up in a rictus of fear. One hand scrabbled at the smooth floor, nails struggling for purchase. "No," he mumbled. "*No.* Where is..." His voice trailed off into incoherency, and then he gave another heartwrenching cry. His chest heaved and his nails chattered against the floor as his hands spasmed.

"Dear god," said Piper. Whatever Galen was seeing, it was clearly horrific. He reached toward the paladin. "Galen, you're having a nightmare—"

"Stop!" Earstripe scrambled toward him. "A human doesn't touch! Stop!"

"What?"

"Where is he?" whimpered Galen. "Where did he go?"

"A human can't touch him. Not during a human's bad dream. Not safe."

Piper stifled a groan. Plenty of people had some misguided notion that if you woke a sleepwalker or shook someone out of a nightmare, you'd do terrible damage to them. It was all ridiculous and not in any way based in science. As far as he could tell, the prohibition against waking sleepwalkers had arisen because of a superstition that their souls might come untethered and a wandering ghost slip inside in its place. *Apparently gnoles have the same thing. Lovely*. "It's fine. It won't hurt him."

"Not him I'm worried about, bone-doctor."

Galen sobbed in his sleep. "I have to do something." said Piper decisively. "He's suffering."

Earstripe tried to grab for him, but he was too late. Piper caught Galen's hand, saying in soothing tones, "Galen. Galen, it's all right."

Galen's eyes snapped open. Dark green stared into brown without a trace of recognition.

"Galen, you're having a nightm—"

He did not finish the word, because the world suddenly rolled upside down as the paladin threw him across the room.

Oh hmm, thought Piper, which was not a terribly useful thought to be having. Then he hit the ground, landed badly, and his shoulder exploded into pain. The world went from rolling to turning gray at the edges.

When it settled again, he sat up and felt for his arm. *Not out of the socket. That's lucky. Right. Don't touch Galen when he's having a nightmare. I should definitely have listened to Earstripe.*

Earstripe was, in fact, standing over him. The gnole's back was to Piper and he was hunkered down, his fur in spikes along his back. A low growl rumbled out of his throat.

"It's fine," said Piper, in pain but also deeply embarrassed. Galen was going to feel horribly guilty in a moment. People always did when they accidentally smacked someone else during a fit, or wandered somewhere unfortunate while sleep-walking. The important thing was to reassure them that you knew it wasn't their fault. "Really, I'm fine."

Earstripe's growl dropped even lower. His ears were flat back against his head.

The sound of a sword being drawn rang through the ivory room.

Galen had risen to his feet. His eyes were unfocused and his hands were full of naked steel.

"Galen?" said Piper.

The paladin screamed.

Earstripe, far stronger than Piper had ever guessed, wrenched the doctor upright and snarled, "Run!" Piper didn't need to be told twice. Galen's scream had not sounded human. It was a long wailing cry, like some animal Piper had never seen and didn't want to.

They ran.

Of course, you fool, the Saint of Steel's paladins were berserkers, that was what they did, *you* knew *that was what they did, why were you so stupid?*

He'd been stupid because he knew the paladins. He'd met them. He'd never seen one of their legendary berserker rages and he'd never had to fit the reality in with the gentle, dutiful men he knew.

More than that, he was a doctor and of course that meant he knew better than anyone who wasn't. *Of* course *it had to be superstition that Earstripe was worried about, not, say, a screaming berserker in the middle of a nightmare. But you knew so much better, didn't you?*

"Did you kill him?" asked Galen, his voice slurring.

"Door!" gasped Earstripe. "Now!"

"But the traps—"

"Open a door, *maybe* we die!"

He didn't need to finish the sentence. Whatever nightmare Galen was caught in, it wasn't letting him go. Piper slapped the door switch and lunged through it, praying the next room wasn't filled with poison gas, hoping that Galen's slow advance would not reach the door in the thirty seconds until it closed.

For a few long breaths, he thought they would make it. Surely twenty-eight minutes would be enough for Galen to snap out of the rage and all he and Earstripe had to do was figure out where the blade would fall or the spikes would drop and live through it and then they could come out and everything would be normal again and...

Galen filled the doorway. He was not a large man, not compared to most of his brothers, but the air around him seemed to vibrate. His eyes still had that terrible unfocused look, as if he had not yet woken up from the dream.

"Galen," said Piper, backing away. "Galen, wake up. Please wake up. You're having a nightmare. It's us. Piper and Earstripe. Whatever you're seeing, it's not really there."

The paladin stepped forward, his head moving back and forth, eyes traveling between human and gnole. Piper could almost see him deciding which one to attack first, not that it would matter one way or the other, because Galen had a sword and all Earstripe had was teeth and claws and all Piper had was a nauseating sense of guilt that wasn't going to do fuck-all against a yard of steel.

Click. The door closed behind him.

Galen spun around at the sound, smashing the pommel of

his sword against the door twice, before he seemed to realize that it was only a door. He turned back toward them, taking another step forward. Piper and Earstripe retreated as one.

Another step forward. Another step back. "Are we halfway?" whispered Piper. "Are we about to set it off?"

"A gnole isn't taking eyes off a human."

Galen's gaze locked with his. Piper took another step back involuntarily. He had no idea what emotion he was seeing in the other man's eyes. Perhaps it had no name. It was deeper than rage, emptier than hate. It made him feel like prey.

Piper's nerve broke and he bolted.

Click.

For a moment, Piper thought he was fainting. The ceiling seemed to fall away. Then he realized that the ceiling was in just the same place, and the floor itself was tilting. Fast.

In a matter of seconds, the far side of the room had dropped several yards. Piper caught a glimpse of another yawning pit...a pit that he and Earstripe were now sliding into.

He flung himself flat on his back and tried to slow his descent, feeling his heels skid on the slick ivory surface. Scraping sounds and gnollish obscenities came from his right as Earstripe tried to dig his claws into the infinitesimal grooves in the floor.

He managed to halt himself for a few seconds, arms outflung, feet flat on the tilted floor. For a split second, he felt relief, and then one of his heels slipped and he skidded another few inches down. *Am I really going to die because I don't have better shoes?*

Somehow, probably because his palms were so sweaty that they stuck to the floor like suction cups, he managed to push himself upward a few desperate inches. He couldn't look behind him to see what Galen was doing. That was irony for you. He'd been running away and now he was desperately trying to scramble backward the way he'd come, probably right onto the paladin's sword. Was it better or worse to die sliced to ribbons in the pit, or be chopped to pieces by a man you were attracted to? *Okay, well, possibly the pit is the better choice in that case...*

Something went clang. Something else grabbed his hair. Piper yelped. It felt like it was being pulled out by the roots, which it probably was. He watched, barely comprehending, as Galen's sword slid past him with a long metallic sound like a draw from the scabbard, infinitely prolonged, and then it hit the bottom and tumbled into the pit. He could feel individual hairs tearing loose from his scalp.

Then a hand tangled in his collar, pulling upward, and the ties on his shirt were caught under his chin and he couldn't breathe and maybe this was how he died, being strangled by a man that he was attracted to, maybe he wasn't going to get a choice after all. His vision was starting to go gray again. He lifted a hand to his throat to try and stop the pressure, imagining Galen's face with his unfocused green eyes and that terrible blank expression, hearing himself choke. He didn't dare lift the other hand but in a second he was going to have to and then he would slide down onto the blades this was it this was how it ended all because he had seen a man in pain and was so goddamn arrogant that he thought he could help or maybe he was still back in the fishing village and he was a fish drowning on dry land and in a minute the vision would fade and everything would be normal maybe this wasn't actually happening at all maybe he was watching the last seconds of someone else's life, not his own...

The pressure on his throat eased. Galen's hand slid under his lifted arm and held hard.

"Hold still," the paladin said in his ear. He sounded almost eerily calm. "I've got you, but if you struggle, we're both going to fall."

Oh god, he's back. He's back. It's over. If Piper hadn't been dangling by his neck over certain death, he'd have cheered. As it was, he couldn't get enough air to speak coherently. He managed to grunt something that he hoped sounded like agreement.

"Earstripe," said Galen, still in that calm voice, "I can probably get one foot down near you. If you grab onto it, I think I can hold you both up."

"Better do something quick," said Earstripe, sounding strained. "Claws aren't going to last much longer."

Piper couldn't see much, but from what he could work out, the paladin was lying flat at the top of the floor. *There must be a lip around the edge,* he thought, *or maybe a little ledge where the edge of the floor is tilted up. But can he really hold both of us up for... six minutes? However long it is?*

"I'm going to move," Galen told him. "I won't let go, but our balance is going to shift. Don't struggle or we'll both go down."

"Yeh..." Piper breathed, unable to nod.

The pressure on his neck changed. He swallowed. Out of the corner of his eye, he saw Galen's boot slide downward. It seemed impossibly far away from Earstripe. Could the gnole even reach it?

One of Earstripe's hind legs slipped. Ivory squealed as the gnole's claws scrabbled along it. Piper heard himself moan in strangled horror.

The gnole lunged upward, grabbing for Galen's foot—and missed.

Galen cursed. Piper felt the grip on his neck snap bruisingly tight. The paladin's foot kicked out into empty space.

With an agility that Piper hadn't known he possessed, Earstripe flung himself upward and sank his teeth into Galen's boot. Piper heard the other man hiss in pain. He felt Galen's grip slacken for an instant, felt himself start to slide—and then the arm around him tightened again.

"Now," said Galen calmly, "I think it would be best if no one moves *at all.*"

"Yeh," panted Piper.

"Auungh," said Earstripe, with a mouth full of foot.

It was the longest six minutes of Piper's life. It felt like six years. His vision began to go gray around the edges from lack of air, and he fought to stay conscious, because if he went limp, all three of them were going to fall, since he couldn't trust Galen to do the sensible thing and let go.

But eventually there was a click and a grind and Galen's body jerked sideways. The paladin rolled into him. Piper had a moment of nauseating terror, but the slope was already decreasing rapidly and he only slid a few inches before the floor snapped level again. Earstripe released his grip on Galen's footwear and all three of them lay flat on the floor, gasping for air, grateful to be alive.

CHAPTER 17

"I'm sorry," said Galen.

"No, it's my fault." Piper waved his hands helplessly. "I shouldn't have—Earstripe told me not to, but I was an idiot—you were yelling and I thought—I'm sorry!"

"No. No. If I wasn't like this...I'm sorry. It's been years." He swallowed. The anguish on his face tore Piper's heart. "I stopped going into the battle tide when I woke up. I thought that was over. Nobody should touch me, still, but usually I don't do any worse than accidentally deck someone. It's been *years!*" His voice rose on the last word, a child crying against unfairness.

"But I shouldn't have—"

"*Both* humans shouldn't have," Earstripe broke in, clearly done with their arguing. "Both humans wrong, both humans don't listen to a gnole, both humans acting like a gnole cub with worms."

There did not seem to be any way to counter that. Piper dropped his head. "You're right," he said. "Wallowing in guilt doesn't help matters." *At least in public*, he added to himself.

Performative guilt doesn't help anyone, and you'd think I'd have learned that, after the first dozen sickrooms.

The silence that followed was horribly awkward, up until Piper noticed the tear in Galen's surcoat and the dark stain underneath. "You're bleeding!"

"Probably," said Galen. "My foot too, I imagine."

"Gnole can't apologize for biting, tomato-man, but a gnole wishes a human's boot had been thicker." He opened his mouth, showing a broad expanse of tongue. "Also that a human's boot had been *cleaner.*"

"Next time we're in a maze of death traps, I'll wear better footwear."

"Shirt off," said Piper briskly. "And sit down. What happened?"

"When the floor tilted, the edge came up against the wall. Made a pointy little ledge about six inches wide. I had one foot and one hand jammed into it. Got both of them out in time when the floor went back into place, but it caught part of the coat and pinched my mail along my ribs."

"Do you feel any breaks? Anything stabbing when you breathe?"

"No."

Piper grimaced. You could never tell with soldier types. Either they wouldn't complain even if their leg was falling off, or they'd whine over every hangnail. He suspected that Galen was more of the leg-falling-off variety, but there was no telling until you actually had one in front of you. "Let me take a look at it."

Galen sighed and stripped off his surcoat and the light chain hauberk underneath. The padded shirt under that was stained with blood. "I suspect it's going to be an impressive bruise, that's all. What I get for sleeping in chainmail, I suppose."

"You're bleeding like a stuck pig."

"Yes, well..." He pulled the shirt off over his head, wincing when the fabric stuck to the wound. Earstripe hissed through his teeth sympathetically. The man's skin was already darkening with a long, ugly bruise, and it looked like the skin had split down the middle. If Galen had less muscle across his ribs, Piper had a horrible feeling he'd be looking at exposed bone.

"Rat's mercy," he muttered. "And me without my kit."

"It'll be fine. I've had a lot worse."

"Hush and let me take a look. And if I press on anything that feels like it impacts your breathing, tell me." He ran his fingers across the man's ribs, trying to focus on possible injuries. Unfortunately, that meant that he was focusing very hard on the feel of sleek muscle over bone and this did not make the job any easier. *Oh my...* he thought, and then, *For the love of god, he's injured and just had an extremely upsetting episode that was entirely your fault. Don't be such an ass.*

Galen inhaled sharply. "Did I hurt you?" asked Piper.

"No." The paladin's voice was clipped.

Right. This might be an excellent time to make conversation. Set the patient at ease. Right. We could talk about...err...there's no weather down here, so...ah...somehow, "How's the ancient death trap treating you?" doesn't seem appropriate...

Piper had started working with dead people because he knew his bedside manner with living ones could use some improvement. He groped for a topic. "So you are prone to extreme sleep disturbances. That's useful to know."

Galen said nothing.

"The literature of sleep disturbance is quite fascinating. We have written records of sleepwalkers dating back nearly a thousand years. While it's more common in children, there are reports across all ages and sexes, and while some theorize that it is caused by stress, particularly in unusual sleep environments, no one really knows the cause."

Galen said nothing, more loudly. Too late, it occurred to Piper that this might be the single thing on earth that the paladin least wanted to talk about right now. Unfortunately, Piper had already committed to this course and couldn't seem to stop talking. "The politician Sang Mar reportedly once gave a speech to a large crowd, while deeply asleep, wearing only his socks." Earstripe made a small noise of either amusement or dismay, Piper wasn't sure. "At the time, the accepted theory of sleepwalking was a form of nocturnal demonic possession, where the demon shared a body with the human soul but could only take control of it when the soul was asleep. The followers of the Dreaming God tell us that this is inaccurate, however, and that they have never encountered a possessed sleepwalker. Also apparently demons do not sleep as such. Indeed, lack of sleep is part of the trauma caused by demonic possession—oh, hmm, I think this rib might be cracked."

"Oh, thank god," said Galen.

"That's not a good thing."

"If it stops our tour of sleepwalking through the ages, I'll take it."

"Sorry. I get going sometimes..." He sat back. "I'd prescribe rest and immobility, but I don't think that's going to happen. I'll clean the wound and we'll bind your ribs. Hopefully it's just a nasty bone bruise." He pulled off his own shirt and the undershirt beneath it, and tossed that aside, then pulled his shirt back on. "Earstripe, can you tear this into strips? And do you still have your waterskin?"

Earstripe nodded and handed over his waterskin and Piper began sluicing the blood off Galen's side. The paladin caught his hand. "Wait, don't do that. We don't have very much water. Don't waste it on me."

"It is *not* a waste," said Piper. "And I'm cleaning this off. You got fabric ground into the muscle here and that will make a truly superlative mess if it's left alone."

"The Saint of Steel's chosen heal quickly," said Galen. "Don't worry about me."

"*Someone* has to." Piper almost added that the Saint of Steel wasn't around to do it anymore, but thought that would be a trifle undiplomatic. "Stop squirming."

"A gnole can go back for more water," said Earstripe, slicing through fabric with a small knife. "And the lantern, and human packs."

"What?" Galen stopped trying to fend off Piper's ministrations. "You'd have to go past the last room again."

Earstripe shrugged. "Now that a gnole knows how, a gnole isn't worried. A gnole gets enough space on ledge for claws, a gnole will be fine."

"Are you sure?" asked Piper.

"A gnole is sure. Besides, could stand to visit the pit again." He gave them a drop-jawed gnole grin. "In private."

"Oh well, don't let us stand in the way of nature's call," said Galen. Piper finished cleaning the paladin's wound and gave the waterskin back to the gnole.

"A gnole will be back," said Earstripe. He stood, looked down at them both, and shook his head. "Humans try not to maul each other with apologizing before then, hey?"

"No promises," said Galen. "It's what we do."

They watched the gnole enter the door, and even though it didn't close behind him, Piper felt himself tense.

"He'll be all right," said Galen quietly.

"I know," said Piper. The gnole had certainly been better prepared than either of the humans. He'd had the presence of mind to grab a knife and waterskin when Galen woke, or he'd been carrying them all along. Perhaps it was simply easier for gnoles to sleep in full kit, with the elaborate cloth wrappings they wore.

Galen was waiting patiently. He shook himself out of his thoughts. "Let me finish wrapping you up."

Galen lifted his arms as Piper bound strips of torn shirt around his torso. His chest was broader than Piper had realized. The man moved like a dancer and it was easy to miss how much power was lurking behind the grace.

"How's your neck?" asked Galen, not looking at him.

"Eh?"

"Your neck. Where I nearly strangled you."

"Oh, *that.*"

Galen gazed at the ceiling, presumably asking some deity for strength. "Yes. That."

"The human neck makes a poor handle," said Piper, "as my anatomy instructor used to say. But you handily avoided crushing my windpipe, for which I am grateful. Don't ask me to look over my left shoulder for a while, that's all." He tried to keep his tone light, because he was certain that there was guilt simmering just below the surface. "And you didn't drop me into the pit, which is the important thing. I'm sorry about your sword, though. Did it have a name?"

Galen looked blank. "Did what?"

"Your sword."

"Why would it have a name?"

"Don't warriors name their swords?"

The paladin stared at him. "Is that a euphemism?"

Piper felt a flush starting. "I didn't think it was, no. You know, the pointy metal thing?"

"...you know they don't come when called, right?"

"Neither do cats, but people name those." His flush was definitely growing.

"Yes, but that's so you have something to yell when they

knock things off the table." Galen rubbed his forehead. "No, I don't name my swords. I'd have to keep thinking of names, for one thing. They break and then I grumble and try to find another one that suits my grip and hand over far too much money for the privilege."

"So all those tales of heroes with magic swords named, oh, Chainbreaker and Blood-drinker and so on?" He finished the bindings and Galen pulled his shirt back on.

"I suppose if you had a magic sword, the rules would be different. Or even a particularly fine one. I'm a berserker, though, as you might have noticed. We're rather hard on weapons." He climbed to his feet, his gaze darkened. "And everything else."

Dammit. For a second there, Piper thought he had managed to distract the man. "That's hardly your fault," he said.

"Don't do this," said Galen. "Don't excuse it. You of all people should have seen it enough by now. A man beats the shit out of his loved ones, and all they can say is, 'but he loves me, he doesn't mean it.' And then he apologizes and eventually they wind up on your slab, because love doesn't fix it."

"It's not the same," said Piper furiously. "You have a *medical condition.* Sleep disturbances have been known to medicine for centuries. Including violence. Sleepwalkers have murdered people and judges found them not accountable because they were *asleep.*"

Too late, he realized that this was the wrong tactic. Galen's face grew even bleaker. "Fat lot of good that did the people they killed. Fat lot it would have done *you*, if I'd..." He couldn't seem to finish the words. So softly that Piper could barely hear it, he added, "I should have killed myself after Hallowbind. I should have known that I was too broken to live around other people. Damn Stephen and Istvhan for stopping me."

"You *aren't too broken!* You said you've lived just fine for years now! Dammit..." Piper stomped forward, grabbed both of Galen's hands in his and brought them to his throat. "Here! Do you want to start strangling me? Are you fighting the urge to kill me right now?"

Galen's nostrils flared and he took a step back. Piper followed, clinging to the paladin's hands. "See? You don't have the least desire in the world to hurt me. This is just a thing that happens to you when you sleep, like...like *snoring,* for god's sake!"

"Nobody dies because you snore at them."

Piper's exasperation was exceeding his ability to keep his emotions in check. "Nobody died today. Stop it. You are *not* a monster."

"You have no idea what I am."

"Maybe not. But I'd like to find out."He risked dropping one of the man's hands so that he could reach up and touch that angular jaw.

Galen froze.

Oh boy. Did not expect to be doing this. Adrenaline aftereffects. How 'bout that. The paladin's skin was just starting to roughen with stubble, the texture slick one way, coarse the other. *Either this is a wonderful idea or I am making a colossal fool of myself. I suppose, that's always the risk you take when you declare your intentions.* Piper moved his thumb gently across Galen's lips and something hot and savage flared in the paladin's eyes.

"You're not afraid of me." His breath was warm on Piper's fingers.

"No," said Piper, which was mostly true, although the look in the other man's eyes was waking something that felt a little like fear and a lot like lust. "No, I'm not."

The paladin moved. He was impossibly fast, catching Piper's arms and pinning him up against the wall. Piper swallowed hard, stunned by the speed and by the sensation of Galen's body pressed full-length against his.

"You should be," said Galen, and kissed him.

CHAPTER 18

Piper had experienced a number of kisses that started tender and turned fierce. He'd never had one go the other way before. Galen's mouth was hard over his, all teeth and tongue, but as soon as Piper began to respond, he softened. His hands slid down Piper's arms. Some part of the doctor's mind registered that he was free, and another part registered that he didn't particularly wish to be.

It was so good. The hardness of the muscles he'd been trying to ignore, just a few minutes ago, the hardness of...well, other things that weren't technically muscle, actually they were spongiform erectile tissue comparable to...*dear sweet Rat, why am I thinking about spongiform erectile tissue right now...okay, well, obviously that's why I'm thinking about it, but...*

The kiss ended. Galen brushed his lips almost apologetically and stepped away. "Damn," the paladin said softly. "Damnit, I shouldn't have done that." He raked his hand through his hair. "I find myself behaving very badly around you. I'm sorry."

"I rather enjoyed it," said Piper, which was possibly the understatement of the century.

Hmm, that's a funny way of saying 'take me, take me now, right here, let's go.'

He told himself to shut up. His inner voice laughed at him.

Galen gave him an anguished look. Piper knew that he was about say something self-flagellating and was almost certainly going to promise to never kiss Piper again and he didn't want that to happen so he opened his mouth and blurted out the first thing that came into his head.

The man was absolutely witless. He had no sense of self-preservation. First he'd lunged into a trapped room to grab a corpse, then he'd been making excuses for a killer who had just come within an inch of throttling him, and now he was sitting here calmly, having just been kissed by said killer, as if that were normal and not really, really messed up.

Well. Perhaps not absolutely *calm.* Piper's face was flushed and he was still breathing hard from that kiss. That terrible, foolish, glorious kiss.

Gods above and below, he shouldn't have done that. He wasn't even sure why he had. Galen never kissed. He preferred encounters where both parties walked away—occasionally a little stiffly, depending on what exactly had occurred—and went on about their day with the warm glow of lust satisfied and nothing else. Kissing felt like intimacy, not lust, and intimacy with someone like Galen was far too dangerous.

Most of the paladins he knew were the same way. Hell, compared to half of the Dreaming God's people, Galen was practically celibate. It was a high-mortality profession, and less than half of them made it to old age. Hardly anybody wanted to leave a spouse or, god forbid, children behind. He'd seen the devastation that Marcus had been through, leaving his wife for her own safety after the death of the god. It was part of why he'd been so surprised when Istvhan had fallen in love up north.

Very well. If Piper didn't have any sense, Galen would have to have sense for both of them. He couldn't be trusted and Piper was a doctor and probably had some misguided notion that he could cure what was wrong with Galen, when it wasn't that something was wrong, it was that Galen *himself* was wrong and broken. The only cure for someone like him was a sharp knife, but he kept staggering onward because the Rat said they needed him and sometimes he was able to fix things.

He doubted he could explain any of this, and Piper would have argued if he tried, but before he could say any of it, Piper said, *"Spongiform erectile tissue!"*

"Err…what?"

"Oh god." Piper put his hand to his face. Galen could see the flush starting at his collar and rising rapidly. "I didn't mean to say that."

"Okay."

"It's…it's what your cock is made out of. Not just yours. Mine. Everybody's." He made a helpless gesture toward his crotch, where Galen noted that there was indeed a definite bulge, apparently caused by the tissue in question.

"I see," said Galen. He knew that he should still be wallowing in shame, and he absolutely was, but there was a tiny part of him that was feeling ungodly smug that his kiss had gotten that kind of reaction. *Yup. Still got it.*

The tips of Piper's ears were blazing scarlet. "It's also present inside the nose."

"Goodness."

"I know I'm babbling, incidentally."

"Just a bit, yes."

"This is what happens to me when I stop trying to be

dispassionate about everything. It's not that I've got a terrible temper or anything like that. It's just that I start babbling."

"I see."

"It's a bit of a problem in relationships."

"I would imagine so."

"And also if I keep talking about this, maybe you won't get all tragic and paladinly and swear that you'll never kiss me again. And I would very much like it if you did. Err, not be tragic and paladinly. The kissing part." His blush wasn't fading. In fact, it seemed to be deepening from scarlet to near-purple.

"*Why* aren't you scared?" asked Galen hopelessly. "You ought to be. I came after you with a sword. Most people don't get over that in five minutes."

This actually shut Piper up for a moment. His color slowly began to return to normal. "I didn't die," he said finally. "I've felt dying dozens of times. You get used to it. If you don't actually die, it just doesn't seem worth bothering about."

"You are going to get yourself *killed!*" yelled Galen, trying not to tear his hair out in frustration.

"This is the most dangerous thing I've done in years," said Piper. "Probably in my whole life. It's not like *my* job is going around fighting people." For the first time, he sounded a bit annoyed. "Unlike *some* people I could mention."

Galen took a deep breath and let it out again. *All right. I probably deserved that. But still! I've got a sword and berserker rage! All he's got is brains...quite a lot of brains, admittedly...and a bone-saw...and gorgeous fingers...*

"Anyway," said Piper, "being in mortal danger is bad, but *surviving* mortal danger is a well-known aphrodisiac. And this place is just nothing but mortal danger after mortal danger, isn't it?"

The blush was starting up again. Galen wondered if the man was still thinking about spongiform erectile tissue.

Saint's teeth, what's wrong with me? Why don't I just fuck his brains out right here and now and be done with it? I've done it often enough, with any number of people. I was completely willing to do it before *I nearly killed him. Why am I making this so difficult for myself?*

Because trying to kill someone ought to matter. Because he *liked* Piper, dammit. Liked him...well, rather a lot. Because it might mean something, and that meant sex might mean something, and that would be far more dangerous than this maze of traps they found themselves in.

It's probably going to kill you, though. And instead of worrying about the future, you could just worry about right now. *And right now, there's a very attractive man coming toward you with an expression like he doesn't know if he's going to the whorehouse or the gallows.*

Piper kissed him, very carefully. A light brush of lips, nothing more, giving Galen time to pull back. Galen...did not seem to be pulling back. Galen seemed to be responding, politely at first, and then with all the pent-up frustration of that first kiss, his hands on Piper's shoulders, feeling the muscle flex as the doctor's arm lifted, his hand going to Galen's face and sliding up into his hair and Galen's cock was standing at attention and thought, furthermore, that Galen was an absolute fool for not tearing the man's clothes off right now, bruised ribs or no bruised ribs, it's not as if you used your ribs when you were on your knees anyway and if he was on his knees, then he could—

The door slid open.

Piper and Galen leapt apart as if they were children discovered with their hands in the cookie jar. *Which is deeply unfair, because I didn't even get my hands anywhere near that particular cookie jar. Dammit.*

Earstripe appeared, holding a lumpy burlap sack over his shoulder. “Good news,” he said. “A gnole has had an idea.”

CHAPTER 19

"You're back," said Piper. "Err...great!"

The gnole looked between the two humans, sniffed a few times, and then raised both eyebrows. "A gnole can come back, if humans are mating," he said.

"We aren't!" said Piper. He was turning scarlet again, Galen saw. *At least that'll pull the blood away from other parts of his anatomy, I suppose.*

"A gnole doesn't mind." Earstripe glanced through the open door. "Twenty-eight minutes until a door opens, though. A gnole can go into the other room?"

"That's quite all right," said Galen.

"A gnole promises not to shout suggestions."

Piper put his face in his hands. Galen gazed steadily at Earstripe, who he suspected was enjoying this far too much.

This is what you get for wasting time arguing. Twenty-eight minutes might not be a great deal of time, but it was long enough to do all sorts of things, if you just shut up and got down to doing them. *Hell, we're both so keyed up right now that five minutes would probably do it for me, if those fingers are anywhere near as skilled as I think they are...*

Perhaps I can convince Earstripe to go back for more water later.

"A gnole doesn't—"

"The moment has passed," said Galen firmly. "Why don't you just tell us about your idea?"

"Ah." Earstripe thumped the sack. "A gnole's idea is apples."

"Apples?" said Galen.

"I'm not following," Piper admitted.

Earstripe held up a finger and went to the next door on the left. He slapped the panel, and when it opened, he dumped part of the sack out. Apples bounced and rolled across the floor. The gnole bent down, picked up a few, and began lobbing them deeper into the room.

"Apples," he said. "An apple is sliced in half, we know a blade is there. An apple vanishes, we know a pit is there. Yes?"

"Earstripe, you are a genius," said Galen fervently. The door slid closed.

"Do we have enough apples?" asked Piper.

"Depends on how many rooms."

Twenty-eight minutes later, when the door slid open again, the apples were all neatly lined up in the center of the room and every single one had been smashed into paste.

All three of them stared at the resulting fruit carnage. Finally, Galen said, "You know, maybe we should try the other door."

They tromped down the hall to the right. Earstripe dumped out yet more of the sack. Galen tried not to think about what would happen if this batch proved equally ill-fated.

"Surely we've got to be most of the way through by now," he muttered.

"If the rooms run straight to the closed doorway we saw before, then we would have three, possibly four," said Piper. "The corridors aren't all the same length, so I couldn't say for certain."

"Three is not *so* bad," said Earstripe, a bit dubiously.

"But that assumes there aren't switchbacks," said Piper, "or that it doesn't turn again, or spiral."

"Maybe we'll be lucky and more of them will be broken," said Galen.

"We've already been incredibly lucky, if you ask me."

"A gnole thinks it would have been luckier not to get caught by a crazy human."

There didn't seem to be much to say to that.

When the door finally opened, the floor was covered in sliced fruit. An apple sitting in front of the doorway had been neatly halved. They all wedged in the doorway, craning their necks. "There," said Piper, lifting his lamp and pointing. "Those in the far left corner are all intact."

"That's where I'll go, then," said Galen.

"But if you cross the halfway point, the trap will trigger."

"There's still got to be a way to get there," said Galen. "There's been a way to get through all the rooms so far."

Piper blinked at him. "That's…ah…"

His expression was simultaneously so sharp and so befuddled, as if he had just had a brilliant but baffling idea, that Galen wanted to kiss him. *Oh hell with it, there's a good chance you'll die. Just do it.* He leaned forward, planted his lips hastily on the doctor's forehead, then stepped back into the room.

"Galen! Wa—"

The door slid shut. The lights came up. Galen saw that the apples in the center of the room were downright macerated. *Not a great sign. Here goes nothing.*

He lunged forward.

There was a click of warning as a blade fell. Galen dove under it, rolled, and kept rolling as a second one came down, missing him by half an inch. A third cut off the route to the safe corner. *Oh shit. Oh shit. Okay, there must be a clear space, we didn't have enough apples to completely cover the floor, maybe if I crouch right here, nothing will land on me.*

He had one moment when he thought he'd avoided the worst of it, and then another one fell, perpendicular to the first two, coming right at his head.

Galen let out what he hoped was a yell, but suspected was a squeak. The battle rage wanted to rise but it had nothing to work with. This wasn't an enemy you could fight. All you could do was dodge and he wasn't going to be fast enough and—

His scalp smarted as the blade buried itself in his hair. He jerked free, leaving several inches of auburn behind. It occurred to him that there might well be another perpendicular blade, and if it was spaced anything like the others, that meant—

He jerked his knees up to his chest, feeling like a turtle on its back.

Click.

There was a little more clearance on this one. It missed him by nearly six inches.

He rolled over. He was trapped in a box about three feet on a side. *Now, will it stay like this or not?*

He didn't dare risk it. The first blades were pulling back into the ceiling now, but he could hear the clicking as another set started up and he had no time at all to get to his feet. All he could do was throw himself forward on all fours, hearing things land behind him with soft, lethal clicks.

His hand skidded on a cut apple and he pitched forward, slamming his chin into the ivory floor and biting his tongue hard enough to draw blood. One of his knees hit the ground wrong and flared with pain, but he couldn't stop. He wasn't going to be fast enough, but he had to keep moving...

He found the far corner by virtue of running his head into it. He stared at it dizzily, thinking for a moment that more blades had fallen around him, but there were no holes in the walls and there was a whole apple between his hands. It was possibly the most beautiful object he had ever seen in his life.

I'm alive, he thought, picking up the apple. *How am I alive?*

He turned around, putting his back into the corner. His knee was complaining. The blades continued to fall from the ceiling, one after another, each offset a little way from the next, like a chef chopping vegetables.

It was nerve-wracking to watch, but Galen forced himself to do so. *I have to get the others through here safely. There's a pattern. It's actually very straightforward. The first blade falls, then the next, then the next. Then each retracts, and then they fall again. If you step forward every time one retracts, to the next one in the sequence, you can walk through to the corners. The perpendicular blades are just the same, you just want to stay as close to one that's already fallen as you can, so the next one misses you.*

It didn't look hard. It *did* look as if it would require iron nerves. If you panicked, you were mince. He had done the worst possible thing by trying to run through it, and the throbbing pain in his knee was proof of that. Nevertheless, just like all the rooms before, there was a way out. It was just that you couldn't rely on the corners close to the door this time. The room had been designed to force people to cross the floor to survive.

It seemed like a lot longer than six minutes before the blades stopped falling. Galen ate the intact apple thoughtfully, trying to time the motions.

When the clicking finally stopped, he banged on the door to let his companions know he wasn't dead, and sat back down, apple in hand, thinking.

Mostly he was thinking about Piper. About having the man

down on his knees, with his mouth and those clever fingers working on Galen's cock, and damn the consequences, because they were probably all going to die. *Do you want to go out horny and frustrated and angry at yourself, or do you want to go out with a smile on your face?*

It all suddenly seemed very straightforward. Probably it had been all the blades falling around him. There was something about having gigantic sharp objects slamming down close enough to cut your hair that really focused the mind on the here-and-now.

You'd think you were contemplating a marriage proposal, not tossing each other off in the corner. You, of all people! Piper's never given the slightest indication that he wants more than that, and you've *never wanted more than that in your life. One quick lay and your mind will clear and you'll part friends. That's how it always happens. Quit fretting like Stephen and get your hands on that man's cock.*

His own spongiform erectile tissue started to respond, and...*dammit, now he's got me doing it. I'm never going to get hard again without thinking about what the tissue inside my nose is doing.*

The inside of the human nose was not a sexy thing to contemplate, except to a select few persons with highly specialized tastes. Galen was not among them, which was why, when the door finally opened, he was able to walk straight.

"Galen!" said Piper. "Galen, I—"

The paladin held up a hand. "You," he said to Earstripe, "are a genius." Then he kissed Piper passionately. *And if that doesn't make your toes curl inside your boots, I am not doing it correctly.*

"Uh," said Piper, when the kiss had finished, probably because Earstripe was tapping his foot. "Uh. I. Uh. I had a... thing. A thought. I was thinking."

Galen waited politely.

"No! Yes! It's not a trap or a torture chamber or a religious thing! I know what it is!" Piper waved his hands, apparently trying to pull his thoughts back in order. "It's an obstacle course."

CHAPTER 20

"An obstacle course," said Galen. He slapped his forehead. "Yes, of course. Like in the army. You run a little way and then you have to go over a wall and then you run another little way and then you have to crawl under something and then there's a dummy with a sword you have to fight."

"Yes! Exactly!" Piper was so excited that he was practically bouncing on his toes. "Only this is an obstacle course for the ancient's machines. Like the clocktaurs, only smaller. Humans were probably never meant to be here. It was all for the machines that we saw broken apart in the pit."

"A machine isn't very good at thinking, though," said Earstripe. "Clocktaurs thought some, but mostly were just big. Clocktaur couldn't run this."

"The clocktaurs we saw couldn't," said Galen. "But those were controlled by demons, and most demons aren't very smart. Word from the Dreaming God's people is that they were *meant* to be controlled by human souls."

Piper grimaced. "Maybe these little machines are, too. Maybe it's some kind of bizarre training ground. Or an entertainment, like a steeplechase. Hell, for all we know, the ancients were shoving condemned prisoners into machines and betting on how far they'd get."

"A gnole doubts it matters *why*," said Earstripe. "A gnole just wonders if it's good or bad for two humans and a gnole."

"It's good," said Galen. "Isn't it? It means that there's always a way out."

"It means there's a way out for a *machine*," said Piper. "Not necessarily for one of us. The poison gas room, for example. Maybe it was a corrosive, and the machine would have had to brace itself against the ceiling."

"Thank you for that little ray of sunshine," said Galen.

"It's what I do." *We're back to banter. Oh thank god. Kissing and banter and no one is dead yet.* Impossibly, Piper felt his heart lift. *We're going to get through this.*

Galen went through the room twice more before he was confident that he'd gotten the pattern down. "It's not hard," he said. "Or rather, it is, but I can walk you through it. There's enough space for two, barely. Who wants to go first?"

"A gnole took an oath to serve and protect," Earstripe said. "A gnole is not a guard-gnole now, but a gnole swore."

"I'm not sure that oath covers obstacle courses of death in a murderer's basement," offered Piper.

"Oaths are oaths," said Galen. "I took one. You probably did as a doctor, too."

"Yes, but it was mostly about doing no harm and not a lot about death traps."

"A gnole would prefer traps to philosophical discussion."

"Right," said Galen. "Now you're gonna stand pretty much on my feet, and move when I say..."

The door shut behind them. Piper fretted, even though he trusted Galen's skills. *And you know damn well that Earstripe is a lot more agile than you are, and a lot less likely to get you both killed.*

He tried to distract himself with more pleasant thoughts,

like the bit where Galen had kissed him. Unfortunately, that led to the bit where he had blurted out, "Spongiform erectile tissue!" which was possibly the least suave thing he had ever said in his life.

It worked, though. He stopped talking about how broken he was and how wrong it was, and started kissing again. I would call that a win.

Are all paladins like this, or just this one in particular? Granted, his experience was mostly limited to a few from the White Rat, but they all seemed rather solemn and brooding. Galen wasn't solemn and didn't *look* like he was brooding, but it was pretty clear that he'd been gnawing over his own unworthiness for a long damn time.

Which was utter nonsense. So the man had a pretty severe sleep disorder, so what? He was also brave, loyal, calm in a crisis, and had a wicked sense of humor. He was the person that Earstripe had gone to when the gnole needed someone to talk to humans for him, and he'd done it while making it very clear that the gnole was still in charge. Piper couldn't think of many of his fellow humans who would do that gracefully.

Also he kissed like he had been about to throw Piper down and ravish him right there. Possibly he would have, if the door hadn't opened at an opportune moment. Piper swallowed, feeling himself starting to get half-hard again just at the memory.

And then he kissed me again. Like he hadn't regretted it. Granted, that may have been adrenaline, but still...

Stop that. Think about something useful. Otherwise you're just going to stand here being frustrated, or you'll try to do something about it and lose track of time and they'll open the door to find you standing here with cock in hand like a teenager.

Sleep disorders. Sleep disorders were not sexy, particularly when they lead to berserker fits. Piper didn't know enough about berserkers to even speculate as to the connection, and it seemed like a touchy topic for Galen. Perhaps he could ask Stephen, when all this was over. Stephen was calm to the point of being morose.

The usual treatments for sleep disorders ranged from the practical, like tying the sufferer's feet together, or having him sleep in what amounted to a drawstring sack, to the cruel, like dousing him with ice-cold water in the middle of the night if it looked as if he were about to start a disturbance. That last seemed *very* unwise with Galen, and not particularly useful in treating the underlying cause.

Fact is, we don't actually know how to treat sleep problems. I know some people dose themselves with laudanum before sleep, but that just gets you a laudanum addiction on top of everything else.

No, in practical terms, Galen was stuck with his condition. But although Piper would never say it to him, it could have been a great deal worse. He didn't sleepwalk, which might have exposed others to danger, and he hadn't mentioned harming himself in his sleep. He just could not be safely awoken from a nightmare.

So he doesn't share a bed with anyone. At least, not for anything other than...dammit, that's what you were not *supposed to be thinking about.*

Still, it was clear that Galen was far more upset by it than anyone else. Half the lovers Piper had had—all four of them, if he was being honest, and a handful of quick encounters—had been uninterested in sharing a bed after sex. One had done so out of a kind of awkward courtesy, but he clearly didn't prefer it, and after a night or two, Piper had made a habit of excusing himself to go home to his own bed.

For that matter, Piper wasn't entirely sure that he wanted to sleep beside another human being himself these days. He kept strange hours and he had his own pillow and his own blankets and if he wanted to get up three times in the night to use the chamberpot, he wasn't bothering anyone.

But how do you convince a paladin of that?

Come to think of it, does he even want to be convinced?

It had been two kisses. That was all. For all Piper knew, Galen wanted one of those quick encounters and then they would go back to the city and Galen would move on to the next encounter and Piper would...would...

Throw myself into my work and feel sad, I suppose. He wouldn't be the first attractive man looking for a notch on his bedpost and nothing more.

This dampened Piper's ardor significantly. He had never been good at casual encounters. Every time he ended up wanting more. Which always felt desperately needy, which left him feeling even more miserable. *All I want in life is to have a sexy man make passionate love to me, eat a nice meal together, and then I'll leave to go chop up corpses. Is that really so much to ask?*

Apparently it was.

Annnnd now I'm depressed. Is that better or worse than aroused? Probably worse. I should be trying to figure out how this ridiculous maze works, not moping around thinking about One Night Stands I Have Known.

He leaned his head back against the wall. Machines. Machines running an obstacle course. Machines like small clocktaurs. *What do you gain by running a machine through an obstacle course?*

With human soldiers, they were supposed to become better soldiers—but no military obstacle course would include endless fatal traps. *Hard to improve if you're dead. But the clocktaurs weren't exactly alive. Though they were run by demons. Were the small machines made the same way?*

No, the ancient clocktaurs had had human souls animating them. The ancients could have put a human soul into the small machines too, presumably, but why? A dying soldier might want a chance to strike at the enemy from inside an indestructible ivory body, but who would want to run through an obstacle course and end up crushed or impaled?

Maybe I'm going at this from the wrong direction. What if it's not about improving individual machines? What if it's some sort of design process? Does machine number one survive the room full of spikes? No? Okay, send in machine number two. Oh no, Two fell into a deep hole and can't climb out again. Send in Three. Three gets past the spikes and the hole, but the horizontal blades got it. Send in Four —oh, Four got stuck on the spikes again. Back to the drawing board.

Of course, that still didn't explain what was animating the machinery. The souls of someone passionately committed to machine design? Tame demons? If Galen had served the Dreaming God instead of the Saint of Steel, he might have been able to tell at a glance. *And also he'd be so good-looking that he probably wouldn't look twice at me. Though Galen's not far off from that, truth be told...* Piper remembered the width of the paladin's shoulders, the sleek muscle under his fingertips as he stroked the man's ribs, and swallowed hard.

And here we are again. I circle this thought like a goldfish circles a bowl.

The door opened and Galen stepped through. "Ready?" he asked.

Piper gulped. Now that the prospect was upon him, he found it much more alarming than he had when it was an abstract trial to be faced somewhere in the near future. He rubbed sweating palms on his trousers. "I suppose."

The paladin smiled at him and Piper's insides melted a little. "I'll be right there with you," he promised. "Come on. It's not hard, really, you just have to stay calm and keep your arms close to your body."

Piper did not feel calm. He felt even less calm when they

entered the room together and Galen tugged him into position, then stood close behind Piper's back, hands gripping his elbows. The paladin's feet were braced on either side of his. *Oh dear god.*

"The trick is not to try and rush through it," Galen murmured in his ear. "Slow and careful. Rushing only gets you in trouble."

Does he mean for that to sound that suggestive?

Click. A blade fell in front of him and Piper squeaked and recoiled. Galen caught him. "Steady now," he said. "I've got you."

On the one hand, there was an ivory wall bare inches in front of him. On the other hand, Galen's chest pressed against his back, and Galen's hips were suddenly tight against his. *Rat have mercy.* He wanted to scream. He wanted to run away. He wanted to lean back into Galen's embrace and feel...everything.

The blade lifted. Galen's knee nudged the back of his thigh. "Walk forward."

Piper tried to make his legs work. They did not want to. His nerves screamed that a blade was going to slice him in half vertically any second now.

"Listen to me, Piper. I'm right here. We're in this together." The paladin pushed him and Piper took a stumbling step forward, then another. "That's good. You're doing good. And... stop here."

Piper stopped gratefully. "Close your eyes," Galen suggested. "That might make it easier. I'll tell you when to move."

It did make it easier, except that if possible, he became even more aware of the paladin's body pressed against his. He could feel Galen's breath against his ear when the man spoke again. "Forward now. Come on. Just a little farther in and then we'll stop again."

He has got *to be doing that deliberately.* And it was working, too. Piper kept his eyes tightly shut but the next step forward was easier. Galen stroked his forearms lightly and that distracted him even more.

Click. Click. A breath of air to his left. Piper opened his eyes involuntarily and saw the wall practically against his nose and another bare inches from his left shoulder. They were in a tiny ivory box barely bigger than a coffin. He sucked in a breath, feeling panic rising in a bubble under his sternum, and squeezed his eyes closed again.

Galen nipped the back of his neck.

Piper's yelp turned rapidly into a groan. *Oh god. Oh sweet Lady of Grass.* He bent his head forward as the paladin's lips moved down his neck. Was he shivering from nerves or from the man's touch? He couldn't be certain.

"Keep your eyes closed," murmured Galen. "There you go. You're doing good. I know this is hard for you. It's hard for me too."

He is absolutely *doing that deliberately. Also, take me now.*

More clicking sounds, but before he could do more than register them, Galen was nibbling on the back of his neck again and Piper was starting to think that if he just kept his eyes closed, he could keep this up for hours, or at least until he had to turn around and tear the paladin's clothes off, which was probably not hours, possibly not even minutes at this rate—

"Last one."

—and Piper took another step forward and another and Galen said, "It's all right, we're through," and Piper opened his eyes and he was facing the corner and quarters were tight but not impossibly so. He turned around.

Warm green eyes looked down into his. Galen leaned forward. "You're lucky," he said into Piper's ear, sliding his hands up the doctor's arms. "What I want to do to you would take much longer than six minutes, so you're spared for a little longer."

"I don't think that's luck," croaked Piper. "I think that's terrible, actually."

Galen grinned at him and Piper barely noticed the wall slamming down behind the paladin. "Well," he said. "Maybe Earstripe's the lucky one, in that case. Not having to walk in on us."

Piper managed a laugh. "He'd just roll his eyes and shout suggestions from the next room."

"I might be able to fuck my way through an ancient death trap," said Galen, "but I draw the line at doing so with gnole commentary."

The word *fuck* did remarkable things to Piper's brain. Maybe six minutes would be enough time after all. He started to lean closer.

The blades retracted. The doorway slid open. Earstripe poked his head through. "Humans still alive? Not chopped like apples?"

"Still alive," Galen confirmed, stepping back.

Piper resigned himself to battling with his spongiform erectile tissue for a while longer yet. "Yes. What's past this, Earstripe? More doors?"

"Not doors," said Earstripe, surprising him. "Long hall. Six alcoves. One door at the end."

The two humans went immediately to the door. Sure enough, the corridor ran much farther than any of the previous ones had, bracketed by three alcoves on each side. *Alcove* was perhaps ungenerous; each one was nearly the size of the sitting room in Piper's apartment. The door at the end was framed with dozens of lines.

"The way out, do you think?" asked Piper. "Are we through?"

Galen shook his head. “No idea. I’m too turned around to tell you.”

“A gnole doesn’t think so,” said Earstripe. “If a gnole is picturing right, last door should be on left wall, not straight ahead. But could be a door to another hallway. Ancient humans liked hallways.” He scowled.

“Or it could be another trap,” said Galen. He rubbed his face. “I know it’s only been a few hours, but I don’t think any of us slept much, did we? Perhaps we could try again? Before I dodge more blades?”

“A gnole thinks this is a good idea.”

They sat down in one of the alcoves and divided out a few apples and the waterskins. “Do you know, I used to like apples?” said Piper, gazing at his wearily.

“Don’t you complain about that apple,” said Galen. “That apple’s brother saved my life.”

“Should I apologize to it?”

“I think that would be best.”

Piper put a hand over his heart. “Dear apple, I did not mean to belittle your family’s sacrifice. Please, forgive me.”

“Humans have lost their damn minds,” said Earstripe, shaking his head. “A gnole knew it was only a matter of time.”

Piper grinned and took a bite of the apple. Galen snickered. “You should just be impressed we made it this long.”

“A gnole is very impressed, tomato-man,” said Earstripe, and ducked the apple that the paladin threw at his head.

CHAPTER 21

Later, when they had eaten as many apples as they could stand and converted the prior trapped room into a de facto privy, the three sat together in the farthest alcove. Galen wished they could have a fire. The lantern gave off a tiny bit of heat and he watched Piper warm his hands at it. Earstripe lay in a boneless sprawl, his dark eyes pensive. Galen wondered what the gnole was thinking. *Planning for the future? What are his plans, anyway?*

"So what will you do, when this is over?" asked Galen. "Are you done with the guard forever? When it comes out that you solved the murders, Mallory will almost have to take you back, but I can't swear that it'll be easy on you."

Earstripe sighed. "Probably done. A gnole spent too long twisting whiskers. A gnole was almost done anyway. Guard always listens to some human before guard listens to a guard-gnole. Even if a guard-gnole is right." His whiskers drooped. "Helped a little," he said. "But didn't help enough."

"But you did help," said Galen. "You made a difference for your people. One you couldn't make anywhere else. You could keep making a difference." He looked at Piper for backup.

"Such a paladin thing to say," said Piper. Galen blinked at him. "It's a noble sentiment, but you can't ask people to pour themselves out for something that doesn't care and can't be fixed and at the end they're empty and nothing changes."

Galen suspected it was a mistake but he said it anyway. "But if nobody tries to change things, they don't get changed. How else can we change it?"

Piper sighed. "I don't know," he admitted. "I just know it's not Earstripe's job to kill himself to fix human mistakes."

"A gnole *would*, if it would fix them," said Earstripe, sounding very tired. "But always more problems. Nothing stays fixed. Another gnole can try, maybe. This gnole is done."

He got to his feet. "And now this gnole is tired. A gnole is going to sleep before next door." He paused, giving Piper a wry look. "If tomato-man screams, a gnole would prefer you *not* try to help."

Piper barked a laugh. It broke the tension, even if the topic was scarcely any less fraught than the previous one. "I promise I'll keep my good intentions to myself."

Earstripe nodded and slouched off to another alcove. Piper leaned back against the wall. Galen studied his profile, the long nose and full lips, the stubble that crept along his jaw, looking deep blue in the ancient light.

The silence had stretched out so long that it had almost ceased to be uncomfortable when Piper turned his cheek against the wall to look at Galen. "I'm sorry," he said.

"What?"

"If I snapped at you earlier. I know you're a paladin, and changing the world is exactly what you're supposed to do. It's just..." He made a meaningless gesture with his free hand. "The rest of us aren't built to quite such a heroic mold. It kills us after a while."

Galen snorted at the thought of fitting any kind of heroic

mold. "Some of us might be heroes." He thought of his fellow paladins, some of whom could undoubtedly rub shoulders with any hero ever born. "I'm hardly one of them, though."

"You are incredibly brave," said Piper. "You go into those rooms first, expecting to die."

"Yes, but that's not heroism," said Galen. "That's what I'm *for.* And don't start with me about how doing your job is heroic under the right circumstances, because I've seen plenty of battlefield medics, too, so you'd be just as guilty of it as I am."

"God forbid." It was Piper's turn to snort. "Why do you think I stopped working with the living? It was too much. Well, fine. Maybe a hero is just what we call someone who doesn't have the sense to stop before they destroy themselves."

"In the army, they'd send kids barely old enough to shave to take forward positions. They knew they'd have thirty, forty percent losses or more. Those kids got told they were heroes, too." Galen sighed, draping his wrists over his knees, letting his hands dangle. "I doubt you can call any of the Saint's chosen inherently heroic. We didn't have much choice, did we? The battle tide wakes up, and there we are. It's not heroic if you've forgotten you're not invincible. Then again, I've known paladins who really *were* heroic. My friend Istvhan, have you met him? And Shane. Shane could go toe-to-toe with a god, if he could get his head out of his own ass first. A couple of the Forge God's people. The Dreaming God's people are positively stiff with it, whatever *it* is."

Piper nodded. "Still," he said finally. "I shouldn't have snapped at you. Whatever I may think, it doesn't matter enough to be sniping at each other while we're down here. In whatever this is."

He was doing it again, Galen thought. Stepping back from emotions as if they were an imposition. It was hard to believe that this was the same man who had argued so passionately on

Galen's behalf—and kissed him just as passionately a moment later.

The memory of that kiss heated his blood. They could be doing so many things other than arguing. Did he need another set of blades slicing down around him to remind him of that?

Piper turned his head and started to say something else—Galen never knew what—and Galen leaned forward and kissed him.

What has come over me? He had never particularly liked kissing and now it seemed like he couldn't get enough of it. Something about Piper's lips against his, about the taste of him, about the look of surprise and delight in the man's eyes...he felt almost drunk with it. He needed more. A lot more.

You need to get laid is what you need. Once that's over, this will all recede and you'll be able to think again.

Unfortunately, when he shifted position to reach for Piper's shoulders, his knee smacked into the ground and the flare of pain made him wince and recoil. Piper's eyes went wide and he pulled away. "Uh..."

"Nothing you did," Galen assured him. "Banged up my knee earlier and it just reminded me, that's all."

The doctor was immediately all cool professionalism. "Let me take a look at it," he said, in a voice that brooked no disobedience.

Galen stifled a sigh, feeling the mood evaporate. He rolled up his trouser leg and Piper ran his gloved hands over the joint. There was a red mark already starting to darken towards blue and Galen grimaced.

"Bend it...good...and extend it toward me...mmm. Stand up and put weight on it?"

Galen got to his feet, back against the corner. Piper continued prodding his leg and having him lift it and the paladin felt a sudden sympathy for horses, an animal he generally could do without. *At least he isn't trying to nail hot metal to your foot.*

"The good news is that you don't seem to have done anything to the tendon," said Piper, concluding his poke-and-prod routine. "Just bruised the kneecap, and you know how knees hurt all out of proportion."

"God, yes."

"I should probably wrap it, though. Knees swell up if you look at them funny." He dug through the pack and pulled out the remains of the shirt that Earstripe had already cut into bandages. Galen leaned back, watching the dark head bent over him, thinking mostly carnal thoughts.

When the job was done, Piper sat back and looked up at him, his assured manner suddenly falling away. "I...uh..."

"Oh, don't mind me," said Galen. "I've been wanting you on your knees for days now. I was just hoping that it wouldn't be my knee you were paying attention to."

The doctor blushed scarlet. Galen opened his mouth to say something clever and flirtatious and then Piper reached up to the front of his trousers and began unhooking the buttons and he briefly lost the power of speech.

Coherent thought did not return until Piper bit the fingertip of one of his gloves and pulled it off. Leather slid over skin for a small eternity. He set the first glove down and reached for the second. "No," Galen heard himself croak, "leave that one on."

Piper raised his eyebrows and smiled a small, devilish smile, despite the blush that hadn't quite faded. Galen dug his fingers into the man's hair and then Piper's mouth and extremely clever fingers were on him and he was lost.

It didn't take long. It was almost embarrassing, how long it didn't take. The sensation of skin and leather and Piper's tongue were too much to bear, and then he made the mistake of opening his eyes so that he could see the other man's mouth on him. He gripped Piper's shoulders and gasped something that might have been his name, or the Saint's, or just a general obscenity. His knees turned to water and he slid down the wall as soon as Piper let him go.

"Good god," he said, when he could think again, "why the hell did we wait so long?"

Piper chuckled, taking a long swig from the waterskin. "Well, we had a few other things on our minds. Death trap, murders, that sort of thing."

"I can't imagine how those could have been more important." Galen rubbed his forehead. "Give me a moment or two to recover, and then I'd be happy to reciprocate."

"Not on your knees you won't," said Piper, frowning at him. "Not with your knee like that."

"Are all doctors this pushy in bed?"

"Only when we think you'll hurt yourself."

Galen grumbled and reached out, drawing the other man close. "Here," he said, pulling Piper more or less into his lap, his legs braced on either side. "Lean back."

Piper obeyed, his back against Galen's chest. Galen could feel the tautness of his muscles and set to work soothing them, sliding his hands in aimless patterns across Piper's arms, then under his shirt to the smooth, flat muscle of his chest. "Relax," Galen murmured in his ear. "You've already had your hands all over me. Allow me to return the favor."

Slowly, Piper's tension eased, and then was replaced with a different type of tension. Galen could feel the quiver whenever his hands slid lower. *It would be lovely to do this somewhere with a bed, where we aren't sitting on hard ivory with our backsides going numb. Ah well. Next time, perhaps.* He stopped teasing Piper and reached down to take him firmly in hand.

The position was a trifle awkward, but they made it work. Piper, Galen discovered, was *not* quiet. He gasped and yelped and moaned, all of which Galen found delightful. *You do like to know you're having an effect.*

He was definitely having an effect. Piper thrashed as Galen stroked him, until the paladin had to wrap an arm around his chest to hold him in place. He could feel the doctor's heart pounding like a drum under his wrist. Galen murmured something—praise, encouragement, obscenities, it hardly mattered what—feeling Piper's body draw tight as a bowstring. He slowed his movements, hoping to draw out the moment, but Piper clutched at his legs and thrust into his hand. *Oh, I see. Well, in that case...* Galen nipped the back of his neck and the doctor let out a final choking cry, hips bucking. Shudders wracked his body until he collapsed back, limp and wrung out and damp with sweat.

Galen rested his chin on the other man's shoulder, listening to the hard rasp of Piper's breathing, and felt the warm glow of a job well done.

"You're right," said Piper finally, when he had gotten his breath back. "We really should not have waited."

"Mmm." Galen kissed the back of his neck, smoothing over the small red mark he'd made. Part of him wanted to start all over again. Another, rather larger part, pointed out that he was middle-aged and that it had been a dismally long day, with only an hour of disturbed sleep earlier. The spirit was willing, but the spongiform erectile tissue was weak.

Still, it was good to sit here with his arms around Piper. It felt...peaceful. Galen could not remember the last time he had felt peace. Since before the god died, certainly. Back then, he had been secure in the knowledge that he was an attack dog on a god's leash, and the god would not let him slip the leash until it was time. It had been easy then. Very little had been easy since.

But this...this was easy. The weight of Piper's body, the way his ribs moved under Galen's arms as he breathed, the prickle of short dark hair against Galen's cheek. The paladin did not have to do anything. He could sit and simply exist and know that Piper was safe and in his arms and he did not have to be afraid.

Eventually, of course, his body began to grumble. Galen let out a jaw-cracking yawn. "As much as I would like to continue this, we should get cleaned up and I should go and fall down somewhere. Will you be all right?"

"Yes, of course." Piper turned in his arms and kissed him. "Hopefully tomorrow we'll be out of this mess and can go somewhere with blankets and an actual mattress."

"I would do terrible things for a mattress," said Galen. "But I will have to settle for doing terrible things to you on a mattress, when the opportunity presents itself." He brushed his lips across Piper's forehead and pushed himself to his feet.

He looked down at the doctor, still flushed and smiling, and did not even dare to dream of curling up around him to sleep. But perhaps he could dream of holding him again.

"Something wrong?" asked Piper, looking up at him.

That wasn't enough. That should have been enough, but it wasn't. I want more of you. "No," said Galen. "Nothing at all."

On the bright side, he thought, going to the next alcove and settling in with his back to the cool ivory wall, *even if I have another round of nightmares, I'll be too damn tired to try to kill anyone tonight.*

CHAPTER 22

Piper woke the next morning—or whatever passed for morning in this place where the light was all the same—feeling both stiff and ungodly smug.

The source of the stiffness was immediately obvious. He'd been sleeping on the floor again, his pillow was now shredded into bandage material, and his back was informing him that what had been acceptable at twenty was no longer acceptable when one could see forty on the horizon.

The source of the smugness took a moment longer, but then he heard Galen's voice and it all came rushing back to him. Galen's hands on his flesh. His hands on Galen's, for that matter. Also his mouth and...well, it had been a good night. Fraught and fumbling and much too fast for both of them, admittedly, but the relief of knowing that the wanting was mutual—that was worth a great deal.

And he said he'd want to do it again. That's worth even more. Assuming we don't die horribly in the next few hours.

Piper believed in the gods, of course. They were obviously there, so not believing in them would be remarkably silly, like not believing in wind. He had reason to be fond of the White

Rat, and most doctors invoked the Lady of Grass, who was well-known as a healer. Generally, though, he believed that gods worked through people rather than engaging in direct intervention.

Still, it couldn't hurt. *Lady of Grass,* he prayed, bowing his head. *White Rat. Please let us get out of this alive. Please don't kill us just when I've found the first man I've been interested in for ages who's also interested in me. It would be very unkind.*

Then he climbed to his feet and went to where Galen and Earstripe were sitting, counting out the remaining apples for breakfast.

"You're awake," said Galen, and smiled up at him. His eyes were warm jade this morning. Piper sat down next to him, closer than he'd ever dared before, and Galen reached out and put a hand on his lower back. "Did you sleep well?"

"Very well."

"A gnole slept well too," said Earstripe sardonically, "*eventually.*"

Heat rose in Piper's cheeks. He hadn't even thought about Earstripe overhearing them. Galen only snorted and tossed an apple at the gnole's head. Earstripe caught it and took a bite out of it.

"Sorry, Earstripe," Piper mumbled.

"Nah, nah." The gnole flicked his ears. "Bone-doctor should not worry. A gnole prefers human mating-yelping to days of humans standing around stinking of *longing.*"

Piper put his face in his hands. His ears felt hot. Galen had the temerity to start laughing. "You can smell that? Really?"

"Surprised humans can't."

"It must be easier for gnoles," said Piper, "being able to tell so easily if someone you like likes you back."

"Eh." Earstripe made an equivocating gesture with one hand. "Awkward sometimes. Mating season, eh, everybody wants, nobody cares. But sometimes a gnole gets mate smell with a gnole who isn't mate, very awkward."

"Like an affair?" asked Piper, puzzled. *I know so little about gnoles. I don't even know if they mate exclusively like humans claim to.*

Earstripe shook his head. "No, like mate. Like...uh..." He seemed to be trying to think of a human equivalent. "A human marries another human, yes?"

"Sometimes, yes." He carefully didn't look at Galen.

"Yes. Humans are mates. But could a human marry another human who didn't marry them back?"

"Uh..." This time he did look at Galen, baffled.

Galen nodded to Earstripe. "Not legally, but yes, I think I understand. If someone thought that they were in a close relationship, but the other person didn't, or didn't want to be, or was trying to get away."

"Yes." Earstripe nodded. "That. Embarrassing. Everyone can smell then. Worse if different caste. A gnole leaves then, usually, goes to another warren far away."

"Maybe it's better we can't smell that well," said Piper, imagining being so deeply in love with someone who wasn't interested. *If I was in love with Galen, say...*

His stomach clenched in a way that he didn't like and he could feel his cheeks heating again. *If I was. If. Not that I am. Not* love-*love.*

Just because he's funny and handsome and intelligent and as brave as a lion and he accepted your weird gift as if it was nothing strange and he acts like he admires you, when he isn't yelling at you for running risks, and he dropped everything to come on this trip because Earstripe asked, just like you, and he understands that gnoles are people and we have to learn more about each other in order to live together and also when he slid his hand over your cock, you thought you'd died and gone to heaven...

He cleared his throat and very carefully pushed all those feelings away, because they weren't going to help but Earstripe could probably smell them anyway. "So," he said. "Are we ready to try the next door?"

"A gnole is getting very tired of doors."

"Maybe it'll be the last one. We're almost back where we started, I think."

Galen stood, then reached down and pulled Piper to his feet with easy strength. "We can only hope," he said. His fingers lingered in Piper's hand for a moment, warm even through the kidskin. "Let's see what we're dealing with."

They stood in front of the door and Galen reached out and tapped the mechanism.

The door opened onto a room full of clockwork bones.

"What happened here?" asked Piper softly.

"Dead machines," said Galen, eyeing the pile of broken ivory that lay ankle deep across the floor.

"Did something kill them? Or did they just stop working?"

"Judging by the marks, they didn't just stop." Galen pointed to a piece of machine-stuff as long as his arm, the end splintered. "But why here, and nowhere else?"

Earstripe tossed an apple into the pile, where it lay forlornly.

"That's an interesting question," said Piper. "Someone must have cleaned the other rooms, except for the pits, which were presumably too hard to reach. Human staff? But why not this room?"

Earstripe lobbed a few more apples in.

"And if they had cleaners, how did they avoid getting smashed to bits?" asked Galen.

"Perhaps there's a way to turn the entire mechanism off,"

said Piper. He gave a short, humorless laugh. "Probably there is, and it's clearly labeled in three languages that nobody reads any more, and it's currently somewhere under the river. But either they didn't clean out this room before whatever event caused them to abandon this place or..." He trailed off, uncertain what the alternative would be.

Earstripe tossed in another apple and said, "A gnole doesn't want to alarm anyone, but a door isn't closing."

"No..." said Galen thoughtfully. "No, it isn't, is it? And it's been more than thirty seconds by now."

"Nearly a minute by my guess."

Earstripe tossed in another apple.

A blade shot out from the pile of bone, and speared the apple in midair. Piper recoiled in surprise. Galen slapped for a sword that no longer hung at his waist.

From out of the mound of debris, a machine began to rise. It was hard at first to tell what was part of the living machine and what were broken pieces of dead ones. Piper had an impression of a body like a slender scorpion, equipped with a blade instead of a stinger. Its legs rose above the level of its back like a spider, and instead of heavy claws, it had two long, thin appendages, like an insect's feelers.

"It's injured," whispered Galen. "Look!"

It was indeed. It had five legs on one side, but only two on the other, and one of the thin feelers was dragging on the ground. It looked as if it had taken a serious pounding at some point.

It must be over a thousand years old. And it's been injured all this time.

The scorpion used its good feeler to scrape the apple off the blade. It turned toward the doorway, and even though it was eyeless, Piper swore he could feel it looking at them.

"A gnole thinks the machines fought here," said Earstripe quietly.

"Like a cock fight," said Galen. "The ones that survive the obstacle course get here and fight the ones that got through before them."

"Cock fighting is barbaric," said Piper, recognizing as he did so that it was a profoundly unhelpful observation.

"You know, the Bishop says the same thing."

The scorpion took a jerky step toward the door, then another one.

Piper's first thought was that it wouldn't be able to go through the door. The other rooms had all been safely enclosed. *But if this is a machine made to run the obstacle course, not one of the traps, why wouldn't it come out? And the door's been open for much longer than a minute.*

"Maybe it isn't supposed to fight humans?" he said hopefully.

"Had no problem fighting apples."

"So what do we do now?" asked Piper, taking several steps back.

"I'm going to fight it," said Galen. "Obviously."

"How is that obvious?!" he hissed, but any answer was lost when the scorpion machine charged.

CHAPTER 23

"Get out of the way!" shouted Galen, dodging to one side of the doorway as the tail-blade smashed into the floor where he'd been standing. "Get back!"

"You don't have a sword!" Piper yelled behind him.

This was true, but Galen was quite aware that a sword made of steel would be only emotional support. Whatever substance the machines were made from was only vulnerable to attacks from other machines.

Fortunately, there was an entire room full of broken machine parts that he could use.

Unfortunately, the scorpion-thing was standing between him and it.

He could feel the black tide beginning to rise, like water swirling around his waist and creeping higher. The taste of iron filled his mouth.

"Don't come near me once it's dead," he grated, his voice sounding strange in his own ears. "Not until I talk to you first."

The scorpion turned its blunt, eyeless head toward him. It seemed to be moving slowly, almost as if whatever powered it was running down.

It's been a few thousand years. Nothing lasts forever.

He had just formulated that thought when the blade sliced at him, missing him by half an inch.

The tide engulfed him, whispering instructions. Galen embraced it. He had done the best he could for his companions. Now it was time to do what he was made to do.

Everything slowed. The scorpion was still terribly fast but he was faster. It was so easy to step to one side as the blade struck at him, to dive forward, past the machine, into the room of bones.

He picked up a large piece of ivory, not quite the size of his lost sword, and swung around. The machine had turned and come after him. It struck at him again, and this time one of the feelers whipped out to slash at his ankles, forcing him to divide his attention. He put both feet together and jumped over it, like a child skipping rope, and blocked the bladed tail with his makeshift ivory club.

The force of the blow almost sent him to his knees. He stumbled but the tide caught him and carried him, even though he had to drop the club from fingers gone numb and smarting. The feeler whipped back the other way and caught his calf, a line of heat telling him that he was bleeding. No matter. Pain was the tide's problem, not his.

Don't block. It's too strong to block. Dodge. Dodge and look for a weakness.

He dove to his right and kept going, snatching up another piece of ivory. The machine spun and then it, too, almost stumbled, as the missing legs on that side failed to keep up.

Take out the remaining legs and it won't be able to move.

He smashed the club down on one of those legs. They looked delicate, but they were surprisingly strong. The club bounced off, but in the moment of the swing, when everything was so slow, Galen saw that the broken legs were dangling useless from the joints. The whip-feeler was coming up again and the blade was coming down so it seemed like a good idea not to be in the middle. He dodged right again and it stumbled again on the turn, so this time he cracked the club down directly onto the joint, just as it was taking the scorpion's weight.

The whole machine staggered and it swung the blade wildly at Galen's face in a sideways slash. The tide flung him down in a sprawl across the scorpion's back, and that was not a good place to be, so he kept rolling and went off the far side, striking at the legs on that side as he went. The angle was wrong, but the machine had apparently learned that if it allowed the human with the club to strike at its legs, bad things happened. It snatched those legs tightly under its body and came crashing down on that side, practically on top of him. Galen's bruised knee hit the ground and it hurt dreadfully but that didn't matter because the tide only rose higher in response to the pain. The blade came at him, as did the whip, and he could only avoid one this time. Another hot line burned across his left arm, almost at the shoulder, although compared to his knee, it was insignificant.

He regained his footing at the same time it did, and tried to circle behind the scorpion. *The range on the blade is all forward. If I can get behind it, maybe it won't be able to strike as easily.*

If it had been a real scorpion, this likely would have worked. Galen brought the club down on another leg joint, felt the machine shudder, and had a moment of triumph, before the entire tail simply swiveled around on a joint at the base and cut at him.

And now I'm dodging the blade and it has a lot more reach because it's not going over the body. Lovely.

He tried to dodge to the side again, but the machine had learned this trick and the blade came down in another sideways slash, forcing him back. A clockwork bone turned under his feet and he fell backward and landed on his bruised ribs.

The battle-tide blunted pain but could do nothing about loss of breath. Galen suddenly couldn't get air in his lungs and that was very bad, that was probably terminally bad, and the machine limped toward him, backward, lifting the blade high overhead and Galen tried to let out a yell of defiance that came out as a gasp and then an apple hit the scorpion in a bad leg joint and it collapsed reflexively again to try to protect its legs.

This time it couldn't quite get up. The part of Galen that was still Galen doubted that the apple was the cause, so much as the pile of bone gears that it had dropped its bodyweight on. The part that had surrendered to the tide noted that there was another party armed with possibly lethal projectiles and he would have to deal with that once he'd finished off the scorpion.

The scorpion heaved itself up again, and then began to rise. It had one working leg on the right side. It flipped its body upright vertically, standing on the good leg and the matching leg from the left side, inelegantly bipedal.

It looked absurd, the thick body and lashing tail-blade balanced on two slender points. His first thought was that there was no way that it could possibly walk around like that.

His second thought was to remember the narrowness of the spaces in the room with interlocking blades. To get past that, it would have had to assume a posture like this.

He got to his feet. His lungs didn't want to work, but they weren't given a choice in the matter. He could hear his own breath wheezing in his ears.

The scorpion lumbered at him, rocking from side to side. Galen dodged, or tried, but the scorpion pivoted on one leg like a swivel, barely slowing at all. The feeler wrapped itself around a narrow piece of ivory and struck at him with it, missing his kneecap by inches and slamming heavily into his thigh.

Someone yelled his name. An enemy, probably, but Galen didn't have time to worry about that. He stayed on his feet, even though he was going to have a bruise the size of a dinner plate. *The legs,* whispered the tide. *It's only got two left. Take out one more leg and it can't walk. One more leg and it's done.*

Arguably Galen *also* only had two legs left, but the tide didn't concern itself with such things. He grabbed the ivory club that the feeler was holding and yanked, hard.

The feeler was strong enough to hold onto it, but not to keep its balance. It lurched toward him and Galen kicked out hard at the near leg. His knee throbbed like a broken star as it connected.

The machine collapsed again, trying to protect its leg, but this time the trick worked against it. It lost its balance and went over. Galen leaped out of the way as it crashed down full length.

The underside looked exactly the same as the upper. Maybe it could reverse direction just as easily—or could have if it had more than two thin legs remaining. It began trying to right itself again, but this time Galen was not having it. As soon as it put its tail down to push itself upright, he snatched up another bone club and brought it down on the last leg, then flung himself free.

The scorpion began to flail wildly. Its tail struck at air, the feeler lashing back and forth, but it could not reach him and it could no longer stand on its own. Galen watched the machine's ratcheting motions, waiting for an opening, then stepped in and slammed the club onto the thinnest part of the tail, just behind the blade. The shock of impact numbed his arm but he heard something crack that didn't seem to be his bones so he hit it again and then again, forehand and backhand, over and over, no longer thinking, nothing but a hand on a weapon, again and again and again and again...

The tide slowly receded. The machine still moved, but only in aimless twitches, the motions of a snake with the head cut off. The blade lay half-severed, the tail joints broken.

"It's dead," someone said from the doorway. "It's dead, Galen. You can stop."

Someone. He knew them. Not the enemy, no matter what the tide might say. Not the enemy. Someone who had been in his arms, breathing against him. Piper. Yes. Not the enemy. The enemy was dead, if it had ever been alive in the first place.

He stepped back and shook himself. The tide never went away, but it receded. Ankle deep instead of over his head. Yes.

Galen turned and saw Piper and Earstripe in the doorway, watching him. The wariness in Piper's eyes hurt more than he expected. "It's fine," he croaked. "I'm fine. It's over."

Piper crossed the distance between them in seconds. Galen wasn't sure if the man was trying to embrace him or trying to keep him from collapsing where he stood. Possibly a little of both. "You're hurt," said Piper, getting a shoulder under his arm. "Sit down, for god's sake."

"Not here," mumbled Galen. "Is the door open?"

"No," said Earstripe, "but a gnole sees a panel." He went to the door, giving the dying machine a wide berth, and pressed it.

For a long, long moment, no one breathed, and then the door slid silently open. Through the doorway, Galen could see another door standing open, and the darkness of the cellar beyond.

"We're out," he said. "We did it. We got through."

As one, they bolted. No one had to voice the thought that the door might close again and trap them. Earstripe was through first, and Piper and Galen hobbled out like partners in a three-legged race.

The wet air of the cellar tasted like fine wine. Galen hadn't realized how dry the air inside the maze was, or how badly his lips and skin and sinuses had dried out. He drew in a lungful and almost didn't care how badly his ribs hurt in response.

"You're hurt," said Piper. "Sit down—let me look at you—"

"Not yet," he said hoarsely. The adrenaline of the fight would last him a little longer, and he knew that they weren't out of the woods yet. "There's still our gracious host to deal with."

"Ah, yes," said Thomas, from the top of the stairs. "I was wondering when you'd remember me."

CHAPTER 24

"I am very, very impressed," said Thomas. "I mean that very sincerely." The tip of the crossbow he held didn't waver. It had a nasty man-killing head, pointing down at the trio. "I never expected that you'd make it through. At best, I thought you might manage another room or two, and I was hoping I could determine how you had died. But this! You got the door open, no less!" He smiled warmly at them, and Piper was struck by the thought that he was entirely sincere.

"He can only shoot one of us," said Galen quietly. "Then he has to reload. We can rush the stairs."

"Don't think you can take another hit, tomato-man."

Galen gave a soft, ragged laugh. "Then let him shoot me. I'm expendable now."

"Not what a gnole meant."

"*No one is expendable*," hissed Piper. He raised his voice and stepped forward. "Anyway, he won't shoot me."

"I assure you, I will," said Thomas. "Regretfully, mind you. It's rare to find someone who appreciates the ancients as I do. But I will shoot."

Piper put his foot on the first stair. Galen grabbed for his shoulder and Piper shook him off. The fact that he *could* shake the paladin off only cemented his resolve. Earstripe had been right. Galen was in poor shape after his fight with the machine. The paladin couldn't take another hit. Certainly not a crossbow bolt. Piper had seen what a bolt like that could do to a human body. If it hit somewhere vital, it would punch a hole and the victim's blood would drain out like wine from a barrel with the bung drawn.

"If you shoot me," said Piper, "I won't be able to tell you what I saw. I've figured it out. What it's for. All of it." Would Thomas buy that? Perhaps not. He gave a self-deprecating cough. "Well, almost all of it. I wouldn't presume to say there's no mysteries left."

Thomas lifted his head just slightly. The lamplight glinted in his eyes. "Have you, now?"

"I have. You let my friends go, and I'll tell you everything."

Galen made a small noise of protest. Earstripe didn't. *Smarter than a paladin. Mind you, when it comes to expediency, paladins aren't known for their wit.*

Their captor clearly considered it. Piper could see him weighing the options, and risked putting his foot on the next stair. Thomas sighed regretfully. "As much as I'd like to hear your conclusions, I fear that you must think me a very great fool," he said. "If I let these two go, they'll just come back here with more men. I can't risk damage to the ruins." He sighted back down the crossbow.

"But—" Piper began.

"If it makes you feel any better, I will aim for your legs. Then you may be able to tell me what you know before you die."

"I doubt I'll be in the proper of frame of mind," said Piper grimly.

"I can't imagine a man of science would let a little thing like spite keep him from passing information on." He smiled. Piper stared upward. Had a shadow moved behind Thomas? Was someone else there?

Well, it hardly mattered. No one was going to save them. They could only hope that the other person didn't also have a crossbow. Piper shook his head. He pretended to turn away, and then, because he had absolutely no idea what to do and because Galen was going to get himself killed if he didn't do something, he lunged up the steps at Thomas.

The crossbow bucked. Something smashed into his side. For an instant Piper thought he'd been shot and was just thinking, *Oh hell, right in the vitals, I'm not going to live long enough to regret this,* and then he hit the railing and Earstripe let out a scream of pain.

Thomas collapsed. Piper clutched the railing, holding himself up and got an arm around Earstripe, who had moved faster than anyone had a right to move.

Earstripe, who had a crossbow bolt sprouting from his thigh.

Oh shit, no, no, if it hits his femoral artery he'll bleed out right here oh no... Galen rushed past him but Piper couldn't spare a thought for any of that. He lowered Earstripe down on the stairs and tore at the gnole's clothing, trying to unwrap his leg. Where was the bolt lodged?

Hell with that, where's the artery? If he was a human, the floor would be awash in blood right now, but he's not and it's not and maybe the bolt didn't hit but if I pull it out, I might tear the artery wide open oh god oh god...

He applied pressure as best he could at the point where the shaft entered the leg. There was a flurry of activity somewhere at the top of the stairs and a metallic sound. It seemed very far away. Did he dare apply a tourniquet? How the hell could he apply a tourniquet when he didn't even know where the artery was?

Someone gurgled wetly and part of Piper's brain said that it might be Galen and he darted a look over his shoulder to find that Galen seemed to have picked Thomas up by the throat. That was all right then. Galen would do what he did best and Piper would do the thing that he was woefully inadequate at, but had to do anyway.

"Don't you dare die," he told the gnole. He'd located the point of the bolt, which bulged obscenely from the back of the gnole's leg, but somehow hadn't penetrated all the way through. Had it hit a bone and been deflected? Oh god, it had. Piper palpated the gnole's leg gingerly and felt the bone move in a way that intact bones should not move. It jiggled, in fact, which was a terrible thing for bones to do.

Shit, shit, there's probably splinters of bone in there, lodged in the muscle, and if any of them hit the artery, it won't matter how much pressure I apply. Oh god, I don't dare move him more than a few inches. It's a miracle I got him to the bottom of the stairs. It's a miracle that I didn't kill him outright. Sooner or later I'm going to run out of miracles.

He needed more pairs of hands. "Galen!" he yelled. "Galen, I need your help!" Belatedly it occurred to him that Galen was probably murdering someone, but that really shouldn't take priority. You could always murder people later, after all.

"What do you need?" Galen appeared at his elbow. Piper couldn't tell if the blood was from his injuries or if he'd killed Thomas, and didn't actually care.

"I need bandages and hot water. Then I'm going to have to push the bolt through, open the leg up and get the splinters out, then try to splint everything back together and get the torn muscle back in place." He took a deep breath. Opening up a wound was a horrible idea nine times out of ten and was just begging for massive infection to set in, but what choice did he have? *Oh god, if only I'd ever had a gnole on the slab, then at least I'd know what I was doing!*

"Do you need me to carry him upstairs?"

"We can't move him until I've looked in the wound. He could be a quarter of an inch from losing all the blood in his body."

"All right." Galen went away again. Piper heard him talking to someone and for a minute he thought that the paladin was sending Earstripe to get the bandages and that made sense because of course Earstripe was fine and walking around and would say something sarcastic shortly. The universe could not be so poorly run that the gnole in front of him was Earstripe. Then Earstripe moaned softly and Piper stopped thinking about it at all.

"It's all right," he said aloud. "We're here. You're going to be okay." Probably that was a lie. He didn't even know what the muscles were supposed to look like when they weren't shredded by a bolt. He applied pressure with one hand and tried to pick apart the wrappings on the gnole's other leg, just to get some point of comparison. Earstripe moaned again, but didn't sound conscious. Probably that was for the best. Nobody wanted to be awake for a bone being set, and Piper's kit with laudanum and powdered datura was in a wagon somewhere. Hopefully somewhere very far away.

He was focusing so intently that he didn't hear Galen returning. "Water's heating. I've got two sheets. What else?"

"Tear them into strips," said Piper. "I need...shit. Everything. Tweezers. Needle and thread. The strongest alcohol and the sharpest knife you can find. Honey if they've got it. And light, more light. As much as you can."

Galen's hand closed on his shoulder and squeezed briefly.

"I'll get it. The housekeeper's on our side, incidentally. She hit Thomas over the head with a poker."

"Good," said Piper absently. That was good, wasn't it? Yes. Probably. Where did he take a pulse on a gnole?

Galen squeezed his shoulder again and went away, leaving Piper holding Earstripe's life between his hands.

CHAPTER 25

"Tweezers and more sheets'll be upstairs," said Missus Hardy. "Check the master's bedroom, and the closets. You'll be faster on the steps than I will, belike."

Galen nodded grimly. He'd asked earlier why she hadn't run, and she'd lifted her skirt to show him two heavy shackles around her legs, the skin rough and red and scaly around them. She could shuffle along, but she could not run. Thomas had made sure of that.

The sight had made Galen want to kill the man all over again, only slowly this time. When he had seen Earstripe knock Piper aside and take the crossbow bolt instead, he had charged up the steps, knowing only that he had to stop Thomas, even if it cost his own life. The tide hadn't had time to rise. Perhaps he'd outrun it. It had been simple human rage and terror that fueled him—that and the guilt that Earstripe had been faster than he was.

If it had been left up to me, Piper would have been the one to take the bolt.

The thought made him break into a cold sweat even now.

Even the feeling of Thomas's neck collapsing under his hands hadn't been enough to slake it.

When he had seen the kitchen and the long chain that Thomas had kept Hardy on when she was cooking—"So that I didn't try anything with a knife, y'see,"—he'd wanted to drag the man's corpse out of the stables where he'd dumped it and stab it a few more times for good measure.

"I told your friend to run," Missus Hardy said. "On the wagon. Was afraid I wouldn't make it back to the house in time, but I warned him off. The master was suspicious, but I said he drove off on his own."

And thank the gods for that. Brindle will bring back help. I hope.

They didn't need any more muscle at the moment, but they sure as hell needed doctoring supplies. It had only taken one look at Piper's stricken face to see that Earstripe was in bad shape.

He found tweezers and a razor in the master bedroom upstairs, balanced on the edge of the sink. Every other room was empty, the furniture gone or hidden under dust cloths. There were more sheets in the closet, and he grabbed an armload of those as well, wondering how many sheets were required to make a bandage at all.

By the time he got back downstairs, Missus Hardy had laid out needle, thread, a bottle of brandy and a jar of honey. "Thank you," said Galen. She nodded, meeting his eyes with her unnervingly flat stare.

"Wasn't able to save any of the others," she said. "Might be able to save your friend."

"You could have gone with Brindle," he said.

She shook her head. "He'd have gone after. And if he didn't find me, he'd like have killed you three. Don't know what happens down there, but nobody comes out but him. Thought maybe if your friend came back with help, they might be able to get you out in time."

Galen nodded in recognition of the grim calculus involved and went to raid the rooms for candles.

By the time Piper was ready to operate, the wine cellar was a sea of wicks and flame. Galen knelt beside him, ready to lift a lantern or hand him items as required. Piper's face was gray but his hands were steady as he took the razor and made the first cut.

"Lady of Grass," he murmured, picking fragments of bone out with the tweezers. "White Rat. Four-faced One. Forge God. Dreaming God..." On and on he went, a litany of the names of gods, repeating over and over. It was as sincere a prayer as Galen had ever heard, and he wondered if the doctor even knew that he was doing it. Occasionally he would interrupt himself to give orders—"Hold the lamp higher." "Pour a ladle of water over the wound."—but then he would start up again within a minute or two. "White Rat...Lady of Grass..."

"I've got as much out as I can," he said finally, sitting back. "We have to push the bolt through and then break the head off. If I've missed a fragment, or if there's another major vein back there, then..." He trailed off, shaking his head. Galen didn't need him to say the words aloud. *Then Earstripe will die.*

Piper took a thimble that Missus Hardy had included with her sewing kit and set his fingers to the end of the bolt. He took a deep breath and then began to push the shaft down. "If he thrashes, hold him down."

Earstripe cried out, a shrill yelp of pain, and his eyes came open. His teeth snapped at thin air. "Just a little more..." said Piper. Galen pinned the gnole down, prepared to use his full weight, but he didn't need to. The gnole's eyes rolled back and he slumped again in a dead faint.

Probably for the best. Nobody wants to be awake for this part. Or any of the other parts.

"There. It's through. Can you break the head off?" asked Piper. "I doubt we've got a very fine saw lying around."

Galen felt for the point and scowled. It was bladed and not particularly easy to grab. He had to wrap his hand in the bottom of his chainmail hauberk and snap the shaft. He opted for speed rather than finesse. Earstripe whimpered as the wood broke, but that was all.

Piper extracted the bolt and flung it aside in disgust, then set to work again. Galen felt anxiety like a live animal clawing at his chest. He infinitely preferred battle to this horrible balancing act between life and death.

"It's as clean as I can make it," said Piper finally. "If there's some fragment lying up against the artery that's going to kill him, I can't see it. Hold his leg and pull when I tell you, and we'll get the bone set."

This bit, at least, Galen had done before. He hauled the gnole's leg straight when told and maneuvered as needed. Piper had to stop partway through and feel Earstripe's other leg to check something. Judging by the almost inaudible cursing, gnoles were built just differently enough to take years off the life of any human attempting to administer first aid to them.

"There," said Piper, at least an hour later, straightening up. Earstripe's leg was shaved to the skin in a thick line, layered with dressings. There was a shorter, matching line on the other side where the bolt had come out, and a splint along the side. "It's in the hands of the gods now."

"He's still alive," said Galen. "You've done wonders."

The doctor looked up at him wearily. The circles under his eyes were as dark as bruises. "I may have killed him trying to save him. The infection will likely be massive, even with honey and alcohol to treat it. He's going to run a fever and I have no idea what to give him for it. Even if I had my kit, the treatments I'd use on a human might kill a gnole outright."

"Are we that different?"

"Physically? We might be. Pigs can eat things that would poison a human. Humans eat things that would kill dogs. If I tried to give him something as simple as willowbark for the fever, it might kill him. I just don't *know.*" His voice broke on the last word, and Galen wondered how he'd ever thought that Piper stifled his passions.

Obviously he was just saving them for the important things.

There was a smear of blood on his cheekbone. Galen wanted to wipe it away, but it somehow felt like a greater intimacy than stroking the man's cock had been. That had only been sex, after all. It couldn't compare to keeping a vigil over the body of a friend.

He did it anyway, with the pad of his thumb. "What do you need?" he asked.

Piper closed his eyes and leaned into the touch for a moment before pulling away. "I need a gnole doctor," he said. "And the nearest one is likely in Archon's Glory."

"I'll go fetch one, then."

Piper made a small noise of frustration. "We're three days away. You won't be back for a week, and I don't know if I can keep him alive that long."

"We're three days away by the world's slowest ox," countered Galen. "That's two days' march in the infantry, and I can shave time off that. And once I'm there, I'll requisition a carriage, and we'll be back in a day."

Piper looked up at him with a sudden gleam of hope. "Maybe. If I can keep his fever down with cold compresses... maybe."

Galen nodded. "I'll carry him upstairs," he said. "Then I'll go at once."

The gnole weighed no more than a large child, but large children tend to be remarkably heavy. He didn't stagger under the weight, but his injured calf throbbed where the scorpion-device had stabbed him. He got Earstripe laid down on a couch in the parlor where they had eaten several hundred years ago. Possibly thousands.

Piper immediately knelt beside the gnole, one hand on Earstripe's chest, muttering softly. "Heartbeat's still strong, I think. But I can't tell if it's fast or slow. It would have to be faster than an adult human, but what's the baseline?" He rubbed his face with both hands and gave Galen a rueful look. "Why on earth did I never ask Earstripe what his resting heartrate was?"

"It's not the sort of thing that comes up in casual conversation."

"It should." His gaze suddenly sharpened. "My god, Galen. You look like hammered shit."

"But *sexy* hammered shit, right?"

That got a rueful laugh out of Piper. "Always. And I doubt I look much better."

"Oh, I don't know. That tunic really brings out the color of the circles under your eyes."

"Nevertheless, you're not going anywhere until I've patched you up. I'm sorry. I should have paid closer attention."

"Yes, between being shot at and having to perform medicine on a different species, you absolutely should have made time for my scraped knee. It's nothing. I'll be fine."

Piper folded his arms, his lips compressed into a flat line. Galen had a strong urge to kiss that line and see if he could soften it. "I appreciate that you're trying to be strong and paladinly, but if that gash on your leg gets full of dirt and you fall down of a fever halfway to Archon's Glory, you won't do Earstripe any good. Now sit." He snapped his fingers. Galen sat, feeling somewhat like a dog.

"You're very imperious when you're being the doctor." Piper didn't reply, being too busy inspecting his calf. He heard the hiss of air between the man's teeth and thought it was probably worse than he he'd hoped.

"How the hell were you walking around on this?"

"The Saint of Steel's chosen tend to be thick-skinned."

"Well, his chosen's going to need stitches."

"I'm sure it can wait until—"

"Sit."

Galen settled back into his seat and resigned himself to his fate.

It was the better part of an hour before Piper certified him fit to leave, and had involved patching the slash on his arm as well, and slapping a dressing over it, despite Galen's protests that he'd had worse, walked it off, and never had any problems.

His bigger concern, honestly, was stiffness. Once the adrenaline of the fight and killing Thomas had worn off, he had been kneeling beside Piper for hours. His knee was swelling against the wrappings, and the bruise on his thigh was turning spectacularly blue. The longer he sat, the worse it was going to be. *If I can just get on the road and start walking, at least I'll shake some of that out.* It was a brutally long trip, to be sure, but he'd done worse at forced march, and that had only been...what, eighteen years ago? Surely he was just as fit as he had been at nineteen. *Yes. Definitely. And absolutely just as capable of going without sleep.*

He rose to his feet, stretched some of the soreness out, and turned to the hall. "Am I allowed to go now?"

"Yes," said Piper. "I should demand you sleep first, but I can't."

"I know." Galen put out his hand and cupped Piper's jaw. The doctor's already pale skin was nearly translucent with exhaustion, his eyes rimmed with red. Galen could see a blue vein beating in the hollow of the other man's throat.

He had a sudden urge to say something utterly mad, like, *I love you.* Which was absurd. They'd known each other for what, a few weeks? He couldn't possibly have fallen in love. *Merely because he is brave and clever and intensely passionate about the things that matter and laughs at your jokes and you laugh at his and he knows the worst about you and doesn't think it's all that impressive...no, for god's sake, don't start down that road.* You *don't get to fall in love. That would be the worst thing you could do to him. You're tired and maudlin and worried and you can't screw his brains out so all that lust is finding ridiculous outlets. Stop worrying.* You *really are turning into Stephen.*

"I'll come back to you," he said instead. "I promise."

Piper closed his eyes and turned his cheek until his lips touched Galen's fingers. "Thank you," he whispered.

Galen turned to go and made it as far as the front door before it slammed open.

CHAPTER 26

Three burly men wearing full battle armor rushed into the hall. Galen slapped for a sword that still wasn't there, felt the tide rise, got as far as, *Go for the first one, he'll block the hall and you can use him for a shield*—and then recognized Shane, Marcus and..."*Jorge?*"

"Well, I couldn't let these two come alone," said the paladin of the Dreaming God. "You know how horses feel about berserkers. I was afraid that if something bad happened, they'd be stranded with no ride in the middle of nowhere and we'd have to send a second rescue mission out for them."

Shane and Marcus rolled their eyes. Of the seven broken paladins, Galen knew that they were the only two with a long history of riding. The others could ride a horse, more or less, if the horse was extremely calm and if the battle tide didn't rise while on horseback, which was a recipe for disaster.

"A gnole could have followed with an ox!" said an extremely indignant voice behind Jorge. "A gnole does *not* approve of being put on a horse in front of a human. A horse did not approve either."

"Has the threat been dealt with?" asked Shane.

"I strangled him, if that's what you mean."

Shane nodded. "Very well. I apologize for having rushed to your aid, in that case, but our gnole friend was most concerned—"

"No, no." Galen held up his hands. "Thank the gods you're here. We very nearly didn't make it. And Earstripe was badly injured and Piper doesn't know how to treat gnoles. We need to get him to a gnole doctor as soon as possible."

Brindle shoved his way past the paladins, ears back. "A gnole is hurt?"

Galen led the way into the parlor. Piper leapt up, startled, then sagged with relief. "Oh sweet Rat, Brindle, I was so worried."

Brindle flicked his ears. "A human warned me. A gnole thought it best to bring sword-humans. But a gnole is hurt?"

Piper nodded. "And I don't have my kit. I've got some headache powders from the back of the drawer, but I don't know what's in them. Even if I could find a local doctor, I don't know what or how much to use compared to a human to keep his fever down."

Brindle put his nose next to Earstripe's wound and sniffed. "Doesn't smell rotten," he said. "But too fresh to be sure."

Piper nodded. "Can your people tolerate willowbark? I could maybe boil some of that, although god knows what the dosage would be like."

Brindle shook his head. "Don't know. Gnoles don't use it."

"Damnation."

"Bad wound. Needs gnole medicine." Brindle scowled. "Not bone-doctor's fault. Gnole not human, human not gnole. Take a gnole to gnole-doctor, maybe a gnole gets better."

"A day long ride with a broken leg, though?" Piper

grimaced. "I don't know how many bone fragments are left in the wound. I'm afraid something will tear and he'll bleed to death."

"If a gnole had an *ox*, a gnole wouldn't worry about it."

"If you had an ox, he'd die of old age before we got back to the city," said Shane.

Galen turned to the other paladins, who were standing around awkwardly. "Can you get us to the river? If we can get him on a boat..."

"Yes, of course," said Marcus. "One of us can ride upstream and hire a boat. There must be a place to make landfall near here, so we can minimize banging the poor fellow around."

The door at the back of the parlor opened and Missus Hardy stumped in. "I heard voices—" she started to say, then stopped at the sight of the newcomers. "Mercy!"

Galen didn't blame her. Three paladins in full armor could really suck the air out of a room. It didn't help that Jorge was a paladin of the Dreaming God and thus incredibly handsome. Shane was close, although he tried to hide it under a regrettable beard, and Marcus, the most normal-looking of the bunch, was still as broad as a barrel and muscled like a bear.

"This is Missus Hardy," said Galen, as all three of the paladins turned, reaching for their weapons. "She's the housekeeper. We'd be in a world of hurt if not for her."

"Ah." Shane took several steps forward and bowed deeply. "My thanks for what you have done for my brother in arms, madam."

"And mine," said Jorge, pushing past him and taking Hardy's hand in his. He bowed over it, because he was like that.

A flush started to rise up the housekeeper's neck. "Weren't nothin'," she mumbled.

"She hit our captor over the head with a poker," said Galen, "while he was holding a crossbow."

"Brave as well as beautiful," said Jorge. Hardy had to clear her throat several times.

"We think we have a plan to get out of your way," said Galen, "but before we go—do you have somewhere to go?"

"I'll go to my daughter's," said Hardy gruffly. "Likely she's been thinking I'm dead, for not having come home all this time. But I'll explain."

"We're getting those chains off first," said Piper.

"Chains?" All three paladins jerked upright, clearly horrified.

Missus Hardy looked embarrassed. She lifted her skirt up to show the shackles, then dropped the hem quickly. "Don't mean to complain," she muttered.

It was Marcus who stepped up to the rescue. "Those look like they're locked with a pin mechanism," he said. "If I can turn up a hammer and chisel, I'll have them off you in a trice. Can you show me where they might be kept?"

He led her away, talking soothingly. You'd never have known he had been a minor noble in his life before the death of the god, Galen thought. *Then again, a few years with the rest of us as berserker infantry and you probably get all the nobility knocked off you pretty quick.*

Jorge and Shane took themselves off on horseback to head upriver and find a boat, leaving Piper and Galen alone with the two gnoles.

Galen began to say something, but was interrupted by a weak sound from Earstripe. All three of them dropped to their knees next to the couch.

Earstripe muttered something in the liquid gnolespeech. Brindle responded. Galen couldn't tell what he said, but it sounded reassuring.

The injured gnole stirred and tried to lift his head, but Piper said, "No!" and held his shoulders. "Don't move," he said, in a gentler tone. "Please. You're very weak from loss of blood and you don't have the strength to spare."

Earstripe opened one eye, squinting against the light. "Alive?" he croaked.

"Yes. We're all three of us alive. And Brindle."

He pricked his whiskers forward and sagged back against the cushions.

"Silly to lay straight," muttered Brindle. "A gnole curls up. But no gnole beds here."

"We'll get him to somewhere with proper gnole beds," promised Galen. "Soon." He glanced at Piper. "Is waking up a good sign?"

"Yes, but not that good." The doctor wrung his hands together. "The real enemy is the fever and infection. He'd almost certainly live through the injury, but bolts aren't clean and there was cloth in the wound and even though we set the bone, it wasn't in good shape and might heal wrong and..."

"Twisting your whiskers, our bone-doctor," said Brindle. "Bone-doctor did our best work, yeah?"

Galen recognized the courtesy in the *our* pronouns the gnole was offering, even if it mangled the sentence a bit. "Piper did amazing work," he said firmly. "He started treating Earstripe when it might have meant a bolt in the back. And he worked for hours."

"I did what I could, but if Earstripe lives, it's entirely because of you, Brindle," said Piper. "If you hadn't gotten away and brought help, it would have been days before we could get him to a gnole doctor, and I might have poisoned him by accident."

Brindle flicked his whiskers and looked away, the gnole equivalent of an embarrassed shrug. "Chained-lady came and told a gnole to get away and bring help. A gnole would have been quicker, but didn't know how dangerous a human was. Thought best to get sword-humans, not try to find local humans to help."

"I don't know if it would have mattered if you were sooner," said Galen. "Thomas would have denied everything, and if Missus Hardy wasn't able to speak to them..." He shook his head. "Getting paladins was the best thing to do."

Piper rubbed his face. "I wonder how many people he killed?"

"Six while I was here," said Missus Hardy from the doorway. She limped in, leaning heavily on Marcus's arm. Galen heard no clinking and guessed that Marcus had found a chisel after all. "He'd advertise for a clerk from the city, a young man who could do writing and figuring, for a project lasting a couple months. Room and board and enough money to make it look good, but not suspicious." She scowled. "The master'd show them the maze, get them familiar with it, and then shut them in a few days later, and advertise again."

"And it's a remote enough place in winter that nobody expected regular messages," said Galen. "Dammit. It was a good plan. And explains the leather shoes, if they were clerks."

Missus Hardy nodded to him. "Somebody came looking for one of them, and the master said they'd never showed up and he was a bit sore about it. And I managed to warn one of the lads off, but the master locked my door at night, belike, and watched me close when they were about. Was lucky that he didn't lock me in while you were here."

"Too many of us, I imagine," said Galen. "He must have been afraid to do anything that might look strange for fear we'd get suspicious."

The housekeeper hung her head. "Should've told you right out," she said. "With him in the room. But I didn't know you, and didn't know your people and I got scared." She looked over to the couch. "Mebbe your friend wouldn't be lying there if I had."

"You probably knocked that bolt askew with your poker," said Piper, "and saved either my life or his. I don't know how good a shot Thomas was, but I'd rather take a chance with a wild shot than an aimed one."

Missus Hardy grunted. She took a step, carefully, then a larger one. "My legs feel so light now," she said, with bleak wonder. "Hips don't quite want to work right just yet."

"It'll come back," said Marcus. "You can put a horse in leg hobbles, but they learn to run again quick enough." He reached out to steady her when she took another large step and wobbled.

"Before we go," said Piper, "may I check your ankles? I don't mean to be rude, but I want to make sure there's nothing you can't fix with time and salve."

The housekeeper crooked up one corner of her mouth. "Been years since so many young men were trying to get beneath my skirts, and now I got two in one day!"

Galen cackled. Piper ducked his head. "I promise to be entirely a gentleman," he said.

"Well, damn," said Missus Hardy, and Galen laughed again.

"I hope Missus Hardy will be all right," fretted Piper a little later, as they prepared to leave.

"She'll be fine," said Galen. "She'll probably strip the place to the rafters before she goes, and more power to her."

"I wish she'd let us send someone to escort her to her village."

"I offered," said Marcus, "but she said that if she did, they'd all be expecting me to marry her when she got there."

"Fine figure of a woman," offered Jorge.

"Already got someone," said Marcus. "But feel free to stay and make the offer."

"Then who would take the horses back while you're all having a pleasure cruise down the river?"

Galen knew, if Jorge didn't, that Marcus had been married before the god died. His wife thought he was dead, but so far as Galen knew, the other paladin had remained faithful in the four years since.

A few days ago, he'd thought it foolish to stay loyal to a woman who believed herself a widow. A few days ago...well. It had been a long few days. He looked over at Piper, who was carefully settling Earstripe into Shane's arms. "Try to keep his leg elevated," he said. "And try not to jostle him. And..."

Galen intervened to rescue his fellow paladin. "It will be fine," he said. "And if it isn't fine, at least it will be quick."

"I know," said Piper. "I'm just worrying, because if I worry enough, maybe it won't all go bad." He flashed Galen a wry look. "This is the other reason I got out of dealing with live subjects."

Galen put his hands on the doctor's shoulders, leaned in and kissed his forehead. Piper blinked at him. "What was that for?"

"For being you."

He led the doctor to Marcus's horse. The other paladin was looking at him thoughtfully.

"What?" said Galen.

"Nothing. Here, Doc, we've got to ride double and I'm the one least likely to accidentally drop you on your head in the roadway." He offered Piper a hand, and between him pulling and Galen pushing, they got the doctor settled behind Marcus.

Galen felt a flash of envy. He'd never liked horses, but having Piper pressed up against his back, being pushed against him with every stride...the image had a lot to recommend it. *And Marcus is only interested in women and celibate besides. What a waste.*

Not that he was riding alone himself. Brindle was already perched at the front of the empty saddle. "Never thought a gnole would say this, but should have brought more horses."

"I will never let you forget you said that," said Jorge.

"Sword-human thinks he is *so* funny."

Galen hauled himself onto the horse. He was a lousy rider. He knew it, the horse knew it, there was no point in denying it. Brindle shifted to try and give him more space, then settled for clinging to the saddle as they set off at a trot.

Fortunately, it was not far to the landing site. The boat was already waiting for them, captained by a round-faced woman in a slouching cap. "Ready and waiting," she said cheerfully to Jorge, and then, catching sight of Earstripe, "Ah, poor little mite. Get him aboard and we'll be at Archon's Glory by midnight."

Galen knew nothing whatsoever about boats. It was bigger than a rowboat and a lot smaller than the big clipper ships that docked in Delta. It had a curved front end, and there weren't eyes painted on it like the ones in Delta had. They all fit in it, except for Jorge, who was staying with the horses.

Their captain had a pole, as did her assistant. The assistant untied the rope from around a wooden post at the landing site, and they dipped their poles in the water and pushed the boat away from the shore. The current picked them up and began to carry the boat downriver, slowly at first, and then, as they pushed the boat toward the center of the river, faster than a man could run.

It was cold on the water. Piper fussed over Earstripe's blankets, then sat beside him in the bottom of the boat, back against one of the low benches. Galen sat down next to the doctor, knowing there was nothing useful to say and so didn't say anything. Their knees touched and neither one moved away, while the banks of the river slid silently by.

CHAPTER 27

"I think he's feverish," said Piper an hour or two later. "Brindle?"

Brindle felt the inside of the other gnole's ears, then peeled back his lip to check his gums. "Too hot, yeah."

"Do we keep him warm or try to cool him down?"

"Cool. Fever's no good for anything but cooking a gnole's brain." Piper dipped a cloth into the chilly river water and Brindle packed it around Earstripe's ears. The injured gnole whined softly, a thin thread of sound, then fell silent. Galen was pretty sure that he wasn't really awake. *Not that that matters. I of all people know that nightmares are usually worse than waking.*

"Brindle," said Piper cautiously, "I know this is a lot to ask, but may I feel your ears? I don't know what a healthy temperature should be, and if I ever need to treat a gnole again and don't have one to help me..."

Brindle's whiskers arched forward in the gnole equivalent of a tired smile. "A gnole will help, bone-doctor."

He sat patiently while Piper felt his nose and the inside of his ears, and even opened his mouth so that Piper could compare the color of his gums to Earstripe's. "Can't always use," he warned. "A gnole has bad teeth, maybe, a gnole's gums go red anyway. But red, dry, hot, all bad for a gnole."

By the time night had fallen, it was obvious that Earstripe was running a fever, even without checking ears or gums. Heat seemed to radiate off the small body. At first, he snapped his teeth and growled at things that only he could see, but as hours passed, he seemed to lose the strength for that. Eventually his only movement was violent shivering, and even Brindle seemed at a loss for what to do next.

It was probably close to midnight when Galen looked up and saw the lights of Archon's Glory shining brightly ahead. The sight filled him with unutterable relief. They were almost to a gnole healer. If anything could be done, it would be done.

He nudged Piper. The doctor had sagged against him in exhaustion and Galen had put his arm around the man's shoulders. Piper had fallen into a fitful doze with his head on Galen's shoulder. *No surprise there. I don't think he's slept since...since...hell. Since before I fought that scorpion machine.* It felt like an age of the earth ago.

"Piper," he said gently. "Piper, wake up. We're almost there."

Piper muttered something and burrowed against Galen's side. Fortunately, it wasn't the side with the bruised ribs. From this angle, Galen could only see half his face—the long, straight nose and the dark curve of eyelashes. There were lamps lit at the front and back of the boat and the light was very yellow, which gave the blue circles under the doctor's eyes a greenish cast.

The paladin sighed and tucked the blanket around Piper's shoulder, feeling a rush of some gentle emotion that was hard to identify. Fondness, perhaps, and a touch of exasperation. The man should have slept before now, but of course he hadn't, not until he was ready to drop.

Galen lifted his head, to see Shane watching him.

"What?" he asked.

"Nothing."

Galen narrowed his eyes. First Marcus, now Shane. "He's very tired," he said irritably. "He was up for hours tending Earstripe before you arrived. I don't think he's slept in over a day."

"I'm sure he's exhausted," agreed Shane. "And how long has it been since *you* slept?"

Galen shrugged. "It's different for us. How many forced marches have we done?"

Marcus snorted. "Too many. Though they were a long time ago, most of them."

"Thank the gods for that," said Shane.

"Yes, of course. But we're not as young as we used to be. I like eight hours a night, when I can get it."

The boat traffic increased as they approached the city. The captain and her assistant used their poles to steer the boat out of the way of the big barges carrying goods, and finally they bumped against a dock on the far side of the river from where the bodies had been found.

Piper stirred and sat up, rubbing at his eyes. "Mm? What? Are we—Earstripe!"

"Not dead," said Brindle, who had been curled up beside the injured gnole. He sat up as well. "Hot, but not dead."

Piper felt his patient's ears. "Is he hotter?"

Brindle nodded grimly. They packed more cold cloth around Earstripe's ears and dipped his hands in river water to cool them, while Shane paid the captain the other half of her fee.

"Good luck to him," she said, nodding to the limp gnole in Marcus's arms. "I'll light a candle to the River Serpent for you all."

"Thank you," said Shane gravely, because Shane was always

courteous. Galen, who was suspicious of most gods these days, except perhaps the Rat, did not say anything. He helped Piper scoop damp cloths in a bundle, to try and cool Earstripe on the way to the gnole doctor.

"How far is it?" he asked Brindle.

"Not far." The gnole paused, smoothing down his whiskers. "A gnole doesn't live in this warren. May need to ask some gnole when we get there. Entrance to a warren changes sometimes, yeah?"

"Lead the way."

Brindle, to Galen's mild surprise, did not take them back into the city proper, but stayed on the far side of the river, heading downstream. Galen knew that there were warehouses on that side, and a shanty town that had sprung up when the Elkinslough had burst its banks several years ago and flooded some of the poorest low-lying neighborhoods. He knew that at least one gnole warren had been flooded as well, but he hadn't realized that it, too, had relocated.

"Built into hillside here," said Brindle, leading them through the narrow makeshift streets. "No flood here. But a long walk for a job-gnole or a rag-and-bone gnole, so more small burrows in the city now, yeah?"

"Makes sense," said Piper. Galen was too busy looking over his shoulder. The tent city he remembered had matured, permanent and semi-permanent structures replacing flimsier canvas ones. There were even scatterings of lamps, burning the very cheapest oil by the smell, but still providing light. Rope-and-board walkways crisscrossed the area at varying levels and Brindle led them up onto one. Looking down at the ground, Galen could see why. Sewer systems were expensive and complicated to install and it would probably be a hundred years until anyone got around to putting one here.

Still, it wasn't the worst he'd seen by a long shot. The slope of the hillside meant that the nightsoil was washed down to the river, so it didn't smell significantly worse than any other neighborhood in Archon's Glory. The smell of the river itself was extraordinary in summer, but there was no getting away from that anywhere in the city either.

There were a fair number of people, both gnole and human, coming and going, as one might expect, even in the middle of the night. The humans gave the paladins a wide berth, clearly not thinking it worthwhile to get involved. Galen heard footsteps overhead and looked up to see more walkways above them, the bottoms hung with slum-weaver nests.

"This area built up fast," he said.

"Available material," said Marcus. "The flood destroyed a great many houses. The people who lived in them scavenged everything that they could, and more washed in from upriver." He had been carrying Earstripe, but he nodded to Shane and handed the gnole over to give his arms a rest.

"I can take him," said Galen.

"You've been beat to shit," said Marcus bluntly. "I wouldn't trust you to carry a bouquet of daisies right now."

"Oh yeah? I'll take you on right now. Bare-knuckle. Let's go."

"*Gentlemen,*" said Piper, sounding exasperated, "we are on a matter of some urgency. You can fight later." He narrowed his eyes at Galen. "*After* your ribs have healed up. And if you tear out those stitches, I shall be annoyed."

Galen sighed dramatically. Brindle rolled his eyes. Shane gazed at the sky, perhaps seeking strength from a higher power.

"Getting close," said Brindle a few minutes later, as they threaded their way higher up the hillside. The amount of human traffic had diminished significantly and the makeshift alleys were darker and quieter. The walkways were no longer board and rope, but cobbled together from packing crates. Galen caught the occasional flash of gnole eyes in the gloom, but there were no lamps here, only the glowing red haze of the sky to see by.

"Wait here," said Brindle. "A gnole will be back." He vanished into a space too small for a human, leaving the four men standing in a knot.

It was very quiet, once the rustle of gnole fur had faded. Much quieter than Galen liked a city to be.

Piper took advantage of the pause to check Earstripe. His face was grim. "Fever's getting worse, I think," he muttered to no one in particular. Galen put a reassuring hand on his arm, although his own nerves had begun to prickle.

"I believe someone is watching us," said Shane quietly.

Galen opened his mouth to say something sarcastic, and then a figure materialized from the shadows.

CHAPTER 28

There were three of them. The woman in front, who seemed to be the leader, looked less like a footpad and more like someone's mother, but presumably baby footpads had to come from somewhere. She was holding a board like a club. The two men behind her were carrying truncheons. None of them looked happy.

Marcus's hand went to his sword hilt. Galen reached for his own, realized yet again that he didn't have one, and cursed internally. *And Shane can't draw because he's carrying Earstripe. I could go for his sword, but dammit, he favors that ridiculous back scabbard that the Dreaming God's people use, I'll take his ear off if I try.* Galen didn't know how they managed the damn things without slitting themselves open from stem to stern. He settled for stepping in front of Piper and getting ready to shield the doctor if it was his only choice.

"I don't know what you're doing with that gnole," said the woman, her eyes narrowed, "but if you think you can come in here and start hunting them, I don't care how big you are, you'll soon learn differently."

Galen felt a twinge of relief. They weren't here for a

mugging, they were here defending the gnoles. *Which...okay, admittedly, four heavily armed men lugging around an obviously dead or injured gnole* is *suspicious. Where's Brindle? If he comes back, he can vouch for us.*

"We mean no harm," said Piper.

"How about you put that fellow down, and we'll see about that?"

"Here?" said Piper, clearly horrified. "No, it's too dirty." Which was true, but perhaps not the most diplomatic thing to say at the moment.

Galen tried to think of how to smooth the situation over but he was so damn tired that he couldn't think of what to say. "It's fine," he said. "It's fine, really."

Judging by the way that the woman and her associates gripped their weapons, they did not believe that it was fine.

It was Shane who saved them. "I think that we share a goal," he said, still holding Earstripe to his chest. His voice was so calm and gentle and soothing that he could have said he was about to fly to the moon and it would probably have sounded reasonable. "This gnole is our friend, and he has been badly injured. We are seeking the gnole-warren here, so that he may be treated by his own people."

The back scabbard wasn't the only thing Shane had taken away from the Dreaming God's temple. Most paladins could do the voice to a certain degree, but the Dreaming God's people had refined it to a high art. Galen watched the two men's white-knuckled grip on their truncheons relax. He felt a stab of envy. He couldn't do the damn voice at *all.*

"You say you're here for a healer?" the blonde woman said, still suspicious but not quite as hostile.

Shane nodded. "We are here with a gnole guide," he said, still in the voice. "He has gone to get directions, but should return shortly. I promise you, we have nothing but goodwill for the gnoles here."

She took a step back. "Been some trouble lately," she said gruffly. "People got word the warren was here. Bully-boys thinking it would be funny to start trouble with 'em."

"I am sorry to hear that," said Shane, and anyone listening could tell that he *was* sorry. "I will inform the Temple of the White Rat that there have been problems."

The line between the woman's eyebrows eased. "You're with the Rat?" Shane dipped his head. "Ah, right then. Good people. But don't let 'em send the guard. We don't want 'em throwing their weight around, understand? We take care of the gnoles and the gnoles take care of us. Don't need to get anybody else involved."

Shane nodded gravely. "You have my word that I shall pass on your concerns only to the Rat."

She nodded, distracted, looking past him. Then her expression changed and she lowered her weapon completely. "Guess you're telling the truth."

"A gnole leaves for five minutes and humans get into trouble," muttered Brindle, pushing his way past Galen. "Gnoles opening up a path for too-big humans now."

The woman said something in halting gnolespeech, putting her free hand up to imitate one ear. Brindle flicked his whiskers sharply and replied, enunciating each word clearly. She nodded and the trio vanished as quickly as they had arrived.

"It is good that the warren has local protectors," said Shane.

"Yeah, I just thought that some of those local protectors were going to try to bash our heads in," muttered Marcus.

Scraping sounds heralded the arrival of more gnoles, pulling aside boards and what looked like a broken door, until they had made a path that was large enough for a human to walk through. Brindle waved for the four men to follow. Marcus took point, with Shane after him and Piper after that. Galen brought up the rear, not because he didn't trust the gnoles but because he didn't entirely trust other humans. *Those three seemed friendly, but if there are people about who think it's amusing to torment gnoles, I'd rather be where I can stop them.*

Fortunately, no one like that materialized. They were led through a dark labyrinth of canvas walls and scraps of board. Galen could barely make out the outline of Piper in front of him. Then a light flared up behind him and Galen turned to see a strange gnole following him, holding a candle on the end of a short pole, probably for the benefit of the humans. Another light bobbing up ahead seemed to confirm that.

It made the going easier. They went down a short ramp and then onward again. Galen wasn't certain, but he thought they were probably actually into the hillside by now. The air smelled less of the river and more of gnole-fur and earth.

The way opened up abruptly and he and the other humans spilled out into a large circular room. The edges were defined by hanging blankets and wooden supports but the roof was made of earth and stone. Tunnels led off in multiple directions, like spokes from a wheel.

Dozens of gnoles lined the walls and peered at them from the tunnel mouths. There were small lights fastened to the wooden supports, casting a much dimmer light than the candles carried by their escorts.

Galen trusted the gnoles completely, but his nerves prickled anyway. Without the lights, the paladins would be completely at the mercy of the warren's occupants. And there were many, many occupants. He could hear breathing and shifting and a soft murmur of gnole voices from every side. *I am going to guess that no one tormenting gnoles ever came in here. Or if they did, they didn't leave again.*

A gnole came forward. They leaned heavily on a cane and

Galen guessed by their gait that one foot was shorter than the other, but they still moved with gnolish energy. A broad white blaze ran down the center of their face, much wider than the usual badger stripes, splashing across the eyes and leaving the nose entirely pink.

"Our doctor," said Brindle, with obvious pride.

The white-blazed gnole chattered at Brindle, but their eyes were locked on the bundle in Shane's arms.

"Ours says to bring this gnole," says Brindle. "Ours says that ours will care for him."

"I would like to speak with your doctor if I may," said Piper. "The more...ours?...knows of the injury the better."

Brindle launched into a rapid explanation, ears and whiskers sweeping as he spoke. Galen caught two or three words, but for the most part, the gnole was talking far too fast for his meager skills to keep up.

The doctor turned to look at Piper warily, and spoke a few curt words. Brindle said, almost apologetically, "Ours does not think that a human can tell ours much of a healing."

"No," said Piper, one corner of his mouth lifting with weary humor. "No, but a human can tell ours what a human did to a gnole, so that ours knows what to undo."

The white-blazed gnole barked a laugh at Brindle's translation, and ours' stance seemed to soften. They nodded curtly to Piper and stumped away down a tunnel. Bays opened off it, marked off with woven blankets. The humans followed, ducking their heads. Shane was practically bent double, trying to avoid crushing Earstripe to his chest.

The gnole doctor swept a blanket aside and pointed. The bay was large, the center a round nest of bedding. A long side table gleamed with instruments, some of them similar to the ones that Galen had seen in Piper's bag, some of them baffling in purpose and design. One of the gnoles with the candles set it down reverently on the side table.

The ceiling here was even lower and Shane gave up even trying to stand. He knelt, and shuffled forward on his knees to lay Earstripe into the nest. He bowed his head to the gnole doctor, and then he and Marcus retreated into the hallway.

Galen stayed, while ours moved around the patient, rearranging his limbs, checking the insides of his ears, and scowling.

"Brindle, can you translate what I've done?"

"Complicated words," said Brindle. "A gnole can try." He looked over at the white-blazed gnole and said something. Ours nodded again and gestured to Piper to join ours beside the patient.

Gnole and human bent over Earstripe together, Piper explaining what he had done, and Brindle quietly murmuring a translation. What struck Galen as he watched was how similar the two looked. The intensity of their gazes, the deft, careful movements as they unwrapped the dressings—these were two of a kind, no matter that one was three feet tall and the other flat-faced and naked-limbed.

Another wave of that odd, tender emotion rolled through him as he watched Piper. This one was stronger than the first, laced with admiration. *He is a good man,* thought Galen, almost wonderingly. *A good man who is good at what he does. He wants nothing more than to help people, and when it began to hurt him too badly, he found another way to help.*

Ours sniffed the dressing and gave Piper another sharp look. "Honey," said Piper. "I didn't know what else to use. It does help sometimes in humans, but I don't know about in gnoles." The gnole doctor cocked ours head, listening to Brindle's translation, then let out another sharp laugh and cuffed Piper's arm in clear amusement. Ours pointed to a clay jar on the table and Brindle fetched it and opened the jar, revealing dark amber honey. Piper laughed too, the tired lines of his face briefly falling into kinder ones, and Galen felt his heart clench in a way that was close to pain.

He leaned against the wooden pillar that marked the doorway, feeling his own weariness catching up with him. *Perhaps I'm just getting maudlin because I'm tired.*

The white-blazed gnole called out the door and two young gnoles slipped by Galen, listened politely, and then left again, returning with damp cloths for Earstripe's ears. One peeled the patient's lips back and the other rubbed some kind of oil onto the gnole's gums. *Probably better than trying to shove something down his throat and getting bit.* Galen lost track of the conversation for a moment, his eyes swimming. When he lifted his head, the two young gnoles had moved aside and the white-blazed gnole was sitting on a stool. *Definitely tired.*

Piper seemed to have gained new energy, talking animatedly with the doctor. He stretched out his own leg and traced a line with his fingers, marking the path of the femoral artery. Brindle was hard-pressed to keep up with the translation, but apparently ours understood anyway because ours slapped their knees and made Brindle stretch out his leg, tracing a different path with one clawed hand. Piper put a hand to his heart in clear relief. "I was terrified the entire time," he admitted, "that the bolt was close to the artery. I wish I'd known."

"Now our gnole knows," translated Brindle. "If our gnole ever works on a human, maybe our gnole won't accidentally bleed them dry."

"Brindle," said Piper, "would it be rude to ask if ours would be willing to teach me a little more about how gnole anatomy works? Not right this minute, of course, but in the near future? I would be happy to return the favor as much as I can. It might help us both to save lives someday."

Brindle considered this. "A gnole can ask," he said slowly. "Ah...ours is...very high-caste. Bone-doctor understands?"

Piper looked at Galen and Galen felt foolishly pleased that he could help. "I believe he's trying to say that ours is an extremely senior doctor, and you would need to treat ours as such."

Piper chuckled. "I am not very senior," he told Brindle. "I promise that I will give ours all the respect I would give one who is far wiser than I. And ours may set the time and place of ours choosing." He paused, then added, "If ours would like to come to my workplace and view human bodies, it's a large part of what I do."

The gnole doctor listened to Piper's relayed request with interest. At one point, ours whiskers flicked sharply, though Galen could not tell if it was with dismay or simple surprise. *Is it the bodies? Grave-gnoles handle corpses and they are the lowest caste of gnole society. Is ours alarmed by Piper doing grave-gnole work?*

When Brindle had finished, the gnole doctor bent over Earstripe, examining his wound again, then barked a few words over ours shoulder. Galen could see Brindle's astonishment at whatever ours had said, and braced himself in case it was a sharp rejection.

"Ours has a name," said Brindle. "Humans would say... Skull-of-Ice, yes? Ours allows bone-doctor to use the human version." He swallowed. "Our gnole says that ours will come to bone-doctor's burrow and look at human dead. Ours says that lives will be saved between you." The gnole shot Galen a pleading look. "Our gnole honors bone-doctor with this, and with our name. Tomato-man, can you explain for a human? Better than this gnole can?"

"You've explained very well, I think," said Piper. He looked over at Galen. "Am I missing anything?"

"I don't think you're missing anything," said Galen. "But I think this may be...ah...somewhat unprecedented. It might be like Beartongue visiting a temple of a different god in another nation. Ours is doing you a favor, but it's a favor that extends to any other humans ours might have to treat, if that makes sense?"

Piper nodded and turned back to Brindle. "Please convey all my gratitude to Skull-of-Ice. Ours is very generous to a human who cannot smell."

Brindle repeated this. Skull-of-Ice cackled, reached out, and tapped a claw against Piper's nose. Galen felt a swell of pride at how well the doctor had handled things. It was a great compliment, he was certain, and Piper had responded in exactly the right way.

Skull-of-Ice made shooing motions toward the humans and to Brindle and gestured to the assistants who were waiting patiently with cloths and poultices. Piper bowed to the gnoles and retreated into the hallway where the other two paladins waited.

"Is everything all right?" asked Shane.

Piper nodded, exhausted but clearly satisfied. "He's in good hands," he said. "Far better than mine."

"But you kept him alive to get there," said Galen.

The doctor made a small noise of acknowledgment. "I suppose there's that." His eyes met Galen's and in their dark brown depths, Galen could see the memory of that long, terrible vigil at Earstripe's bedside.

No stranger to vigils himself, he wondered how many Piper had kept, over the living and the dead. But the doctor had come through his kinder and fiercer in defense of the living. Galen had only come out older and more broken. *As exhausted as we are, his first thought was to ask if the gnoles could help him to save more lives. That's what he does.*

And I think I'm in love with him.

He had to look away. Piper's eyes were too bright. The doctor might be able to read Galen's thoughts in them, and that would be far too dangerous.

He looked down at his hands instead. Hands which had killed more people than he could even remember. Hands which he'd briefly wrapped around Piper's throat. A man he loved.

Oh gods and saints, thought Galen, *I've got to let him go.*

CHAPTER 29

"Well," said Piper, as they stood outside the gnole warren. "Well." He swayed a little on his feet. "I suppose all we can do now is wait for word."

"I will see you home, then," said Galen.

Piper gazed at him for a moment, then smiled. It was a sweet, unguarded smile, bright with relief, and Galen's heart clenched. *Let me steal a last few minutes. Then I'll have to end this. The sooner the better.*

"We'll all see you home," said Marcus. "If somebody tries to jump you, Galen's going to be about as much use as tits on a bull."

"Marcus, I will *absolutely* fight you."

They walked out of the warren together. Galen took Piper's arm and they leaned against each other and it felt good and correct and he wanted more and his heart ached with it. He wanted to walk more slowly so that they did not reach the end of their journey. He wanted to store up the warmth of Piper's shoulder against his, the way the light woke red highlights in Piper's dark hair, the sound of his laughter, hoarse with exhaustion, when Marcus said something particularly outrageous. *Oh*

Saint, why didn't I pay closer attention when we were in the maze? I should have committed every bit of him to memory.

But eventually, no matter how slowly Galen went, their feet led them back across the river and into a familiar part of the city. *It's almost over. You must do this and be done with it. Quick, before it has time to hurt even more.*

"I'm just down here," said Piper, gesturing to the street. He looked awkwardly at Shane and Marcus, then over to Galen. "Ah..."

Galen tried to think of a polite way to tell the other two paladins to make themselves scarce. Unfortunately, at the moment all he could think of was, "Get lost, you bastards," and that seemed undiplomatic.

"I think I'd like a beer," rumbled Marcus. He looked at Shane. "And so would you."

"I would?" said Shane, who rarely drank at all.

"Yes. You would love one."

"Subtle, your friends," said Piper, watching the two paladins retrace their steps to a small tavern on the corner of the street.

"They mean well," said Galen with a sigh. "But we were mostly called in to be killing machines."

Piper's lips tightened a little, which only solidified Galen's resolve. *He's a healer, and I'm truly no different than that scorpion thing I bashed to death. He needs to be with someone else entirely. Someone whose only purpose isn't putting more bodies on the slab in front of him.*

This is for the best.

He bit down on the sudden rush of anguish at the thought, and followed Piper down the street to his door.

His apartments were cool but not chill, the brick of the small fireplace radiating heat. Judging by the warmth of the chimney, the neighbors had been cooking recently. Piper wanted to fall down and weep with relief, or possibly just fall down. He had never been so glad to be at home in his own rooms.

"Come inside?" he asked Galen nervously. The paladin had been silent the entire walk down the street, and Piper could feel tension growing in his gut. Something was wrong. Something had been wrong since they left the gnole warren.

Galen stepped inside the door and stood in the entryway, very obviously not coming any further inside.

"Would you like tea?" Piper asked, because he had to say something. Galen shook his head, and Piper could read something about the set of his lips that set off even more warning bells. "It's funny," he said, rushing to fill the silence, "it seems like we did everything in the wrong order. We know all the important things about each other and none of the small things. I don't even know if you like tea. Maybe you're allergic to it."

"Piper..."

"You could stay here tonight, if you wanted. I don't mean for —I mean, we're both exhausted, obviously. I could make you up a pallet in here. If you wanted."

You're babbling again because you're afraid of what he'll say if you let him get a word in edgewise. Because no one ever has that look in their eyes when they're about to say, "This is interesting, let's see where it goes."

"Piper," said Galen, a little louder.

You're an adult. This is not the first time you've been rejected. You can handle having a man say he doesn't want to see you anymore. Yes, a very sexy man, yes, a brave decent man who saved your life several times over, but it's not as if you've known him for more than two weeks. Try to keep what little dignity you have left. Piper began filling the kettle resolutely.

"I think," said Galen, very carefully, "that it would be best if we do not continue seeing each other."

He'd been half-expecting it but it still landed like a blow to the chest. "Ah," he said, and pressed his lips tightly together to keep anything else from escaping. He focused on pouring water from the jug into the kettle. He might not have dignity, but at least he would have tea.

When he was absolutely certain that he would not babble or weep or cling to Galen's ankle, he said, very carefully, "May I ask the reason why?"

Even with his eyes locked on the kettle, he could feel the paladin wince.

"You're a good man," said Galen. "You deserve better."

"Ah," said Piper again.

From anyone but a paladin, he'd have considered that one of the classic lines, up there with, "I'm just not ready for anything serious" or "I'm sorry, I have suddenly been called to the priesthood." The hell of it was that Galen might actually mean it.

He took the kettle over to the hearth and began trying to start a fire. It would have been easier if his hands weren't shaking. *It was two weeks and one quick toss in a corner. There's no reason to feel like your heart is breaking.* He pushed the emotions away, the way he had become so skilled at doing. *When you're both on a slab, none of this will matter anyway.*

"You are also a good man," he said. He sounded calm, which was good. All that practice finally paying off. The wound might be mortal, but there was no sense letting the patient see you panicking. "I can accept that you don't want to see me in particular, but don't give up just because you have an inflated sense of your own unworthiness."

He heard the paladin move closer, and his nerves prickled with awareness of the other man's closeness. Stupid nerves. What did they know about it?

He finally managed a decent spark onto the tinder and breathed gently onto the flame. It flickered, nearly going out, and if he were a different sort of man, he'd think it was a metaphor but Piper was a lich-doctor so he took a deep breath and thought about a burn victim he'd seen on the slab. *No matter how you feel, you're still doing better than they were.*

This was less comfort than one might expect.

"You don't understand," Galen grated. "There's no happy ending. I can never sleep beside another human being again. I'll always be dangerous."

"So what?" Piper finally turned to look at him. "My god, man, great love poems aren't written about how lovers get eight hours of sleep a night and no one steals the covers. So maybe we fuck and then go to separate beds. *So what?*"

He wished immediately that he hadn't mentioned love. It wasn't love that he felt. It was much too soon for love, wasn't it?

The cold knot in his chest made him horribly afraid that it wasn't.

Galen opened his mouth, closed it again, and then looked away. "Piper," he said, almost gently, "you are kind and you care very much about people and you don't give up even when things seem lost, and that means that you wouldn't give up on me. And I am already a lost cause. All I could do is drag you down with me."

"Ah," said Piper, for a third time.

The silence stretched out, beyond strained into unbearable. "Perhaps you should go," said Piper finally.

"I didn't mean to hurt you."

"I believe you."

Galen let himself out. The door clicked quietly behind him. Piper sat in front of the hearth and made a cup of tea and didn't drink it until long after it went cold.

. . .

"I am going to guess by your face that it didn't go well," rumbled Marcus, as the three paladins walked toward the Temple of the Rat.

"It went fine," said Galen. *Was that a lie? Maybe. What did you expect Piper to do, smile and nod and say, "You're so very right, let's never speak of this again?"*

You could never make him happy. You could only make him as miserable as you are. You'd run roughshod over him. He hasn't got the steel to stand up for himself against you.

The memory rose unbidden of Piper darting into the trapped room to touch the corpse there. *That isn't the same,* he argued with himself. *That was recklessness or courage or some combination of the two. I've got that.*

"Fine," said Marcus. "Yes. I believe that. That is why you take five minutes to answer a question and look like you swallowed a weasel."

"It wouldn't have worked," said Galen. "Him and me. It's better this way."

"I thought that you two seemed quite close," offered Shane.

"And you're both snarky bastards," agreed Marcus.

"No," said Galen. "I mean, yes, we are, but he's...nice. If you scratch him, you get all this caring and decency. If you scratch me, there's just more me."

"You are *literally* a paladin sworn to defend the innocent and downtrodden," said Marcus.

"You both know as well as I do what that's worth these days."

Marcus looked as if he might argue the point. Galen glared at him. "You of all people should understand. You walked away after Hallowbind too, didn't you?"

The other man inhaled sharply. Shane, who had been walking a little behind them both, stepped forward and quietly inserted himself in the middle. Marcus fell back a step, but not before Galen saw the slash of anguish across his face.

There, you see? That's what I'll end up doing to anyone who cares about me. Marcus is as tough as an old boot and I still hurt him. Piper's got no defenses against someone like me.

He was right. He was most definitely right. So why did he feel as if he'd made a terrible mistake?

They reached the Temple. Galen wanted nothing more than to go inside and fall down and sleep for a year, god willing without dreams.

"I will make a preliminary report to Beartongue," said Shane. "She'll want to grill you in the morning."

"And then the guard will want to grill me again," said Galen wearily. "Yes, I know. If I can get a little sleep, I'll manage."

Shane nodded and turned away. Marcus stayed behind, setting one hand on the doorframe of Galen's room.

"I shouldn't have said that," Galen said. "I didn't mean to throw that in your face. It's just that you know, and no one else does. No one else was at Hallowbind."

"I know," said Marcus. He was staring into the distance. Galen wondered what he was seeing. *His wife? Or what scraps were left of the dead at Hallowbind when we were done with them?*

"I think about her every day," said Marcus finally. "She's the first thing I think about when I wake up. I can't let it go."

"But she's safe," said Galen.

"I hope she is," said Marcus. He focused on Galen finally, and his deep brown eyes were bleak. "I hope she's happy. But sometimes I wonder if she's thinking about me when she wakes up too. Maybe all I've done is condemn us both."

He stepped back and let the door close. Galen stripped off his clothes, sponged the worst of the dirt off himself, then fell down on the bed and let exhaustion stop his mind from self-recriminations.

CHAPTER 30

Piper slept for nearly two days, waking only to use the chamberpot, drink water, and on one heroic occasion, stagger down the street to a food cart and buy something. It was mostly onions and beans, but there was a piece of fish in it that gave him a bad moment until he managed to spit it out, his mouth tingling with a remembered hook.

When he finally seemed to be awake for good, he got dressed and went to a public bath for a quick shave and a long soak. The hot water made him feel close enough to human that he started to feel guilty about his replacement, who was probably frantically trying to keep up with the bodies coming in and wondering when Piper would come back to relieve him.

The world goes on, he thought grimly. *Even for those unlucky in love. And hopefully for those shot with crossbow bolts.* He wasn't sure if he could find the gnole warren again. Hopefully someone would think to send him a message when Earstripe woke. If he woke.

He tried to think of something else, but the only other thing he could think of was Galen, which didn't help at all. Sleep had dulled his misery but consciousness seemed to be sharpening it to a point. He walked to work with his shoulders hunched, staring at his feet.

"You look like hell," said Kaylin, the guard on duty.

"Thanks," said Piper. "How've you been?"

"Knee hurts like hell in this weather." She slapped her left leg, which was missing from the knee down. Kaylin was one of three guards stationed at the top of the steps to make sure no one came down to bother the bodies. She was married to a baker who sent along vast quantities of pastries every feast day, apparently convinced that Piper was going to starve to death if not given enough fruit pies.

"How long have you been married?" he asked abruptly.

Kaylin's eyebrows rose. "Nineteen years," she said. "Why?"

Two weeks. You don't get to sit and mope because you knew someone for two weeks. Nineteen years, now...that would be worth moping over. He shook his head and turned away, but she'd known him too long. "There's someone out there for everyone," she said. "Even nice young doctors who spend all their time chopping up bodies."

Piper grumbled something as he started down the stairs. "I've got a nephew about your age," she called after him. "Sweet boy. Strong stomach."

Piper snorted. Ironically, a strong stomach really did have something to recommend it. There had been more than a few men over the years who had been very interested in getting to know a doctor, right up until they found out exactly what sort of doctor he was.

Yes, but how does Kaylin's nephew do with death traps created by the ancients?

Does he have red hair and jade eyes and strong arms and can he make me laugh?

He opened the door to his workroom and his replacement looked up. "*There* you are! Lady of Grass have mercy upon me, where have you been? I was afraid I'd have to hire someone to replace me replacing you."

"Sorry, Sanga. Things got very dicey."

Piper suffered through a one-armed hug. (The other hand was holding a bonesaw.) Sanga had dark skin, broad shoulders, a big beard and an even bigger laugh. He also had one of the most delicate touches with a scalpel that Piper had ever encountered. If anyone working at the guard or the government noticed that Piper was gone, it was probably because the quality of the work had improved significantly.

Sanga held him at arm's length and frowned. "You look terrible, my friend. Just how dicey did things get?"

"Very, very dicey." Piper went to a drawer and pulled out a fresh set of gloves. "A very nasty fellow was kidnapping people and feeding them to ancient machines in his basement."

"Lady of Grass! Were you hurt?"

"No, but my friends were. They're recovering. Hopefully." He was going to have to find some way to check on Earstripe. Perhaps he could go to the Temple of the Rat and ask for Brindle. *And risk running into Galen? Do you want that?*

He didn't know what he wanted. The thought of seeing the paladin again was like a knife in his chest, and yet he was desperate for a glimpse, even though he knew that it would hurt.

He set to work on the next body on the slab, reading the notes and throwing himself into work. He knew that Sanga was watching him, but the other doctor said nothing, only continued his own job. Between them, the backlog began to go down. By the end of the day, when Piper called for the grave-gnoles to come and take the bodies away, the morgue was empty.

He wished he could speak to the grave-gnoles and ask them about the warren, but while the shrouded figures had made it clear that they understood some human speech, they would not speak. Piper's communication with them consisted of the locations where the bodies were to be taken, "hello," "please," and, "thank you." The one time that a particular graveyard had been closed due to rising water, the gnole had communicated the matter entirely in mime. "Can you take me to the gnole-burrow on the other side of the river so that I can find out if my friend is recovering" was a fairly complex concept to express in mime. He vowed again to find a gnole dictionary somewhere.

Sanga clapped him on the shoulder. "You should call it a night," he said. "You still look terrible."

Piper sighed. He was surprised at how tired he was, for having slept for nearly two days. "Perhaps you're right," he said. He led the way up the steps, waved to Kaylin, and opened the door to the outside.

—into ivory and watery green light and soon he'd hear the click and the blades would fall and he would never get out none of them would ever get out—

His heart seized and he jumped back, gasping. Sanga put out a hand to keep from running into him. "Piper?"

He shook his head. There was no ivory. There was only the late evening sky in a band above the buildings, shading from darkness through shades of blue and finally to a faded greenish light over the river. It must have been that quality of the light that had tricked his brain. He had never even noticed it before.

Oh god, he thought wearily, *am I going to panic now every time I see light that color? I live in a city on a river. Does this end with me pulling up roots and moving somewhere else? Charlock, maybe, so I am in a desert instead?*

This seemed rather ridiculously excessive. He realized that he was standing in the doorway still and flushed with embarrassment.

"Piper, is something wrong?" Sanga asked again.

"No," he croaked. "I'm fine. Just...uh...go on without me." He flattened himself against the wall to let the man pass him.

"I'll come by tomorrow," Sanga said, eyeing him worriedly. "If you need to rest more."

"I'll be fine."

"Sure. Lady of Grass watch over you."

Piper nodded.

"It'll go away in a minute," said Kaylin behind him. "Just breathe. In through the nose and out through the mouth. Count 'em if you have to."

He turned back to her, startled. She was watching him with compassion but no pity. "The breathing helps," she said. "Try it."

He did. He counted ten breaths and it did seem to help. The sky was just the sky and he'd startled himself for no reason. His hammering heart slowed.

"How did you know?" he asked.

One corner of Kaylin's mouth crooked, though there was no real humor in it. "You had the look. We all know the look."

Piper swallowed. He knew the look too. The war with Anuket City had been over a decade ago, when he was young and the ink was barely dry on his medical certificate from the College of Physicians. He'd never been anywhere near the front lines, but like nearly every doctor in Archenhold, he was pressed into service treating soldiers and refugees injured by the rampaging clocktaurs. He'd seen the eyes of men who had left some part of their soul on the battlefield, the stare into the distance. But those men had been in battles, facing impossible enemies, for days or weeks at a time. Piper had spent two days in an ivory maze, and less than an hour total in actual danger of falling blades. What right did he have to it?

"I can't have the look," he said. "I didn't...it wasn't bad enough. I shouldn't be jumping at shadows. Not over this."

Kaylin snorted. "I knew men who could stand toe-to-toe with a clocktaur and not turn a hair, who'd lose their damn minds if they were locked in your morgue overnight. Brains don't care about *bad enough*." She slapped her stump. "I hardly ever think about the fight where I lost this. Doesn't bother me. But there was one time where we were all in a tight pass, trying to stop a clocktaur. This was back before we ever really knew what they were. Damn thing charged straight through us. The brass didn't know yet that you couldn't slow them down by throwing bodies at them." Piper winced. "The ones who survived either hunkered down against the walls or got behind it in the first charge. That one...yeah. I still have nightmares about that one."

"I'm sorry," said Piper. He thought of Galen's screaming nightmares and wondered again what he saw in his dreams that led him to attack everything around him. *What have I been through that could compare with that?*

"Don't have to be sorry," said Kaylin. "Just saying. Wherever you've been for the last week, that was bad enough. If it's coming back once, it'll come back again. Just breathe." Her eyes sharpened. "And you tell me if you get to thinking of doing anything stupid, you hear?"

Piper blinked at her, wondering what on earth she meant, before finally putting two and two together. *Ah. Yes.* "I won't," he said. "I mean, I will talk to you. But I won't. It's not..." He made a meaningless gesture. He'd never contemplated ending his life and couldn't imagine starting any time soon.

"Good. But the door's open." She nodded to him, then pushed herself to her feet, grabbing her crutch from beside the door. "Come on, doctor. I'll walk you out to the street, at least, and you can tell me about the week you had."

. . .

Piper got home feeling, if not better exactly, at least a little comforted in his misery. He opened his front door and the walls were *not* ivory, they were just a little dingy from burning candles and lamps all the time, they needed a new coat of whitewash, that was all. He took a deep breath. *See, there's the painting you bought when you first moved in. The one with the ducks and the cattails. You've lived here for most of a decade.* He stood on the threshold and told himself this until he believed it and stepped through.

I suppose I should be grateful that it's doorways that are getting to me. I go through them so often, I'll have to get over this in short order. I won't have any choice. If it was something else, it could linger for years. Like night terrors, say.

He grimaced. He wished he could talk to Galen about it.

No, if he was being honest, he wished that he could feel Galen's arms around him, feel those hard shoulders ready to take on the dangers of the world. He'd felt safe then. They'd been in a maze of traps, they'd nearly died a dozen times, and yet he'd felt safe.

You'll feel safe again. It just takes a little doing. You have friends. You aren't alone, no matter how it feels right now.

Granted, most of his friends were also incredibly busy and he hadn't spent time with one that wasn't related to work or a court case in...ah...well, a long time. *Still. And there's people like Kaylin, and Sanga and the other lich-doctors. I don't have to be isolated if I don't want to be.*

Someone tapped on the door at gnole height.

Piper's first thought was that it was Earstripe, but that was ridiculous. Earstripe wouldn't be able to get out of bed. *Assuming he's even alive. Oh god, please let this not be a gnole sent to tell me that he's dead.*

He wanted to run and throw himself on the bed, away from the knock, but he didn't. He opened the door instead, and sure enough, there was a gnole standing there, a small brown-furred one, looking up at him with bright eyes.

"A gnole has a message for Bone-doctor?" they said.

Piper swallowed. "That's me."

"Our gnole says to tell Bone-doctor that a gnole called Earstripe lives. A gnole's fever is broken, yes?"

Piper sagged against the doorframe. "Oh, thank the gods," he whispered. *Rat and Lady of Grass and Four-Faced God and Forge God and all the rest of you, thank you. I will go to every temple in the city and put something in the poor box. Well, maybe not the Hanged Mother. But everyone else.*

"Bone-doctor understands?"

"Yes." He nodded. "I understand. Please tell Skull-of-Ice that this human is grateful for the message." He paused. *When in doubt, ask.* "Is that the right thing to say? A human does not want to give offense to Skull-of-Ice."

The small gnole grinned up at him. "Close enough. A gnole will say it right to ours."

"Thank you." Piper dug a coin out and offered it. "May I pay you for your trouble?"

Nimble fingers made the coin disappear. "A gnole does not require payment to carry a message from ours...but a gnole will take a gift for translating for a human." The gnole waved and scurried back down the stairs, humming to itself. Piper closed the door and latched it, then went into his bedroom and lay face down on the bed and cried for a little bit from sheer relief that he hadn't killed his friend after all.

CHAPTER 31

Galen was dripping with sweat and had reopened the cut on his calf and was finally starting to relax.

Wren, a round woman who barely came up to his collarbone, stepped back, lifting her wooden practice sword. "Had enough?"

"You've both had enough, I think," Stephen said from the sidelines.

"I can take more," said Galen.

"So can I," said Wren, "but you're bleeding pretty good and I don't much feel like having the healers yell at me." She glanced over at Stephen, who nodded.

Galen sighed. He knew it was for the best. It was rare enough that the Saint of Steel's chosen worked out against each other instead of sword drills against inanimate objects, and they always had a third paladin to watch them if they did. Otherwise there was always the chance of the tide rising for one or both and driving them to murder. If they did train against another paladin, they did so carefully and they stopped early.

I can hardly fault Stephen for caution. I broke his arm once in the early days. If Istvhan hadn't strangled him into unconsciousness in his usual friendly fashion, I'd have been in palm-sized bits.

It frustrated him, though. He wanted the silence inside his head that came with fighting. Pell work wasn't the same. If you didn't have to dodge, didn't have to worry about the next blow, you found yourself thinking, and the last thing that Galen wanted to do was think.

He had made his report to Bishop Beartongue, and then he had made it again, to two guards with expressions that could have curdled milk. He'd taken pleasure in dwelling on Mallory's malfeasance and giving Earstripe all the credit for tracking down the murderer, watching their expressions grow sourer and sourer, until curdling water was not out of the question. *That'll put a flea in somebody's ear, that's for certain.*

And then everything had gone back to normal. He had rested for a day or two and then he was right back on duty, escorting healers, standing around in court, and generally doing all the things that the White Rat asked scary men with swords to do.

Normal, except that he could not stop thinking about Piper.

At first, it was to wonder if he was as tired as Galen was, if he had gotten enough sleep, if someone was making sure he ate. Galen even thought of sending Marcus or Shane to check on the man, but he knew that was ridiculous. *Saint's teeth, I'm turning into as much of a mother hen as Stephen.* But as the days fled and he found himself walking and standing guard and walking and standing guard and very little else, the thoughts evolved. When a healer's patient had a difficult childbirth, Galen thought of Piper's frustration and wondered what the doctor would have suggested to make it safer. When the healer reached into his bag and pulled out instruments, he wondered if Piper used the same kind or if he had any opinions about forceps the way he had had opinions about scalpels.

But even that was preferable to nighttime, when Galen laid in his solitary bed and thought of Piper's mouth on him, those long fingers stroking him, his body aching. He could not even bring himself off without thinking of Piper, and so he stopped because he had no right to pleasure himself while thinking of the man he'd hurt so badly.

Because that was the image that came to him the most. It overlaid everything. It drove into his skull at odd hours. Piper's face in profile as he knelt by the hearth, his lips set and bloodless, his hands shaking as he tried to strike the flint. He hadn't looked at Galen, not once, but he didn't have to.

You miserable thoughtless bastard. He was completely exhausted. You spent days in that damn maze and then he spent hours keeping Earstripe alive, and all he had was half a catnap in the boat. He was dead on his feet, and you couldn't wait even a day to be done with him. You had to drive him off right that minute. So noble. So self-sacrificing. So paladinly, *giving someone up because they're too good for you. Not thinking that maybe he'd handle it better when he wasn't half-dead.*

Not thinking that maybe in a day or two, he'd have wanted to give you up on his own.

Stephen snapped his fingers in front of Galen's face. "You in there?"

"What? Yeah. Sorry." He shook his head. "What were you saying?"

"I was saying that we're going to get you re-stitched up," said Stephen.

"It's nothing."

"Sure." Stephen didn't touch him, but he maneuvered Galen toward the door anyway, rather like a herd dog with a truculent sheep. Galen grumbled but went along.

"You're brooding," the other paladin said.

"I suppose you're the expert," Galen muttered.

"I am, actually. I am a superb brooder. You, however, make bad jokes and then go to a tavern looking to get laid. Except now you're brooding instead."

Galen grunted.

The healer clucked her tongue, glared, muttered something about paladins, and set to work. Galen grimaced at the pinprick pains. He'd been thumped and whacked and stabbed any number of times, but needles were different somehow. He'd born up to Piper sewing him up because...well, mostly because it was Piper doing it. He hadn't wanted to watch the actual stitching, so he studied Piper's face instead, the narrow lines of beard blurred by stubble, the frown of concentration as he worked, the...

Stephen pinched him.

"Ow!" Galen rubbed his arm. "What was that for?"

"What are you thinking about?" asked Stephen, looking even more inscrutable than usual.

"I'm thinking that my brother-in-arms has started pinching people for no reason and it's a little disconcerting."

"Before that."

"I...uh..." He coughed. "Nothing."

"You're a terrible liar."

"I'm better at it than you are," said Galen, which was true.

"The bar is not high," said Stephen, which was also true. "What were you thinking about?"

Galen looked down, saw what the healer was doing, and looked away again hurriedly. "Piper," he mumbled.

Stephen gazed at him steadily for nearly a minute, then said, "I never thought that I would utter these words in my lifetime. The gods have mercy upon us. Galen, I am afraid that you're in love."

"I am *not,*" he said, which was definitely a lie, but maybe if he said it out loud, it would become true.

From somewhere near his knee, the healer snorted.

"How many times a day do you think about Piper?"

Galen swallowed. *Just once, but it lasts the whole day.*

Apparently his silence was enough, because Stephen rocked back on his heels and gazed up at the ceiling. "Saint's teeth. No wonder you haven't been visiting taverns looking for entertainment."

"I thought about it," admitted Galen. The thought had no appeal. He didn't want sex. Well, he did, obviously, but not with some random stranger who he'd never think about again. *I should never have kissed Piper. That's where it all went wrong. I never kiss any of those other men, for a damn good reason. Kissing is dangerous. It's probably too near your brain or something.*

Or your nose. That's probably it. Spongiform erectile tissue. That's what gets you in trouble.

He considered explaining his new theory of nasal erectile tissue as gateway to the soul to Stephen, realized that it would make absolutely no sense, and wished that he could run it by Piper first.

The healer slapped his leg as if he were a horse. "All right. You're done. Now quit tearing it open! You're going to have a scar as it is, and if you end up back here again, I'm going to write 'jackass' in stitches across it, and serve you right."

"Did you know that there's erectile tissue inside your nose?" asked Galen.

The healer stared at him as if he'd lost his mind. "Is yours giving you trouble?" she asked finally.

"I'm honestly not sure."

"Remember when I was an endless font of facts about ambergris?" asked Stephen.

"God, yes. You wouldn't shut up about whale vomit for nearly three days. Then you started talking about castoreum and we made you eat lunch by yourself. Why?"

"I'd fallen in love with a perfumer. Everything she did was fascinating. I wanted to learn more about it. Still do, actually, but now I can talk to her about it." Stephen examined his nails. "And now you have a sudden interest in human anatomy."

"I've always been interested in human anatomy," said Galen stiffly.

"Not usually the bits inside the nose."

The healer snorted again. "You two get out of here," she said. "Otherwise I'll be tempted to go up *your* noses and check." The paladins left hurriedly.

Stephen was silent as they crossed the temple compound and entered the small corridor of rooms where the paladins of the Saint of Steel lived. In the common room at the end, Galen could hear the sounds of the others comparing the day's assignments. He half-expected Stephen to make for it, but instead the paladin paused in the hallway and simply looked at him. He had a particularly penetrating Look. Galen was convinced that the man could peel paint with it if he stared long enough.

Unfortunately for Galen, merely knowing this did not grant him any kind of immunity. "Fine," he muttered. "You don't need to give me the eye. Yes, all right. I'm in love. I admit it. It doesn't matter."

"Doesn't it?"

"No, it doesn't." Galen flung his hands in the air in frustration. "So what if *I'm* in love? That's the worst thing that could happen to him! I'm too much of a bastard, and far too broken. I'd eat him alive and he isn't mean enough to stop me."

"You're saying he doesn't have a spine?"

Galen glared at him. "He's got *plenty* of spine. He went through that horrible death trap without panicking and he worked on Earstripe for hours to keep him from dying. He's got more guts than any ten paladins."

"But not enough spine to stand up to you."

"It's not about that. It's...dammit. Look, Piper's kind and decent and he deserves someone who won't hurt him on accident. And that person is not me."

"Mmm." Stephen leaned back against the wall, arms folded. "I suppose there's no point in telling you that you're a decent human being and all that?"

"Would it work on you?"

"Good god, no." The corner of Stephen's lip twitched up. "No, I'm entirely unworthy. I'm just lucky enough that Grace persists in not noticing that fact."

And you're one of the best people I know, Galen thought but didn't say aloud, *so what hope does someone like me have?*

"Well." Stephen pushed away from the wall. "Maybe you're right. Maybe you aren't worthy of him."

"That was the worst attempt at reverse psychology I've ever witnessed."

"No, no." Stephen held up his hands. "It wasn't. But Galen, if you were worthy of him—if he was more of a bastard or you were less of one—*would* you want him?"

Yes. By all the gods, yes. *Saint's black and bloody tongue,* yes. *I would go to the ends of the earth. I would fight armies. I would wrap myself around him and never,* ever *let him go.*

Galen was spared from the fact that he could not say any of this aloud by the sudden appearance of a gnole in the doorway. "Are you Tomato-man?"

He turned away gratefully and went to one knee. The gnole wasn't one he recognized. They were smaller than Brindle or Earstripe, although from youth or build, he didn't know.

"I suppose I am," he said. "Can I assist you?"

The gnole dipped their head. "I have a message for Tomato-man," they said. Galen was impressed at how well they managed the patterns of human speech, although it would have been rude to comment. *Perhaps the younger generation of gnoles is growing up with human speech as well as gnole. I wonder if any human children are doing the same. That would certainly make Earstripe's job easier.*

He nodded. The gnole drew themself up and said, "Our healer says that the gnole you call Earstripe is recovered enough to see humans. Would Tomato-man like to see him?"

Galen leapt to his feet. "Yes! Most certainly! This is the best news I've heard all week!"

The gnole had jumped back when he moved, but smiled again. "I will take you to him."

CHAPTER 32

He should have realized that Piper would be there. *Of course he is. Skull-of-Ice probably sent word to him before me.* Galen came around the corner behind his guide and saw the doctor standing beside Earstripe, who was sitting on a barrel in a patch of sunlight.

Earstripe looked surprisingly normal. Galen was familiar enough with gnoles to guess that the fur covered the worst of things. The bones on his muzzle were in sharper relief than before and there was a crutch leaning against the barrel, but otherwise he did not look much different than the gnole who had set out from the city with them, a week and a lifetime ago.

Piper, though...

Is no one looking after him? He looks like he's been dragged behind a horse. Saint's teeth, who do I have to pummel to make sure the man is eating?

He would swear that the doctor had lost weight in the last week. The dark circles under his eyes hadn't gone away and his skin, already pale, was ashen. The neatness of his trimmed beard could not hide the hollowness of his cheeks.

It occurred to Galen suddenly that he had six other paladins and a small army of healers, nuns, and functionaries to look after him. And Piper had...what? The dead?

I know he has friends. He's mentioned names once or twice. Where are they? What are they doing? Why aren't they making sure he eats?

Earstripe saw him and waved. Galen waved back, fighting for calm. *Don't go charging in. You've already made a hash of things. You'll only make it worse.*

Piper turned his head. Something crossed his face when he saw Galen, but it was gone too quickly for the paladin to catch. The cool, passionless mask settled into place.

"Earstripe!" said Galen, with heartiness he didn't feel. "You're looking so much better."

"A gnole hopes so. Bolt in a gnole's leg does nothing for looks."

"Skull-of-Ice is a miracle worker," said Piper, not looking at Galen. "That was a bad break on top of everything else. I wasn't sure you'd walk again."

Earstripe slapped his bad leg. "May have a limp, but may not. Ours says a gnole will feel it when it rains, though."

"Welcome to the club," said Galen. "If the barometer drops in Morstone, I feel it."

Piper opened his mouth to say something, then closed it again. Earstripe looked from Galen to Piper and back again, frowning. "Something wrong between bone-doctor and tomato-man?"

"Nothing of consequence," said Piper.

That hurt. It shouldn't have hurt, but it did. Galen felt as if someone had taken a chisel and gouged a line out of his sternum. *Nothing of consequence.* He'd been lying awake and tormenting himself for days over nothing of consequence.

Earstripe's ears flattened. He sniffed the air and Galen wondered what the gnole could smell. *Probably what he talked about before. One person smelling as if the other's their mate, and the other not. For me, it's love. For him, it was nothing of consequence.*

It had been more than that. He knew it had. Piper's face when Galen had broken it off, the way his hands shook on the flint—*no, he felt something too, I know he did, that's the problem. If it didn't mean anything to him, he wouldn't have looked like that. He wouldn't look like he does now.*

Galen could see muscles flex as Piper's jaw clenched. He wanted to set his lips against it. *He's shaved. It will be smoother than it was, not rough like it was in the maze. And the spot just behind his jaw, he shivers when I breathe on it. I remember that.*

"Humans can't smell," muttered Earstripe.

"No, we can't," said Piper, "which is why you have to tell us when you're getting tired."

The gnole smiled. "A little, yes, bone-doctor. But tell me, tomato-man, the dead humans in the river, are they known now? Can human families be told?"

"I told the guard everything," said Galen. "You know how well that works." The gnole grimaced. "But the records are with the courts, and they'll do what they can."

"The important thing is no more bodies," said Piper firmly. "You did that. You should be proud."

Earstripe nodded. "A gnole is," he said simply. "And a gnole is glad that a gnole is the one who was shot." When both Galen and Piper began to object, he held up a hand. "No. A gnole brought humans along. A gnole was responsible. If a human is badly hurt, a gnole is responsible, is guilty, and a gnole cannot forfeit caste or status, a gnole cannot name a human among kin-obligations—a gnole cannot *fix* anything. So it is better that a gnole bears the hurt." He smiled. "Easier, too."

"I would prefer that *no one* had been shot," said Piper testily.

"But if bone-doctor had been shot, a gnole could not heal him. Works out better this way." He slid down from the barrel and picked up his crutch. "A gnole will heal."

"You'd better," said Galen. "Otherwise I'm going to make sure you eat nothing but apples for a month."

The gnole made a rude gesture and both of them laughed. "A gnole rests now, before ours growls." He looked from doctor to paladin. "Humans sort human things, yes?"

"Yes, of course," said Piper.

Earstripe looked unconvinced. "Mmmm." He waved and hobbled away.

"Well," said Piper. He spoke aloud, but he wasn't looking at Galen. He might have been talking to himself. "I'm glad he's recovering well." His voice was clipped and professional. He nodded once, sharply, then turned to go.

"Wait!"

Piper paused, though he didn't look around. "Can I help you?"

No, you can't help me. That's the point. Galen didn't know whether to laugh or scream. Very well, he was reaping what he'd sown. Still, he was a paladin. "You came alone?"

"Yes."

Galen felt a pang of annoyance at the man's recklessness. This was not a great neighborhood. They'd already been set on once, by people with no apparent fear of multiple armed men. "I'll escort you to the river, then."

"That is not required," said Piper, his voice still clipped. "A gnole guided me in, but I can find my own way back."

"It's not safe," said Galen to the man's back.

Piper finally turned to look at him. His face was a cool, passionless mask. "It is not your concern, sir."

Sir. Saint's balls.

And now the damn fool wants to walk out and possibly get mugged because of 'nothing of consequence.'

"Piper..."

"You've made it abundantly clear that you do not wish to see me. I am giving you what you require."

"I'm not asking you to suck my cock. I'm trying to keep you from getting mugged." Galen realized he was clenching his fists and consciously relaxed them. "Either I walk you to the river or I'm going to follow you to make sure you aren't set on by foot-pads anyway. It's less awkward if you just let me walk next to you."

Piper's lips thinned. Without speaking, he turned and strode away. Galen stretched his legs to catch up. "I see that civility is off the table, then."

If he hadn't been watching for it, he would not have seen Piper's wince. "You are right," the doctor said after a moment. "I am being rude. I apologize. You have done nothing wrong."

"It doesn't feel that way."

"It was one night. No promises were made. You owe me nothing."

"I could have chosen a better moment," said Galen. "When we weren't both half-dead."

Piper shrugged. "Some things are best done quickly, I suppose."

Galen should have felt better at that, but he didn't. The silence between them was still fraught and horrible. They reached the area with the suspended boardwalks, still without speaking, and Galen felt the frustration bubbling in his chest like tar. They were going to reach the river and not say anything and then either one of them would say "goodbye" or one of them wouldn't and it would be even worse.

Damn us both to the lowest of hells.

He had no right to be angry, and yet *nothing of consequence* still rang in his ears like a curse. It was his fault. He'd been the one to end their relationship before it had even really begun. He'd had to, because he was the fool who'd fallen in love.

It was all hurt pride, of course. He knew that. *If you're going to be all noble and self-sacrificing and immolate a chance at happiness on the altar of your own personal unworthiness, you hate to think that the sacrifice wasn't actually worth anything.*

"Have you made a report to the guard?" Piper asked, breaking into his thoughts. The doctor sounded almost normal, and perversely that made it worse, because maybe it really had meant nothing, if Piper was getting over it so quickly. *Or perhaps he's being kind again. That's why it won't work. Because he's kind and you're a murderous bastard, remember?*

"Yes," said Galen. It was his turn to sound clipped. "Have they contacted you?"

"No. I wondered if perhaps you had tried to leave my name out of it."

Galen cast his mind back. "I mentioned you by name," he said. "Perhaps they thought it was nothing of consequence."

God, you really are a bastard.

Piper stiffened. "I'm sorry," he said, his voice chilly, "did I offend you by saying that? Would you prefer that I had flung myself at you and wept on your neck?"

Yes. "No, obviously not."

Piper stopped walking. Galen took a step or two further, realized he'd stopped, and turned around.

"Just tell me what you want," said Piper. The dark circles under his eyes were so pronounced that he looked half-gnole himself, and they were rimmed with red. *Saint's black and bloody tongue, has he been weeping?* "Tell me what gets this over with so that we can stop thinking about it. Do we pretend nothing happened at all? Are we colleagues? Do we avoid seeing each other? Pick something and I'll do it, but you'll have to tell me what the hell it is you want, because damned if *I* know."

His voice cracked on the last word and Galen took an involuntary step forward and put his arms around him.

Piper sagged against him and Galen felt the catch in the other man's breath. But he also felt the width of Piper's shoulders, the wiry muscle of his arms and chest, and a part of his heart he'd been trying to bury for days leapt up and began to sing.

"I'm sorry," he murmured, bending his head. He could see the dark curve of eyelashes on the doctor's cheek, feel the shakiness of his breathing. "I'm so sorry. I never meant for any of this."

"I know."

Galen put his fingers on Piper's chin and tilted his face up. He was close enough to kiss and Galen knew that he should not, knew that it would tear open all the wounds that hadn't even begun to heal. And yet...and yet...

His lips brushed across Piper's and it felt right and Piper's body against his was right too.

Piper took a deep breath and pushed him away.

Surprise took him for an instant, long enough for Piper to pull free and draw himself upright. Galen actually saw the moment when cold calm settled over the man's face, like a glaze of hoarfrost on fallen leaves. The sensation of someone chiseling away at his sternum hit again, colder now, as if the frost was falling on his bones.

"We're nearly at the river," said Piper. "Are you satisfied that I will not be murdered in broad daylight here?"

Galen nodded, not trusting himself to speak.

"I think," said Piper, "that perhaps we should not see one another again. At all."

"Piper—"

He held up a hand. “In the interests of preserving what little dignity I have left,” he said, still in that hoarfrost voice, “I think it is for the best.”

And he turned and walked away, and Galen watched him go and felt as if he was being torn in two.

CHAPTER 33

Piper told himself that he wasn't thinking about Galen, and then, after about ten minutes, told himself to stop thinking about Galen.

You were right. You were absolutely right. He knows you were right. And you owe him nothing and he owes you nothing and you were the one mooning around after he'd made it perfectly clear what he wanted. Or didn't want, as the case may be.

This was all quite true and Piper repeated it four or five times while staring at the painting on his wall without seeing it, living in the memory of that soft, apologetic kiss by the river's edge.

He could not get that kiss out of his head. *For god's sake, you actually sucked the man's cock, you'd think that would be what you're obsessing over, but no, it was a kiss that lasted less than a second. That's what you can't forget.*

Everything else was lust, he argued with himself. *That felt like more.*

And that and a ha'penny will buy you a pint at an establishment where the dysentery is included free of charge.

This was inarguable.

He went back and forth a hundred times a day. He would go and see Galen. He would avoid Galen forever. He would. He wouldn't. The choice played in the back of his head while he worked, until the words lost all meaning and became a stream of *IwillIwon'tIwillIwon't* like a mosquito buzzing inside his skull.

Eventually, he went to prayer and the bottle, the two great comforters of humanity since the discovery of gods and yeasts. He spent his day off getting spectacularly drunk, which didn't help anything much. Prayer didn't seem to help either, but at least it didn't come with a hangover the next day.

His thoughts were so jumbled that he hardly knew what to pray for, so he settled on a general, *Do you see this whole mess, gods? Please just fix it! I'm begging You!* He had a suspicion that most priests would have confirmed this was a very common prayer indeed.

That state of affairs continued for nearly a week, and then the door to Piper's workroom was flung open and Galen burst through it.

The paladin looked wild-eyed and almost panicked and for a horrible moment Piper thought perhaps he was berserk. His chest was heaving as if he had been running. Then he took a shuddering breath and said, *"Piper."*

Piper wanted to go to him. He wanted to wrap his arms around the man. He wanted to slam the door in his face. He wanted to scream or kiss him or fall down. He had no idea what he wanted, so he stood there, still with one gloved hand inside a corpse, and heard himself say, "I thought that we agreed not to see each another again."

Galen shook his head, slumping against the doorframe, and Piper dared to hope that the paladin was here to tell him that it was all a terrible mistake, that he wanted to try again, that he had been miserable thinking about what he had thrown away.

Instead, Galen licked his lips and gasped, *"Earstripe."*

Piper jerked his hand free. The corpse's liver wasn't going to get any worse, and it had already been a mess even before he'd started poking it. "Is he hurt? Did his wound reopen?"

"No. No." Galen shook his head. "They've arrested him."

"What?"

"The guard. Vigilantism, they said. For killing Thomas."

Piper stared at him. "But that was outside the city. The guard doesn't have jurisdiction. And you're the one who killed him."

"I know, I *know.*" Galen's voice was a rasp. "That's why they arrested him. If he was acting as a guard, he was outside his authority. It's my fault." He raked his hands through his hair. "I told those damn guards that Earstripe was in charge, that it was all his idea. I was so goddamn *smug* about giving him the credit."

Piper's breath hissed through his teeth. He stripped off his gloves and apron and washed his hands. "But they didn't arrest you."

"Of course not. I'm a paladin." Galen gave a harsh crack of laughter. "If they arrest *me,* Beartongue will come down on them like the wrath of god. But if they arrest Earstripe, that's an internal guard matter. She's got no jurisdiction until it goes to the courts."

Piper thought of Earstripe, not yet recovered from his injuries, thrown in a jail cell by guards who were more than a little angry to have been shown up by a gnole. His stomach lurched. "But he left the guard!"

"Assuming Mallory wants to inform them of that. He's the one most embarrassed by the whole thing. It was one of his people, on his watch, who solved a crime that he'd told them to drop."

Piper dug his fingers into the soap, leaving white half-moons under his nails. He stared into the water and said, "If he was human, they'd have given him a medal."

"I know."

His fist slammed into the metal tray beside the basin, sending instruments scattering. Piper stared at it as if it belonged to someone else, some furious stranger. He was never furious. He was cool and dispassionate. His knuckles were white.

This will not help.

You can fix this. Earstripe isn't dead. The dead are beyond fixing. The living aren't.

"Right," he said. His voice sounded very calm in his own ears. "Get Stephen. We're going to start with Mallory, and then we will go higher. Clear to Commander Tamsin if we must."

Galen frowned. "None of them will even talk to me."

Piper felt his lips stretch in a smile. "They'll talk to me," he said softly. "I know where all the bodies are buried. I've dissected most of them."

Galen arrived at the guard station with Stephen in tow, five minutes before Piper arrived in a hired ponycart. While there were theoretically sidewalks in this part of town, they were not well-marked or maintained, so the driver pulled directly up to the stairs and Piper jumped out. Galen moved instinctively to catch him if he stumbled, but the doctor's footing was sure.

Galen's eyebrows went up when he saw Piper's clothes. So did Stephen's, but probably for somewhat different reasons.

Neatly pressed tan robes fell around him, adorned with a plain black stole. The severe lines flattered him and brought out the darkness of his hair and the coldness of his eyes. Galen had never seen Piper in anything but a bloody apron or increasingly battered traveling clothes, and hadn't realized how much he'd been missing. He swallowed hard.

"You look..." *Magnificent. Impressive. Regal.* "...very formal."

"What I wear to give testimony in court," said Piper. "I thought I'd remind the guard that they are not the only law in Archenhold."

"Good choice," said Stephen.

"Very," said Galen.

A faint smile briefly warmed Piper's expression. "We'll see how far it gets me. I'm sorry that took so long. I sent word to Skull-of-Ice, telling ours what we know and promising that we will do our best to get Earstripe back, and the return messenger caught me just before I left."

"What did ours say?" asked Galen, half-dreading the answer.

"That humans talk to other humans best and that it was a serpent dance. And there was something else that I don't think translated well, that since Earstripe was my patient once, we were kin, and kin stood for kin, even against humans. But I don't know if that was ours ordering me to succeed or offering a gnole army against the guards if I didn't."

"I suppose we'll find out," said Galen.

"No chance of sweeping this under the rug, then," said Stephen.

"Would you want to, even if we could?" asked Piper.

Stephen frowned. "I worry for the gnoles," he admitted. "They're the ones that come out on the short end if we force a confrontation."

"Which is why it's up to us to handle it," said Galen.

Piper nodded to him. "And the gnoles will know much better than we will where the pain points with the guard will be. Hopefully the Rat can intercede, although at this point, that might just make it worse."

"That's Beartongue's fear," said Stephen. "She'd swoop in with the cavalry if she could, but she's afraid that any show of interest will put the gnoles in the crossfire." He glanced to the door of the guard station, three steps up. The stone was dark and still bore the stains of flooding from two years earlier. "The two of us probably shouldn't even go with you, truth be told."

"We're going," said Galen. He heard how harsh his voice sounded, but didn't try to soften it. The thought of letting Piper go in alone, of the doctor being arrested and thrown in a cell for his part in stopping Thomas, made his gut churn. *I'm the one who killed him. Me. And yet I walk free because a paladin in pursuit of his duties is exempt from murder charges, while others take the blame.*

"I'm glad to have you both," said Piper. Was there a trace of warmth in his eyes as he glanced at Galen? Galen wanted to think so, even as he knew that he didn't deserve it. *Nothing's changed. You'd still eat him alive.*

But Piper, in his court robes, with his face as cold as chiseled marble, did not look like he would be easily devoured.

"Very well," said the doctor, and swept into the guard station as if he were the Archon himself.

CHAPTER 34

"Doctor Piper?" said Captain Mallory, rising to his feet. "How can I..." He trailed off, seeing the two paladins that had shouldered in after him. His expression, which had been professional and polite, soured significantly.

There was a guard on the desk who was supposed to keep people from wasting the captain's time. Piper had simply stalked up and informed him that he was on official business and the guard had taken one look at his outfit and hastily waved him through. Stephen and Galen walked in after him, and when the guard had protested, Stephen said only, "We're with him."

"Oh," said Mallory, "it's you." He sighed heavily. "I have nothing to say to you. Doctor Piper, is there some reason that you've brought these...gentlemen...to my office?"

"Constable Earstripe has been assisting me with my research," said Piper crisply. "These gentlemen have informed me that he has been arrested."

Mallory's eyes flicked between the three men. Galen wondered if he was recalling the long ago pretense of being lovers. *Either way, he's dividing the world into Us and Them and I believe that Piper just firmly became one of Them. I wonder if that'll make his work harder in the future.*

I wonder if he cares.

Judging by the coldness radiating off Piper, the doctor did not care. His eyes were flat and every motion bespoke tight control. If Galen had seen a man walking toward him who moved like that, he would have reached for his sword.

"Earstripe is helping the guard with its inquiries into a difficult matter," said Mallory.

"From inside a jail cell," snapped Galen. Both Mallory and Piper ignored him, their eyes locked.

Piper stepped forward and sat down in the chair in front of the desk. Stephen took the other chair. Galen looked around, found a third chair, and hauled it into place on Piper's other side, so that they flanked him like an honor guard.

Confronted with the fact that apparently the trio was not going to be leaving, Mallory's lips thinned. "I have other matters that require my time."

"As do we," said Piper, in that hoarfrost voice. "The sooner that this matter is cleared up, the sooner we can be on our way."

Mallory clearly weighed the benefits of sitting versus calling for the paladins to be thrown out of the office. *I suppose he could charge us all with trespassing, but he has to know that it would never stick in court, and that one of the Rat's lawyers would take great pleasure in making him look like a fool before the judge.* He sat.

"This is an internal investigation of the guard," said Mallory. "The Rat has no business interfering."

"Do the courts?" asked Piper silkily.

Mallory's eyes narrowed at the reminder of Piper's status. "Once the investigation has been completed, if charges must be brought, perhaps."

"And how long will an injured person sit in a jail cell while it is being completed? Earstripe was near death several weeks ago. Are you willing to let him die while you investigate?"

"I didn't write the arrest order," snapped Mallory. "I don't know what you hope to gain by coming here. I'm not the one conducting the investigation. Don't blame *me.*"

Galen had an answer for that which would have involved Mallory, his anatomy, and the anatomy and legitimacy of many of his relatives, but before he could start, he felt Piper's boot nudge him sharply in the calf. He glanced at the doctor, who flicked his eyes to Stephen. Galen shut his mouth and waited.

"We are not seeking blame," said Stephen, in his deep, sad voice. "We are seeking responsibility."

"Responsibility," said Mallory, with venom. "With the Rat? Don't give me that shit. It's so goddamn black and white for you people. The rest of us have to live down here.""

Galen would have had a lot to say about that as well, but Piper's foot was now pressed down hard on his.

"We've worked together closely before, Mallory," said Stephen. "I have always believed that you were a good man."

Mallory tried to meet the paladin's gaze. Galen could have told him that it wasn't going to work. Stephen in full more-in-sorrow-than-in-anger mode was a force to be reckoned with. Galen would much rather the other paladin came at him with a sword than with that disappointed voice. *And this is why Piper had you bring Stephen. Good thinking. I would have gone in hot and gotten us kicked out of the guard post.*

To his credit, Mallory held out for nearly fifteen seconds before he crumbled. "Maybe I'm not the man you think I am," he muttered. "But you and that damned bishop have made it impossible to do our damned jobs any more. You expect us to sit back and let hardened criminals go free, when you know damned well they'll end up right back in front of a judge for something worse next time."

"We are not talking about a hardened criminal," snapped Galen. "We're talking about *Earstripe.* He hasn't done *anything.*"

"The internal investigation will turn that up, then," said Mallory.

"If you'd listened to him to begin with, you wouldn't need an internal investigation. He'd have caught the killer and you'd give him a medal. But he did it anyway and he wasn't even a guard at the time! You fired him, remember?"

Mallory wouldn't meet his eyes. "That's as may be."

"You *did* inform the investigation that he had been fired, did you not?" asked Piper coolly.

The captain hesitated just a fraction too long. "It doesn't matter. Guards can't simply quit their jobs, go after a criminal as a private citizen, and then be reinstated. Your precious bishop would have our necks."

"But it wouldn't be an internal matter," said Piper. "Would it?"

Mallory fiddled with papers on his desk.

"Captain Mallory..." said Stephen.

"They didn't ask me," muttered Mallory.

"And if this was any other one of your men, you would have moved heaven and earth to correct that," said Stephen. He had a way of speaking quietly that somehow made him louder than everyone else in the room. "I know you. You are loyal to your people. Why didn't you protect Earstripe as well?"

"Is it because he proved you wrong?" asked Piper coldly. "Or simply because he's a gnole?"

Mallory winced. He didn't speak for a long moment, and when he finally did, something in his voice had shifted. He sounded tired. "This all happened above my head, all right? They really didn't ask me. Everybody's been pissed at

Beartongue for months and then one of her pet paladins goes stumbling in—" he jerked his head at Galen, leaving no doubt as to who the pet paladin was, "—and kills the bastard and she sends around one of her oh-so-fucking-polite letters rubbing our noses in it, and it was the last damn straw."

"If they can prove that it was improperly handled, or that Thomas was not killed in self-defense, they save face," said Piper. "They can say, 'Leave it to the guard next time.'"

Mallory nodded.

"You have no jurisdiction over paladins outside the city walls," said Stephen. "But if Earstripe is a vigilante, using one of us as his weapon, then the guard will have jurisdiction over him."

Mallory nodded again, his shoulders sinking. "I'll deny everything if you repeat this," he said, "but some of the higher-ups aren't that happy about gnoles. They weren't happy about a gnole in the guard to begin with, and the thought of a gnole executing a human has them completely riled up."

"Earstripe saved my life when Thomas tried to kill me," said Piper. "Galen killed him to keep him from shooting us with a crossbow. Again."

The guard captain blinked. "That wasn't exactly in the report."

"I begin to think that I would very much like to see this report," said Piper.

Mallory rubbed his forehead, then reached into his desk and pulled out a form. He scrawled a half-dozen words and sealed it with wax. The three men waited while he stamped it with a seal the size of Galen's thumb.

"That'll get you in to see Tamsin," he said, still not looking at them. He tossed it across the desk to Stephen. "You tell him what you told me. I don't say he'll listen. He'd like to see the bishop put in her place as much as the rest of us. But that gets you five minutes with him, and that's as much of my neck as I'm willing to put on the line for you."

"Thank you," said Stephen gravely. "I knew that I had not been entirely mistaken in you."

Mallory grunted. The trio rose to leave, Piper leading the way. Seeing that Stephen had lingered, Galen paused in the doorway. Whatever the paladin said to the guard captain, he didn't catch it, but Mallory grunted again. Stephen joined them, his face serene but his eyes sadder than usual.

"You can't save everyone," said Galen gently.

"No. No, but we still try, don't we?"

"We have someone much more important to save," said Piper, his voice still cool and clipped. "Let us go speak to Commander Tamsin."

CHAPTER 35

The guard headquarters of the city of Archon's Glory was in one of the older districts inside the walls which had become unfashionable over the years. It had certainly not started life as a guard building, judging by the grand architecture and the ornate carvings, but it was in decent repair. Compared to the post in Mallory's district, it was positively luxurious. When they stepped inside, they were greeted by a spiral staircase and marble floors. Granted the floors were badly scuffed and the front desk looked as if teething puppies had gnawed on the wood, but even the shadow of its former grandeur was impressive.

Piper, resolutely unimpressed, strode to the desk and said, "I have come to see Commander Tamsin on a matter of some urgency."

This particular guard was not as easily cowed as Mallory's. He glanced at the trio and said, "The Commander is busy. You can request an audience and it will be scheduled when and if appropriate."

"It is, as I said, a matter of urgency."

The guard wore glasses. He pushed them down now and

looked at Piper over the rims, a fighting move that Galen had seen reduce strong men to jelly, particularly when deployed by nuns or lawyers. He wasn't sure if he should jump in front of Piper to take the full force of the glare or not.

Piper met the glare with one of his own. *He handled Mallory. This is his world. Just be ready to call for a healer in case one of them combusts.*

"Commander Tamsin does not see civilians except by appointment," said the man in the glasses.

Piper produced the letter with Mallory's seal and held it up. The guard reached for it, but Piper did not relinquish it. "Captain Mallory has requested that we be given an audience," he said, hoarfrost creeping into his voice again. "This is a judicial matter and I have neither time nor inclination to wait."

The guard looked from the seal to the formal robes that Piper wore. Galen discovered that he was holding his breath.

A sour expression crossed the guard's face and he sat back, pushing his glasses up on his nose and acting as if he had not lost. "If Mallory sent you, I suppose we can make an exception. The Commander can decide if he will see you or not." He jerked his chin toward the staircase. "Up. The door at the end of the hall."

"Thank you," said Piper coolly, and swept toward the stairs.

To give Tamsin what little credit that Galen was able to muster, his office was no more luxurious than the rest of the building. There was a rug on the floor and the walls had been whitewashed, but the furniture had the same battered look. A secretary looked up at them, frowning.

"The Commander—"

"Will see us," said Piper, holding up Mallory's seal.

"Will I?" asked a dryly amused voice from the next room. Tamsin appeared in the doorway beside the desk. He was a short, deceptively affable looking man, with a heavy mustache and thinning hair.

Piper turned to him. "Indeed. I am Doctor Piper. I believe we have met in passing, Commander, though it has been some years." He bowed from the neck, a very different gesture from a nod.

"You're the lich-doctor who figured out how the smooth men worked," said Tamsin.

"I am."

"That was fine work."

Piper bowed again.

"And you two..." Tamsin's eyes flicked over Galen and Stephen. Galen suspected that the man had registered every weapon they carried, down to the knife Galen used to trim his fingernails. "Paladins of the dead saint, aren't you?"

"We are," said Stephen, giving no sign at the tactlessness of the description.

"You work for the White Rat now."

"It is our honor to serve as we can."

Galen had a vague urge to smash something or scream loudly, just to break up the formality of the occasion.

Tamsin held out his hand and Piper relinquished Mallory's letter. The commander cracked the seal, read the words there, and snorted. "You may have five minutes, then," he said, gesturing them into his office.

There were only two chairs. Piper took one. Galen took the other, while Stephen stood. As the tallest of the three, he could loom rather effectively, and at this point, Galen thought they probably needed any psychological advantage they could get.

Tamsin tossed Mallory's letter carelessly on his desk. Galen read the words upside down.

. . .

They're above my pay grade.

- *M*

He contained a snort. *Typical. Accurate, but typical.*

"We've come to discuss the release of the gnole Earstripe, who has been unjustly detained."

"Ah. I had guessed that a Rat or two would be over, but I did not expect the lich-doctors to involve themselves."

"I believe that you will find that there has been a grave misunderstanding," said Piper.

"Perhaps we will," said Commander Tamsin, folding his arms. "Nevertheless, it's an internal guard matter. We police our own, and we do not countenance vigilantism."

"Earstripe wasn't in the guard. Mallory dismissed him," said Galen. "He didn't quit. He was made to leave, but he had enough of a sense of duty to try and stop Thomas from killing again." He wanted to slam his fist on the table in frustration but he knew that it wouldn't help.

"That runs counter to what is in the report, as I recall," said Tamsin.

"Captain Mallory will speak to the truth of it," said Stephen. "He was not consulted adequately in the matter."

"Then it will doubtless be resolved once further investigation is made."

Galen wanted to erupt at that, but Piper set his foot over the paladin's and he contained himself. Piper leaned forward, elbows on Tamsin's desk. "I fear that you may be laboring under a lack of information, Commander. Earstripe was grievously injured by the murderer and is at grave risk of relapse if he continues to languish in a jail cell. To keep him there would be inhumane."

Tamsin looked unimpressed. "I am certain that adequate care will be provided if that is the case. We are not barbarians."

No, because most barbarians have strong codes of honor around injured enemies, you smug bastard. Piper's boot heel was grinding into his toes, and a good thing too.

You can take him, whispered the tide. *It would be easy. You don't even need the sword. Go over the table and knock his chair over, kneel on his chest, beat his head into the floor a few times. The easiest thing in the world.*

"May I see the report?" asked Piper.

"It is, as I said, an internal matter."

Piper's gentle smile should have caused frost to form on Tamsin's eyebrows. "Then if you would be so kind as to check the report and confirm the charges against Earstripe?"

"There are no official charges yet. He is merely being held securely until full inquiry is made."

"Then you will be giving nothing official away."

Galen could actually see Tamsin debating what would get them out of his office sooner. If it had just been the paladins, he likely would have ordered them out, but Piper was an unknown quantity. Lich-doctors worked with the guard, but were not under their jurisdiction.

Finally, the commander reached into his desk, thumbed through files, and removed a stack of paper. "Very well." He ran his finger over the careful copperplate. "The report states that on the third of the month, Constable Earstripe left the city limits and went in pursuit of a criminal. He was not in hot pursuit at the time, and he was accompanied by a paladin of the dead saint, called Galen." He glanced up at Galen. "I assume that's you."

Galen nodded, not trusting himself to speak.

"The suspect was located and Constable Earstripe took it upon himself to apprehend him, a struggle ensued, during which time Paladin Galen murdered the suspect. The body was left at the scene, and both returned to Archon's Glory, where Earstripe made no attempt to contact his commander and inform him. Fortunately, Paladin Galen *did* make such a report, through civilian channels, where he emphasized that he was acting under the constable's orders. As such, guards were dispatched to locate the body and Constable Earstripe has been remanded to custody until a full internal investigation can be conducted."

"Of all the goddamn lies—"

Piper's heel applied itself savagely to his shin and Galen shut his mouth with a snap. Tamsin's careful lack of a smile managed to convey more than a broad grin would have.

"So there you have it," said the commander. "The constable appointed himself judge and jury, and employed Paladin Galen as the executioner. While paladins are, of course, exempt from such charges while performing the work of the gods, I am afraid that those who serve the Saint of Steel exist in something of a gray area in that regard. Isn't that right, Paladin Stephen?"

Over the desk, hands around his throat, move fast, he's probably got a knife but if the chair goes over, he'll waste a second off-balance...

Stephen, who had once been arrested for a berserker rage within the city, said, "The temples have upheld the right of the Saint of Steel's chosen to act on their own discretion, subject to review by a triumvirate of representatives from the Dreaming God, the Lady of Grass, and the White Rat."

"Outside the city," said Tamsin softly.

This man hates us, realized Galen. *Oh god. We should not have come. We should have sent someone from the Dreaming God or the Forge God to back him up. Stephen told me that the guard was irritated at us, but he genuinely despises us.*

"Indeed," said Stephen. "But we were speaking of outside the city, were we not?"

Tamsin was undoubtedly a good poker player. "That we were," he said, quite pleasantly. "Now, gentlemen, if there is nothing more..."

"I fear," said Piper tranquilly, "that there is rather more that I must bring to your attention. Your report has omitted several key facts. Earstripe did not, in fact, give an order for the suspect to be killed. He was unconscious at the time, and could not have done so."

Tamsin's eyebrows snapped together. "How do you know this?"

"Because I was present at the time," said Piper. "Is that not in the report?"

Tamsin glanced down, then checked several pages. "It may be in an addendum," he said, somewhat stiffly.

"Indeed. In fact, at the time of Thomas's death, I was attempting to staunch the bleeding from a crossbow bolt that Thomas had fired at Earstripe. It was perilously near the femoral artery. Earstripe lost consciousness almost immediately. I believe you will find, based on the time of death, that Paladin Galen was acting in defense of himself and a local woman, who was being held against her will."

"We have only your word for this," said Tamsin.

"On time and cause of death?" Piper ran his gloved fingers down the long black stole draped across his shoulders. "I am one of five lich-doctors certified by the courts of Archenhold. My word is accepted as fact by the court. Are you challenging the word of my colleagues and I on such matters?"

There was a kind of silky menace in his voice that Galen had not known Piper was capable of. He wanted to stand on the chair and applaud.

Commander Tamsin had been threatened by murderers

and professionals and on several occasions, professional murderers. He did not crack visibly, but Galen could practically hear the wheels turning in the man's head. Piper had just upped the stakes considerably. The guard could bring a man in and claim that they'd seen him stab another man, but if the lich-doctor said the victim had died of food poisoning, the court listened. You couldn't even refuse to use a certain lich-doctor because they were assigned by city district. Piper, who did his work practically in the Archon's basement, had been called in on several high-profile cases, including the smooth men. Discrediting him would be difficult.

No, there was absolutely no benefit to the guard in making an enemy of Piper, and a great deal of potential embarrassment.

Tamsin made one last stab at turning Piper aside. He tapped the papers in front of him. "I'm sure you can see why the guard must police itself in matters that smack of vigilantism, Doctor."

"Naturally," said Piper, still in that silken voice. "However, as has been made very clear, Earstripe was no longer a constable. Nor was he responsible for the death of the criminal involved. It was a clear case of self-defense, occurring after Earstripe was injured while saving *my* life." He ran his fingers down the stole again, as if he was the priest of some peculiar god of morgues. "I am certain that if you have preserved the body, my colleagues would be happy to provide corroboration as to the cause of his death, and to the nature of the injuries sustained by Earstripe in my defense. We are always...most concerned...for the health of one of our own."

That was *definitely* a threat. Angering the lich-doctors as a whole would be career suicide and Tamsin knew it. His gaze flicked to Galen.

Galen actually waited until Piper nodded to him before

speaking. The last thing he wanted to do was undo the doctor's good work. "I killed Thomas," he said. "I've testified to that repeatedly. I strangled him, in fact. If you've got the body, you can easily see by the marks that it was human hands on his neck and not a gnole's."

"I would imagine that your men would have recovered the crossbow and the bloody bolt along with the body," Piper said. "The lich-doctors will be more than happy to compare the two."

Tamsin looked down at the papers and Galen knew that he didn't have the crossbow and he likely didn't have the body either. *And after all this time, what kind of shape would it be in, anyway? No, somebody made a report and left him holding the bag, and he's not very happy about it.*

"Furthermore," said Piper, "a paladin of the Dreaming God can provide testimony as to my presence, Earstripe's injuries, and the nature of the local woman's imprisonment. I am certain that he would be happy to do so. The Temple of the Dreaming God, as you know, are *deeply* committed to serving the community."

Galen had almost forgotten Jorge and kicked himself. Sure, the paladin had arrived long after the fact, but that didn't matter. You did *not* mess with the Temple of the Dreaming God, not unless you wanted to find yourself ass-deep in demons. *Not that they would ever stop capturing demons just because the guard was rude to them, but their political power is up there with the Rat and everybody's scared to cross them, just in case they* do *stop.*

What must have seemed like a straightforward enough way to tweak the Rat's whiskers and remove a minor embarrassment was rapidly ballooning out of control. Galen watched the commander weighing the options. "You say that this gnole had left the guard?"

"Indeed. Captain Mallory has indicated his willingness to correct the record."

"And he will not be rejoining?"

"I think," said Piper, with absolute truth, "that he has no interest whatsoever in doing so."

Tamsin leaned back in his chair. "I can see that mistakes have been made with this report, Doctor Piper. It is possible that in our zeal for self-policing, several critical facts were overlooked. I thank you, doctor, for bringing this to my attention."

Piper inclined his head graciously. "It is upon all of us within the court system to make certain that justice is done."

"In light of this information, I suspect that the former constable can be released until such time as the report can be amended to include these new facts. Of course, he will need to be available to answer our inquiries."

"We stand ready to answer any inquiries that your investigation may have," said Piper. "*All* of us. Meanwhile, I am empowered by my counterpart among the gnoles to effect his patient's release, if you would be so kind as to write the release order?"

"My secretary shall see it done," said Tamsin. He rose and opened the door, calling to the man at the desk to write the release papers. "Now. Is there anything else that I may do for you gentlemen?"

Galen was just enough of a bastard to want to lounge around the office for a few minutes to aggravate the guard commander, but he suspected that would be counterproductive. Stephen bowed to Tamsin, and Galen did the same, albeit shallowly. Piper stood by the desk while the secretary added Earstripe's name and the date to the pre-written release and offered it to the commander for his seal.

"A pleasure, Commander," said Piper, taking the form. "I am glad that you could make time to handle this matter."

"The pleasure is mine," lied Tamsin with a straight face. "I am certain I will see you again, in the course of our respective duties."

If that was also meant as a veiled threat, Piper did not react to it. He smiled and said, "We lich-doctors do see everyone... eventually. Good day, Commander." And swept out, his heels ringing on the marble floor, while Galen and Stephen flanked him and Galen tried very hard not to laugh.

CHAPTER 36

"You're worried you'll break him, eh?" murmured Stephen, as they made their way down the steps to the entryway.

Galen grunted, his eyes on Piper's back.

"Because I've got to tell you, from where I'm standing, he does not seem particularly fragile."

Galen grunted again, because he didn't have an answer. He had never dreamed that Piper had such stone-cold ruthlessness lurking inside him. It was impressive. It was effective. If the stakes hadn't been so high, Galen would have been getting hard just watching him. His spongiform erectile tissue was definitely thinking about it. *I never used to find competence so arousing. Probably because there's so little of it in the world.*

Maybe it's the robes.

They reached the door. Piper pushed it open, letting a blaze of late afternoon light into the room. It seemed like an age of the earth had passed, but apparently it had only been a few minutes.

The three men stepped outside and Piper ran his fingers through his hair and said, "Well. I nearly shit myself a few times, how about you gentlemen?"

"You did *not* look it," said Stephen. "At all. I would think you politely threatened commanders every day."

"Oh god." Piper rubbed his hands over his face, looking suddenly much less like a marble statue and rather more like someone that Galen had kissed on multiple occasions. "I was so afraid he'd call my bluff."

"Was it a bluff?"

"Mostly. I have no idea what Jorge would say, and nobody could tell timing on a death and an injury that close together. And I know people are far more worried by lich-doctors than they ought to be, but there's not really anything the lich-doctors could do to him. We're not going to lie about causes of death. I suppose we could arrange to drag out the paperwork for—mmmff!"

Galen did not ever find out what the lich-doctors might do with the paperwork, because he was busy picking Piper several inches off the ground and kissing him.

After the initial shock, just when Galen was starting to think that he had made a terrible error, Piper's lips parted and he kissed back with enthusiasm.

Stephen moved several feet away and gazed politely at the architecture.

"I am an absolute fool," said Galen, setting Piper down before he strained something. "I am the world's most blithering idiot. I have no idea what I was thinking. You are incredible and I am convinced that if I get out of line, you will have absolutely no problem defending yourself from my stupidity. I don't know why I thought otherwise. Have I mentioned that you're incredible?"

Piper was flushed and breathing heavily. "I...uh..."

Galen clutched his head. "I should have apologized first. Before the kissing. Do you want to yell at me? You can. You should. I definitely deserve it."

"He absolutely does," called Stephen.

"Are you sure?" asked Piper.

"That I deserve to be yelled at? Yes. Absolutely."

"I have done entirely too much yelling today," said Piper. "I really don't enjoy doing it. No, are you sure about the other bit?"

"I have never been more sure of anything. I should have known better. I am so sorry. I will probably be sorry for the rest of my life."

"Lovely friezes around here," said Stephen, to no one in particular. "Or are those bas reliefs?"

"You did all that because you were afraid that...wait, what?"

Galen groaned and dropped his head. "I was convinced that I'd hurt you terribly and you would be too good and kind and decent to stop me."

"I believe that's an allegorical representation of something. Commerce, I think, but I'm not sure what the centaur is supposed to be."

Confusion, offense, and amusement warred across Piper's expression. "And now you *don't* think I'm good and kind and decent?"

You're handling this beautifully. You should definitely keep talking. Galen took a deep breath. "I think you're good and kind and decent and also terrifying when you put your mind to it. I should have known better."

"Yes, you should have."

"I hurt you terribly because I was trying not to hurt you terribly. Can you forgive me? Would you even want to be seen with someone as dim as I am?"

There was a long, long stretch while Piper studied him coolly and Galen felt like a body laid open on the slab, as if the doctor's eyes were flaying him open and looking for something that he might not even have. Then...

"Oh god yes," said Piper, and kissed him again.

"The centaur might be to indicate prosperity. He's got a sheaf of grain, that usually follows. Or possibly the artist just liked carving centaurs. Hard to say, really. And I can't tell if that woman over there is supposed to be Justice or Innocence."

"Stephen," said Galen, disentangling himself briefly, "if you do not shut up about the carvings, I will beat you over the head."

"I didn't want you to think that I was being a voyeur."

Piper stepped back, though his obvious reluctance made Galen feel rather better about it. "We have to go spring Earstripe. We can do this later."

"I'll hold you to that," said Galen. "And that's a promise."

"How do we get a prisoner released anyway?" asked Piper. "I've never done it."

"You haven't?"

"By the time I see someone, they're usually not a prisoner any more. Or, y'know, alive."

"I'll handle it," said Stephen. "Give me the form."

The building housing the records was across the street. Like the guard headquarters, it was the remnant of a grand building, but far less money had been poured into fixing it. The floorboards were so slanted that if Galen had dropped a ball at the entryway, it would have rolled through multiple rooms and changed direction at least twice before it came to a stop.

The woman at the front desk wore her hair in a severe bun, and the collar of her plain gray dress came up to her chin. Galen guessed she was one of the nuns working on the transcription project.

"Well!" she said, as Stephen came up to the front, "aren't you a tall, handsome one! What can I do for you, love?"

Galen revised his guess and chided himself mentally for making assumptions.

"I have a release order for a prisoner," said Stephen, "but I don't know where he's being held. Is that something you can help me with?"

"Sure, love, we can work it out. When did he come in?"

Galen spoke up. "Late last night, as far as I know."

Piper's guts twisted at the thought of Earstripe in a cell for most of a day. The jails in Archon's Glory weren't the worst things in the world, but they were hardly the place for someone with a healing injury. *Please let him not relapse.*

Please let some bastard not have gone after him for just being a gnole.

"Then you're in luck. Records came in at noon, right as rain. Follow me."

They entered another room that resembled an extremely cramped scriptorium. Four women were bent over papers, making copies in neat handwriting, while a woman in the habit of the Dreaming God looked over their shoulders and made occasional corrections. Galen fought the urge to take a step back at the sight of the habit. He'd spent several months traveling with a group of very particular nuns and his instincts screamed that he was about to be given a chore and a solid helping of disapproval.

"Sister, if you could help these gentlemen? They're looking for a prisoner that came in last night, but they don't know the house."

"Most certainly," said the nun. "Polly, will you consult the book?"

With the aid of Polly—who had definitely not been a nun at any point in her life, and had a saucy tattoo across her décolletage—they were able to determine the guard post where Earstripe had been taken. It was not the closest one to the gnole warren, which was both unsurprising and infuriating.

"They didn't want Mallory to intervene," said Stephen, as they emerged onto the street. "It seems they are not quite certain of him either."

"They'll be a lot less certain once he testifies that he fired Earstripe," muttered Piper.

"Oh, it won't come to that," said Stephen.

Piper looked surprised. "You don't think?"

Stephen had worked more closely with the guard than any of them. "I think that the report will be quietly buried and those who pushed for it will get a stern talking-to for having embarrassed the commander. And Mallory, I fear, will bear the brunt. It will be decided that he is responsible for not having stopped the process, even though he had no way to do so. I suspect that he will not be a captain much longer. Possibly not even a guard."

"You'll forgive me if I don't have a great deal of sympathy," said Galen.

Stephen sighed. "I do," he admitted. "He was a good man, I think, when he started. I feel badly for that man, if not for the one he has become. I suspect that man would be horrified by what he is now. Perhaps he will yet find redemption."

Galen started to say that he didn't believe in redemption, and then Piper took his hand and he realized that he hoped quite desperately that redemption was possible. *At least for some of us.*

Once they arrived at their destination, Piper released his hand. It was full dark now, and the lamplighters were walking with candles on long poles. Two gnoles were waiting in the shadows outside the guard post.

"I suppose we could have just asked you where he was held," said Piper. "I should have thought."

"No worries, bone-doctor," said one, and grinned with all his sharp teeth. "Ours says that a healer-human is coming to free a gnole from a guard burrow. Gnoles know to wait."

"Ours had more confidence than I did," muttered Piper.

"I never doubted," said Galen, which was not actually true.

One of the gnoles gave him a look, and Galen was fairly sure the gnole could tell he was lying, but the gnole didn't call him out on it.

They squared their shoulders and went in. Stephen presented the release paperwork and the guard on duty reached for it, read the name and nodded. Galen was prepared for another fight, but the man was crisp and professional. "He's been placed in the solitary cell," he said.

"Solitary!" Piper's outrage blazed off him. "What could he possibly have done?"

"Possessed a skull narrow enough to fit through the bars of the other cells," said the guard. "Our facilities were not built to handle gnoles. Would you care to accompany me, sir?"

"I would, yes," said Stephen.

Piper moved to follow and Galen caught his arm. The doctor might be familiar with death, but there was enough suffering in such a place to wound him, no matter how impressively competent he had proved himself to be. "They'll be out in a moment."

"If he's injured..."

"Then we will know in short order."

It was a minor eternity before the door opened again and Stephen emerged with a familiar striped figure. "Earstripe," said Piper, flinging himself to his knees. "Are you hurt? How's your leg? Was it very bad?"

The gnole actually laughed. "Nah, bone-doctor, a gnole is well enough. Stiff but not hurt. A gnole went quietly."

"I am so very sorry," said Galen, also dropping to his knees. "It was all my fault."

"Guard-humans arrested a gnole, tomato-man. Tomato-man does not work for the guard."

"Yes, but..."

"Perhaps we might discuss this on the way back to the warren," said Stephen gently. "And not in the middle of the floor."

"Yes, of course." Piper took Galen's hand as the paladin pulled him up. "Do we need to call a coach? Can you walk far?"

"A gnole is not made of straw and bird-bones." Earstripe rolled his eyes at Galen. "Do all healers act this way? Gnole, human, all the same."

"All the ones I've met," said Galen, squeezing Piper's hand.

Earstripe seemed far less troubled by his ordeal than Piper had expected. "Quiet cell," he said cheerfully. "Dark. A gnole caught up on sleep. Not as good as a burrow, but not bad." His crutch had vanished somewhere, but one of the waiting gnoles moved to act as a brace if he needed it. Piper tried not to fret.

Galen explained what happened and what they had learned from Mallory and Tamsin. Earstripe listened soberly, his ears intent, not flicking aside to catch the sounds of the city. "A gnole would like to be surprised," he said finally. "But a gnole is not. Not really."

"I'm sorry," said Piper. He wanted to apologize for all humans everywhere, even knowing how foolish and futile and self-centered it was, but it would do no good. *And what right do I have to inflict my need for absolution on him?* "What can we do?"

"A gnole is free. Bone-doctor has done more than gnoles could have done."

"Based on the message I got from Skull-of-Ice, I didn't dare fail," said Piper dryly. "I was afraid ours would have my skull on a pike."

"Nah, nah," one of their gnole escort piped up. "Pike is fish, yes? Gnole burrow hangs from posts, put light in skull."

"Very decorative," said the other.

All three gnoles laughed rather more than the joke seemed to warrant. Piper wondered if there was more to it in gnole-speech. *I absolutely must find a dictionary. Tomorrow.*

Earstripe's own story was much shorter. "Guard-humans come to outside burrow. Humans come, tell us guard-humans are there. A gnole goes out to meet them. Was a guard-gnole, yes, should know how to talk to guard-humans. Guard-humans say a gnole comes with them, guard has *inquiries.*" He lifted his lip to show one fang. "A gnole remembers what *inquiries* involved. But humans from near burrow are there, so guard-humans do nothing. Not so bad."

Piper remembered the armed trio who had warned them away from the gnole warren before, and suspected that they might well have saved Earstripe from some casual violence. He grimaced. It had been too damn close. *And what might have happened to him if he'd sat in that cell too long? Or if the guard on duty had been a little less professional?*

"We were lucky," he said.

"A gnole is lucky in his friends," said Earstripe. He glanced at Piper and Galen's hands. "Glad friends have stopped twisting their whiskers, too."

"Yes, well." Galen ducked his head. "What can I say? I can't smell."

The gnoles thought that was hilarious as well.

On the far side of the river, they stopped. "A gnole thinks perhaps gnoles go alone," said Earstripe. "Too many guard-humans lately. Some gnoles nervous, yes?"

"Completely understandable. Please give Skull-of-Ice my regards. Or...err...whatever is polite there." Piper coughed. "Ours scares me a little."

"Human really can't smell if ours only scares him a *little.*"

"Please let the Temple of the Rat know if we can help in any way," said Stephen gravely. "Gnoles are part of the city and if they have a problem with the guard, the Rat will do their best to solve it."

"Mmm." Earstripe flicked his whiskers. "A gnole *was* a solution. See how well that worked! But a gnole understands." He looked at Piper. "Skull-of-Ice said our gnole would call on a doctor, look at dead humans, understand how humans work. Maybe start there, eh?"

Piper wasn't sure if human corpses were the best place to start negotiations with another species, but it was what he had to work with. *Couldn't be any worse, anyway. At least nothing hurts the dead overmuch.* "Ours is welcome at any time."

The gnole nodded. And then the three of them melted into the shadows and left the humans standing alone beside the river.

"Well," said Galen, and sighed from his toes.

"Well," said Piper.

They were still holding hands. Piper looked down at their clasped fingers, then up at Galen. Brown eyes met green and held for a long, long time.

"Now this architecture," said Stephen, rather loudly, "is a style that doesn't really have a name, but I suspect we will end up calling it something like "Post-Flood Revival," and seems to be characterized by—"

"Stephen, I am going to make you *eat* that architecture."

"Fine, fine." The tall paladin held up his hands. "I think I'll be heading home, then. It has been a very long, if ultimately productive day." He glanced between the two. "I'll leave you to escort the doctor home, shall I?"

"Yes," said Piper, still looking into Galen's eyes. "I think that would be for the best."

CHAPTER 37

The sheets were wrecked. Piper didn't know how they'd managed to completely unmake the bed, but they had. Half the bedding was on the floor and his legs were on bare mattress. The room stank of sex and Piper was already envisioning the knowing look that the woman who did the washing was going to give him when he brought her the mangled sheets. There was a dark stain from the oil they'd used and he was going to have to tip the washerwoman generously to get that out again.

It had been entirely worth it. The feeling of Galen moving inside him, that long red hair falling down over them both...no, he had absolutely no regrets about the sheets.

"You look smug," said Galen, idly running his fingers through Piper's hair.

"Smug." Piper considered this. "Smug is probably a good word for it."

"I hope it was worth the wait."

"Fishing for compliments?" asked Piper, arching one eyebrow.

Galen chuckled. "No need. You made more than enough noise to let me know how I was doing."

"Oh god." Piper put his hands over his face. "Did I?" He'd tried to keep quiet out of respect for the neighbors and the thinness of the walls, but Galen's hands on his body had been almost too much to bear. The paladin had been careful and tender enough to drive him half-mad with frustration, and then just when Piper was ready to pin the man to the bed and do the work himself, Galen had murmured, "Now?" and Piper had said something—"Yes," probably, or maybe just, "For the love of god, fuck me."

That first hard thrust had been shocking and incredible and then something more than incredible and then the world had practically dissolved and when he could think again, his throat had been raw from shouting.

Galen propped himself up on one elbow and watched Piper's face intently.

"What are you doing?" he asked, embarrassed. Galen had white eyelashes mixed with the dark red ones. Somehow he'd never noticed that before. *Probably because you close your eyes when you kiss.*

"You're blushing again," said Galen.

"I am *not,*" said Piper, despite the fact that he could feel his ears getting hot.

"Dare I ask what you are thinking about?"

"You, obviously." This was true, but did not lessen the blush at all.

"What fascinating thoughts you must be having."

Piper dropped his head against the paladin's shoulder and muttered something. Galen chuckled and lay back, wrapping an arm around him. Piper closed his eyes, feeling pleasantly exhausted.

"I dreamed about doing this," Galen said. "Every day."

"If we do this every day, neither of us is going to be able to walk."

Galen chuckled. "Not *quite* that. Well, all right, a great deal of that. But mostly I dreamed about being with you."

A cool wash of relief went through him. *He means it. He's serious. He's not going to get that look in his eyes and leap up and flee.* Piper settled himself a little more securely against Galen's chest. He could hear the even beating of the other man's heart under his ear.

"I never thought about anyone else like that," Galen said musingly. "Sex, yes, but not just...being around them. I would hear something interesting and I'd want to talk to you about it. I wondered where you were, and what you were doing. I believe I'm in love with you."

He delivered that last line in the same calm tones as the rest, and for a moment, Piper thought he'd misheard. "I'm sorry," he said, turning the words around in his head and failing utterly to find something that sounded similar. "Did you just say that you were...?"

"In love with you. Desperately. Terribly." He still sounded light and amused, but Piper felt his heart beating faster and knew what a risk he was taking.

He's the paladin. Of course he's the one who takes the risks.

For a moment, Piper thought of pulling back. Galen had hurt him once already. Walking away now would be agony, but it would heal. Much more time in the paladin's arms and that would change. He wouldn't be able to push those feelings aside any longer. If Galen drove him away again, that wound would scar instead.

Galen's fingers stroked through his hair again, and Piper threw the dice. "Oh good," Piper said. "Because I am quite hopelessly in love with you as well."

It did not quite ease the tension in Galen's body. Long auburn hair fell over his face as he sat up, and he pushed it out of the way. "I'm terrible at this," said Galen. "I don't know how to be in love any more. Hell, looking back, I don't know if I was ever any good at it. I'm going to screw up and hurt you and the thought of doing that kills me. All I can do is hope that I don't fail you completely."

"That's how it works," said Piper gently. "You hurt each other and you apologize and you learn better."

"I'm a bastard. And a berserker. I've killed so many people. You have no idea."

Piper put two fingers over Galen's lips. "I've died a hundred times. I spend my life with corpses. I'm not afraid of you."

Galen's tongue flicked out across Piper's fingertips and Piper inhaled sharply. There was a wicked gleam in the paladin's eyes now, for all his solemnity.

"It may not work," Piper said, determined to say his piece before Galen succeeded in distracting him. "In a month we may be sick of each other. You might decide that I'm horribly annoying and I might decide that you're far too noxiously noble—"

"Ha!"

"—hush. You are relentlessly noble, even if you try to hide it. But we won't know unless we try. And I'm willing if you are."

Galen's breath was warm against his fingers. "Even if you never get to sleep next to me?"

Piper surveyed the room, lingering on the disaster that had been the sheets. Tomorrow, he would apologize to both the washerwoman and the neighbors. "If there was only one thing that we could do together in bed, I have to say, I would *not* choose sleeping."

The paladin laughed and wrapped his arms around Piper's shoulders, and what they did for the next hour had nothing to do with sleeping.

EPILOGUE

Six Months Later

It had been a dry summer and a drier autumn. The horses kicked up dust and the coaches traveled in a pale cloud. Dust got into Piper's eyes and mouth and stuck to his clothes and he hated it, but he did not complain.

The three paladins in the coach were as silent as the grave. Even Galen had said nothing for the last ten miles. Shane and Wren might as well have been carved in stone, and Wren, at least, was usually as chatty as her namesake.

If you knew how to look—and Piper had learned quickly—you could see the signs of strain. Shane's forehead had beaded up with sweat. Wren's lips were set and white. Galen's fingers were laced with Piper's and he had been rubbing his thumb mechanically over Piper's wedding ring. Piper had taken his gloves off in the heat and was beginning to think he should put them back on, if only so that Galen didn't wear the engraving off.

Piper had been stunned when Galen went to one knee, in

the finest romantic tradition, and begged for his hand in marriage. Moreso because he'd been holding a bonesaw at the time and there was a body open on the slab in front of him. "I... I...Galen, really? Are you sure?"

"It's been five months," Galen had said, looking up at him. "And I have come close to ruining it at least three times because I'm an absolute idiot. I expect I'll probably come close again. If we're married, at least I'll have a chance to throw myself at your feet and apologize before you tell me to die in a fire."

"That's a terrible reason to get married," Piper had said.

"How about that I don't deserve you and I don't deserve to be as happy as you make me, but I'm just enough of a bastard to try to grab onto something I don't deserve?"

Piper had gulped and dropped the bonesaw. Kaylin had come down the stairs and was in the doorway, grinning. She had nudged Galen with her crutch. "Tell him you love him, you redheaded numbskull."

"Did I not say that bit yet? Piper, I love you. I love you more than I love life. A lot more, actually. Would you like me to die for you? That might be easier than living with me, honestly."

"No dying."

"You don't actually have to live with me. I thought we could maybe get a larger place with separate bedrooms, but I'm flexible. I know I'm hard to live with."

"Your cooking is terrible," said Piper around the lump in his throat.

"There, you see? And I have never learned not to drop my clothes on the floor. I know. I'm dreadful. Please marry me anyway. I love you. Did I mention that?"

"Mention it again," Kaylin suggested.

"I love you, Piper. I want to have the right to worry about whether you're eating enough and to tell you that you're working too hard and to fuck you all night—"

Kaylin cleared her throat.

"—and I know that I'm a lot to deal with but I can't get enough of you. Please marry me, Piper."

"Yes."

"I'll dedicate my entire life to making you happy. If you have any enemies, I'll kill them. Then you can dissect them if you like. Would you like that? I'll do it. Just marry me."

"Yes."

"If you marry me, I swear I'll—"

"He said yes, you dolt," Kaylin said, nudging him with her crutch again.

Galen blinked. "You did?"

"I did." Piper tried to pull him to his feet. "Yes. I'll marry you. I don't know why you want to, when you're so much more...everything...than I am, but I will."

"You will?"

"Yes."

"Oh thank god," Galen said, and swept him up in his arms, ignoring the blood and the corpse and Kaylin snorting in the background.

It had been a small ceremony, or as small as it could be, when the Bishop of the White Rat was the person presiding over it. Seven paladins had attended. Istvhan, that huge bear of a man who had worked with Piper on the problem of the smooth men, had given him a rib-cracking hug. "I told him to propose," he had informed Piper. "He'd bought a ring a month ago and was dithering. Dreadful thing, dithering."

"Thank you," Piper had said, trying to regain his breath.

Now, sitting in the carriage, Galen rubbed his thumb over Piper's ring again. Piper glanced at the side of his face and saw that the paladin's eyes were closed and his lips were trembling.

It was good that Istvhan had come down from the north to speak to Beartongue, and not just for the wedding. Barely a week later, word had come from Anuket City that the ruins of the great temple of the Saint of Steel were being cleared at last.

"But it's been years," Piper had said. "I thought they'd have done it years ago."

Galen had shaken his head. "Cursed ground," he had said. "The high priest burned it when the Saint died. Said that he wanted to make a pyre fit for a god. I thought it would lie in ruins forever."

It made sense. Anuket City was built on profit. If anything, Piper was astonished that the temple had not been cleared within a week to put in a warehouse.

"We are all going," Galen told him. "All of us. One last pilgrimage, to lay the dead to rest." He swallowed. "Will you come with me?"

"Of course."

And so here he was, in this stifling coach, coated in dust, with three paladins pretending to be calm. A round dozen of them—seven paladins, Stephen and Istvhan's partners, a functionary of the Rat and Jorge of the Dreaming God. And Piper himself, of course.

The coach stopped. When it became obvious that none of the three were going to move, Piper flipped open the shutter and looked out onto an expanse of burnt stone. "We've arrived," he said.

They stayed statues a moment longer, and then Shane let out a long, long sigh and opened the door. They stepped out into the cool autumn sun. Piper no longer paused involuntarily at doorways, but he went last anyway.

The other two coaches had also stopped. Piper watched as the paladins emerged, and one by one, they turned to some unknown point in the ruins, like iron filings aligning to a magnet.

"The altar," murmured Galen.

Stephen squared his shoulders. "All right," he said. "Jorge, Clara, you know what to do. Brothers and sisters, let us end this."

Galen squeezed his hand and stepped away. Piper gazed after him, wondering if he should follow, when Jorge tapped his shoulder.

"Come with me," said Jorge quietly. "We've made preparations. Just in case."

Piper frowned. "Preparations?"

He followed the Dreaming God's champion to the third coach. Stephen's partner Grace and the Rat priest were already inside it, and the other two drivers were standing on the board at the back. Clara, an enormous woman as large as Istvhan, stood outside with her arms folded. She nodded to Piper, though her eyes were still on the seven paladins. "All right," she said softly. "In the event that something happens to set them off, we'll have seven berserkers to deal with. You, Grace, and Zale will stay in the coach, and Matthias here will get you the hell away from here."

"What about you?" asked Piper, frowning.

Clara smiled. "Jorge and I will stay and watch and clean up after."

Piper looked her up and down. She was very large and powerfully muscled, but she wasn't even wearing armor. "Are you sure?"

"I'm sure."

He looked at Jorge for confirmation. Jorge nodded. "I've fought two of these men before," he said quietly. "I didn't enjoy it, but I didn't lose."

"We don't expect trouble," said Clara. "But we're planning for it anyway."

Piper looked past her, to where the paladins had threaded their way through the ruins. They stood in a semicircle around a vast, fire-blackened stone slab. As he watched, one by one, they went to their knees.

They waited. The vigil kept at the coach could not compare to the one at the altar, but it felt like vigil nonetheless. Piper swallowed repeatedly. Jorge tapped his foot. Grace wrung her hands. Zale, the slender solicitor-sacrosanct from the Rat, kept pushing their hair out of their eyes, whereupon it would immediately fall back down.

At last, Istvhan rose. He turned toward the coach and lifted a hand in acknowledgment. Clara let out a long sigh of relief.

Would she have fought the man she loved? Somehow Piper thought she might. There was a hard practicality to Clara.

The others began to rise. Only Marcus and Galen stayed kneeling for a long time.

Stephen made a beckoning gesture. Clara pushed away from the coach and nodded to the others to follow.

The stones turned underfoot. Weeds had sprouted between blackened tiles. Even now, Piper could smell burning.

It had been a very large temple. It took a long time to reach the altar, and still Marcus and Galen knelt before the stone.

"Speak to him," murmured Stephen to Piper. "I'll take Marcus."

Speak to him? What could Piper possibly say to a man in mourning for a god? He swallowed hard and nodded.

Galen's shoulders were drawn tight. Piper winced in sympathy for how his legs must feel, kneeling so long on the uneven terrain. He reached out and put a hand on Galen's shoulder, and the paladin flinched.

"Galen," he said softly. "Galen, I love you."

"He's dead," said Galen.

"I know."

"Something that big shouldn't die. It's like the ocean or the wind dying. It doesn't make sense."

"I know."

"It'll never make sense."

"I know."

Galen's hand came up, slowly, and squeezed Piper's. Piper waited.

Finally, the paladin took a deep breath and rose to his feet. "Thank you," he said.

"Of course."

Galen turned away. Piper looked past him to the altar stone. Nothing but a chunk of stone in the middle of a burnt-out ruin. A strange thing, to have such power over men.

You were the center of Galen's life, Piper thought, to the absent Saint of Steel. *I cannot forgive you for what you did to him, but perhaps you had no choice. And you made him the man he is, and I love that man very much.*

Thank you for my husband.

He reached out and laid his fingertips on the broken stone in gratitude and reverence. Bare skin touched sun-warmed stone.

And suddenly Piper knew what it felt like when a god died.

ABOUT THE AUTHOR

T. Kingfisher is the vaguely absurd pen-name of Ursula Vernon, an author from North Carolina. In another life, she writes children's books and weird comics. She has been nominated for the World Fantasy and the Eisner, and has won the Hugo, Sequoyah, Nebula, Alfie, WSFA, Coyotl and Ursa Major awards, as well as a half-dozen Junior Library Guild selections.

This is the name she uses when writing things for grown-ups. Her work includes horror, epic fantasy, fairy-tale retellings and odd little stories about elves and goblins.

When she is not writing, she is probably out in the garden, trying to make eye contact with butterflies.

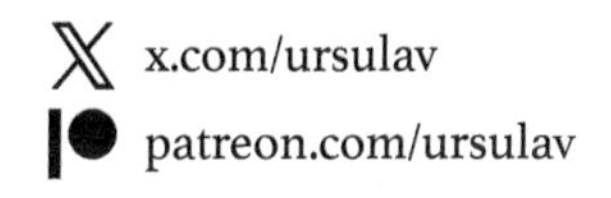

ALSO BY T. KINGFISHER

As T. Kingfisher

A Wizard's Guide To Defensive Baking

Paladin's Grace

Swordheart

Clockwork Boys

The Wonder Engine

Minor Mage

Nine Goblins

Toad Words & Other Stories

The Seventh Bride

The Raven & The Reindeer

Bryony & Roses

Jackalope Wives & Other Stories

Summer in Orcus

From Saga:

The Twisted Ones

The Hollow Places

As Ursula Vernon

From Sofawolf Press:

Black Dogs Duology

House of Diamond

Mountain of Iron

Digger

It Made Sense At The Time

For kids:

Dragonbreath Series

Hamster Princess Series

Castle Hangnail

Printed in the USA
CPSIA information can be obtained
at www.ICGtesting.com
LVHW021800251024
794703LV00012BA/345